THOSE WHO WILL NOT SEE

Lauren Woodcock

LAUREN WOODCOCK

THOSE WHO WILL NOT SEE

© Lauren Woodcock
All rights reserved.
First edition published on Kindle Direct Publishing 2012.
Cover illustration by Sarah Hill.
Title, and character and place names are all protected by the applicable. This book is a work of fiction, therefore names, characters and events are all fictitious and any resemblance to an actual person, living or dead, or any actual event is purely coincidental.
All rights reserved. No part of this publication may be reproduced, stored in a retrieval system, or transmitted in any form or by any means, electronic, mechanical, photocopying, recording or otherwise, without prior permission from the copyright owner.

LAUREN WOODCOCK

DEDICATION

For my brother, Joel, who proves every day how life's hurdles are designed to be overcome. And for my husband, Nathan, who taught me never to give up on my dreams.

LAUREN WOODCOCK

ACKNOWLEDGEMENTS

With special thanks to Ashley and Sarah, without whom this would not be possible.

LAUREN WOODCOCK

Matthew Pickering
November 2008

The flash is like ten daggers in my eyes. I shut them as tightly as I can, but the daggers are now stabbing my ears. The rain is hitting my window very fast, and very heavy. It sounds like it makes a thousand pinging noises every second, but I don't think that is possible. The water collecting on my roof is speeding down the drainpipe on the outside of my bedroom wall, making a loud 'whooshing' noise, and there is very loud dripping onto my window ledge. I can hear the branches from the big tree outside my bedroom waving about in the wind, and scraping against the glass in my window. The screechy noise they make makes me feel like I want to be sick.

Hannah is telling me that everything is okay and that it is just a storm, but I already know that it is just a storm. She is telling me that it is only a bit of rain and that it won't hurt me, but it is hurting me already, because it is like daggers in my ears and in my eyes. I can hear a rattling and a scraping, and I think that Hannah has closed my curtains, because that is the noise that my curtains make when you close them. She says, "It's okay, Matty, you can open your eyes now; the storm has gone," but I think that she is telling me a lie, because I can still hear the storm.

Hannah's voice is making even more daggers hit me in my ears, and I press my hands over them as hard as they will press. I am pressing so hard that I think I might squash my brain if I didn't have a skull, so it is a good thing that I do have one. I push my bottom up against the wall behind me and let it slide down to the floor. I curl my knees up to meet my head, which makes me feel a little bit safer, but not a lot. I close my eyes even more tightly in case the flash comes again, because I know that even my curtains cannot protect me from the flashing daggers. I put my head through my knees to protect me even more.

The noise is quieter now because I have covered my ears up as hard as I can with my hands, and with the inside of my legs; but it is still there. I breathe in a big breath, and then let it out in quick bursts through my teeth so I sound a bit like a steam train. I feel a little bit calmer straight away.

Some hands land softly on my shoulders. My eyes are still closed, but I think that the hands must belong to Hannah, because she is the only one in the house with me. I think that she should use her hands to protect her own ears from the noise daggers, but Hannah is different to me, and she can make a scary storm go away just by closing the curtains.

My body starts to feel more relaxed as I make my train noise. I let my eyes go a bit less tight, and I can see that the eye daggers have gone. It is very dark in my bedroom tonight because I think the daggers reached our electricity cables and gave us a power cut, which means that the lights will not turn on. I can no longer hear the rain, or the whooshing or the dripping, because I can only hear my train noise now. I keep my hands on my ears, and I keep blowing.

Then suddenly, the daggers come back. A big crash happens, and I think it must be thunder, and at the same time the bright flash comes back. Now my eyes and ears are stabbing again, and burning too. My head begins to scream.

The screaming in my head is too loud; I cannot stand it. I lift my head up out of my knees and make the scream come out of my mouth instead, as loudly as I can. I scream again and again, but the screaming inside my head is louder than the real life screaming so it doesn't help. I throw my head backwards until it hits the wall behind me. I think I hit it hard, but it didn't hurt. I want to get this loud scream out of my head, but it carries on. It carries on inside my head, and it carries on coming out of my mouth. I throw my head backwards again and I feel it hit the wall. It must have hit it very hard, because my whole body bounces back a little bit.

Hannah's hands have moved to the back of my shoulders, and I can feel that she is trying to pull me forwards, away from the wall. But Hannah is a girl, and she is three and a half years younger than me, so I am a lot stronger than her, and she does not move me at all. Through the sound of my screaming, and the rain, and the dripping and the whooshing I can hear that Hannah is crying, and she is shouting, "Stop, Matt. Stop." I wish she knew that when she cries and shouts at me to stop, she is only making even more noise daggers go into my ears, which makes me want to carry on.

I throw my head backwards again and it hits the wall. The back of my head feels a little bit wet and sticky when it hits, so I think that it must be bleeding, but it doesn't hurt.

Hannah's hands move to the back of my head and I hear her screaming, and then crying even louder. It is hurting my ears, and it is hurting my brain.

I push back fast against Hannah's fingers and manage to hit the wall hard, but I don't feel it because her hands are in the way. I feel her fingers crunch behind my head, and I hear some cracking sounds.

Hannah screams, and then I can feel her let go of my head.

I scream loudly, throw my body forwards, and then backwards as hard as I can. I can feel my head hit the wall again, and my body shakes back. My whole body feels funny. The screaming in my head goes blurry, and the screaming from my mouth stops. The world that I can see through my eyelids changes from black to white with flashes of pink. My neck doesn't feel like it can hold my head up anymore. It feels like it is made of rubber, and so does the rest of my body. My head begins to fall forwards, so I lift it up again, which is very hard to do. It rolls onto my right shoulder, and then, as my white and pink world turns back to black, my whole body falls forwards.

* * *

I think that the storm has stopped. I cannot hear any dripping, or whooshing, or any other ear daggers any more. I can hear some talking, but it is very quiet. I suddenly realise that I am not on the floor of my bedroom any more, but I am lying somewhere that is very soft. I am lying on my back, and my head is on a big pillow. That is when I notice that my head feels funny. I have got a very bad headache, and it feels like somebody is squeezing it tightly.

I open my eyes.

It is quite dark, but I can see that I am in my bedroom because I can see lots of number eighteens hanging on the wall where I keep all of my birthday cards. I can also see a Scream Mask hung next to them, because it was Halloween day on my eighteenth birthday, because my eighteenth birthday was on the thirty-first of October, and so I wore my Scream mask to scare everybody. That day was a month ago, but I like to keep my birthday cards up on my wall every day of the year because it reminds me of my birthday, and I really like my birthday because I get presents on that day.

I can see that my bedroom door has been left open a little bit because there is some light coming in from the landing. That must mean that the daggers that cut our power off have gone away now, because our electricity must be working again.

I can hear Mum and Ian Hobson talking on the landing outside my room, and even though they are talking very quietly I can still hear what they are saying. I can hear that my mum is crying, but it is not hurting my ears because it is not very loud. "How could I let this..." I can hear her saying, but she doesn't finish her sentence because she starts to cry instead.

Ian Hobson says, "Come here, Sweetheart. It wasn't your fault. You had to prioritise, and tonight your mother had to come first."

"But how could I... how could I think that it would be okay to leave Hannah with him? She's so young." Mum starts to cry again.

"She's almost fifteen, Susan; that's practically an adult these days. Don't be down on yourself like this. Nora needed you."

All I can hear for the next minute is Mum crying, and Ian Hobson making a 'shhhh' noise.

I do not know what my mum and Ian Hobson are talking about. I look at my Scream mask, and I make a little bit of a laugh because I remember how many people I made frightened when I wore it.

"John must... John must think I'm the worst mum in the world. Anything could have happened. And I knew there was going to be a storm, they said so on the news, and I still went and left them alone." Mum's voice sounds very sad, but she isn't crying any more. I wonder why John, who is my dad, would think that she is the worst mum in the world.

"Why do you care what John thinks? He's not going to win father of the year himself, is he? And you had to go; you couldn't leave your mother in that state."

"I know he's no angel, but to get a call like that from his daughter at that time of night... Oh, my poor baby. My poor babies. I hope they're okay. Why didn't I just call you to watch them? I didn't want to bother you at work, but if I knew..."

"You didn't know; you couldn't have known."

"Well, I should have known. I can't believe I was so stupid as to put my poor babies in that position." Mum isn't talking quietly any more, but she isn't talking loudly enough to make my ears hurt.

I rub the back of my head, where it is hurting the most, and I can feel that there is a bandage wrapped around it. I wonder if someone put this on me after I banged my head. I think that they must have done, because I have been asleep since then, and I don't think it would be possible for me to have done it to myself in my sleep.

Now I can hear Ian Hobson talking. He is saying, "Look, Sweetheart, Hannah's fine. John promised to phone as soon as he knows any more from the hospital. At the worst she will have got a couple of broken fingers. Your mother would have been much worse than that if you hadn't gone to her. And Matthew's fine, I've seen to him."

"My son bangs his head so hard that he blacks out, and you think he's fine?"

"I know how to handle a bit of concussion, Darling. Twenty-five years of medical practice teach you a couple of things. I promise you, he will be fine in the morning."

"But he won't, though, will he? Yes, the concussion might have gone, but the problem won't have. Why does he keep doing this to himself? He's covered in bruises, bumps and cuts, and now he's hurt Hannah too. I just... I don't know what to do any more."

"We'll find him some help. I know a few people he could talk to – counsellors; but there's nothing we can do tonight. Come on, let me pour you a nice glass of red and we can wait up for Hannah."

I can't hear any talking for lots of seconds, but then I hear Mum's voice again. "Okay, make mine a really big one and I'll be down in a minute," she says. "I just want to look in on Matty."

I hear a kissing noise, and then Ian Hobson says, "Okay."

"Ian...?" Mum says after a quick pause. "I can't do this anymore; I need help. It's twenty-four-seven, and I just can't do it."

There is a pause.

"So you'll look at the care brochure?"

Another pause.

"Am I a failure?"

"You're a human. I'll get you that wine." I hear Ian Hobson's footsteps walking downstairs.

I think my mum is coming into my room now, because more light is coming in as she opens my bedroom door wider. She stands still at the door and looks at me. I hear her sniff.

"Mum?" I say.

She makes a loud breathing in noise, and walks up to my bed. She leaves the door half open so it is a little bit light in my bedroom, and she sits on the chair next to me. She strokes my face with her fingers. "I'm here."

I say, "My head hurts," because my head does hurt.

She smiles at me a little bit. "It will do, you hit it very hard, Matthew; there's blood all over your wall."

I say, "I'm sorry, Mum," because I don't want her to be cross that I made my bedroom wall messy.

She strokes my forehead again. "It's okay, my baby, as long as you and Hannah are all right. Ian said you should feel better in the morning."

"Where is Hannah?"

"Sweetie, she's at the hospital; you really hurt her fingers."

"I'm sorry," I say again, because I did not mean to hurt my little sister's fingers.

She smiles. "I'm sorry, too. I should never have left you."

There is a ringing, and Mum takes her mobile telephone out of her pocket and answers it. "Hi," she says, "how is she? -

Oh my poor little angel. Are you bringing her home to me? Put her on the phone -

Oh-

No, it's fine; let her sleep. Just bring her round as soon as she wakes up in the morning. Look, John, I'm really sorry you had to deal with this. Did Hannah tell you about Mum? It's no excuse really, but I needed to go to her-

She's a bit better now, but you know the score; the next phone call could be ...-

Don't be nice to me, please. I don't deserve it-

You have to stop saying things like that. We've been through this *so* many times; you know I'm married to Ian -

Of course he's supportive; don't be ridiculous-

Well, he had to work, didn't he? -

Look, I'm not having this conversation now. I'll see you in the morning -

Yes, I'm fine -

That's not your job anymore; Ian's perfectly capable of looking after me -

Stop talking, John, I can't handle this right now. Matty's with me, and Ian's right downstairs -

Well you know how I feel, but it's not right so just leave it. I have to go. Give Hannah a big kiss, and bring her home to me the minute she wakes up -

Okay, bye."

She presses a button and puts her mobile telephone down on my bed. Then she looks at me and makes a loud breathing out noise. "You broke three of Hannah's fingers," she says.

I feel sad that I broke three of Hannah's fingers, because I did not want to hurt my little sister. "I'm sorry, Mum," I say.

Mum is still looking at me. "It's Hannah you need to be sorry to."

"I am."

She is looking at the scars on my hands and arms, and is saying nothing to me.

My eyes are feeling heavy now, like I am very tired.

Mum makes a noise like she is about to say something, so I look at her with my half closed eyes. "What are we going to do with you, my baby?" she says to me, and she has a sad face on. "I just don't know what we are going to do."

I say, "I don't know," because I don't know what they are going to do with me. Then my eyes start to close, and I am falling asleep. My bedroom goes even darker through my eyelids, as I hear my mum tiptoeing away from me, and the door clicking closed.

Matthew Pickering
August 1995

Me and my mummy have come to a place called The Children's Hospital today. A lady called Doctor Waterstone is talking to Mummy, and I am playing with some of her toys. Doctor Waterstone is looking at me a lot and I don't like it. Right now, I am playing with a toy that is like a bendy wire, and it has got lots of different coloured beads on it. Some of the beads are green, some are yellow, some are red and some are blue. The blue beads are my favourites, because I am a boy and boys like blue.

I make one of the blue beads move along the bendy wire, and then I move it back again. The hole in the bead is about one and a half times as wide as the wire. I think that is so it can easily move along it. I look at the bead closely. I think that it is made of wood, because there are very tiny splinters at the edge of it, and my daddy says that you get splinters on wood. I think that the wood must have been painted blue though, because wood comes from trees, and trees are not blue, trees are brown. I flick the bead so that it spins around the wire. It turns four times, and then slows down, and stops. I do it again. This time it turns five times. I can count how many times because I am clever at counting, because my Nana Brady teaches me counting and spelling when I visit her at her flat. I spin the bead again.

There is a lot of noise in this room in The Children's Hospital, and I don't like it when there is lots of noise because it hurts my ears and makes me confused. There is a funny, spinning fan on the ceiling of the room, which is making a loud whizzing noise as it goes around, and I can hear Doctor Waterstone and Mummy talking to each other, and lots of talking and footsteps on the corridor outside. When I spin the bead around on the wire it makes a funny rolling noise, which makes the other sounds seem a little bit quieter, so I do it again.

I don't know why me and Mummy have come to The Children's Hospital today, because I am not poorly, and Mummy is not a child.

I spin my blue bead again.

"Matthew," I hear somebody say.

I spin the bead around again and it makes a rolling noise.

"Matthew."

I move the blue bead along, and pull a red bead into the middle of the wire. I spin that one, but it only does two spins and it jolts about a lot. I look at the hole in the bead, and it is smaller than the hole in the blue bead. Maybe that is why it would not spin as fast as the blue one.

I can see that Doctor Waterstone is standing up and walking towards me. She sits down on a chair across from me on my little table and says, "Hello, Matthew."

I do not look at her. I spin the red bead again, but it still only spins two times.

"Say hello," says Mummy.

I say, "Hello." I am not looking at Doctor Waterstone, because I am looking at the red bead, but I can see her a bit in the background.

"That's a cool watch you have on," she says, pointing to my train watch.

It is a very nice watch, because it has got the face of Thomas the Tank Engine on it, but it is not a cold watch. I look at her because I think she is a bit silly, but then I look away again.

"Who is that on your watch?" she asks me.

"Thomas," I answer, because it is Thomas on the watch. I like watching Thomas the Tank Engine, because it is very good. "You know just where to stop, Thomas," I say.

"Do you like Thomas?" Doctor Waterstone asks.

I say, "Yes," because I do like Thomas. "You know just where to stop," I say again, "you rotten engine."

I hear Mummy say, "That is all we ever get out of him," but I don't know what she means.

Doctor Waterstone says, "Repeating from television programmes?"

"All the time," Mummy says. "Usually from Thomas, but sometimes I have no idea where it comes from."

Doctor Waterstone puts her hand onto the toy I am playing with, and spins one of the green beads.

I look at her, and she smiles at me. I look away.

She spins a bead again.

I lift her hand away from the toy, and then I pull it closer towards me.

I hear Mummy say, "Sorry," but I don't know why.

Doctor Waterstone says, "It's fine, don't be silly."

"I am not a silly boy," I tell her, because I am not a silly boy.

Doctor Waterstone says, "No, you are not a silly boy."

I am glad. I spin the red bead again, but it is harder to see it now because I pulled it closer to my body.

The doctor says, "Do you like that toy?"

I say, "Yes," because I do like it.

Then she says, "Does he ever let you or your husband play with him? Or other children?"

I do not know what she means, so I do not answer her.

Mummy says, "No, never, he just does that; pulls the toys away from you if you try to join in. The only other living thing he will play with is my mum's greyhound puppy; he absolutely adores that thing and will chase her around the garden for hours, but when it comes to other human beings he's just not interested."

My mummy's voice is very quiet, and it is hard to hear her over all the other noises in the room. I can hear an ambulance siren outside, and I do not like it. I cover my ears up and blow air quickly through my teeth so I sound like a train, like Thomas. I can see that Doctor Waterstone is looking at me, so I close my eyes. When I can hear that the siren has stopped I open them again and pull my hands away from my ears. I stop my train noise.

Mummy is still talking. She is saying, "...even the slightest noise and he does it. I don't understand. Why does he cover his ears up and then make even more noise himself?"

Doctor Waterstone says, "It's a surprisingly common coping strategy, actually. He can block out unexpected external noise with something that he is in total control of. Lots of children do it."

"Children with autism, you mean?"

"Well, children who are overly sensitive to sound."

"But, you do think he has autism?"

The doctor is quiet for a few moments and she is looking at me, but I am spinning a green bead now, which spins very well. "Well, I will say that he is exhibiting a lot of the common characteristics, but we will need to do a few more tests before I can tell you anything more conclusive."

I hear my mummy take in a very deep breath, and I can see that she has made her head drop forwards, even though I am looking at my green bead.

Doctor Waterstone stands up and walks over to the chair near my mummy, and then she sits down again. She picks up a box with some tissues sticking out of the top from the big table, and puts it on my mummy's knee.

"I'm sorry, Mrs. Pickering. I know it's difficult, but try not to worry; nothing is definite yet."

My mummy doesn't say anything for a lot of seconds, and then she says, "You think he is though, don't you? Autistic? And so do I. I think I always knew it, really."

"It's perfectly understandable for you to be upset. Would you like to talk about how you are feeling?"

Mummy is quiet for another ten seconds. "John doesn't - John my husband - he doesn't seem to think there's anything wrong, he just thinks he's a naughty little boy." She takes another big breath, and I can see her putting one of the tissues up to her face.

I spin the green bead again.

"But he's not a naughty little boy. He's my little angel."

Doctor Waterstone says, "How is Matthew's relationship with your little girl? She's eighteen months, isn't she?"

"Sixteen," my mummy says. Then she pauses before she speaks again. "He hates her." She makes a funny noise, and lifts the tissue up to her face again.

"Take your time."

"I didn't mean that," Mummy says. "He doesn't hate her, I know he doesn't; he loves her. And she loves him, too... mostly." I can see that she is lifting her head up a little bit. "But he hates it when she cries; he can't stand it. It's not so bad now she's growing up a bit, but when she was newborn it was all the time. She would cry, and then he would scream, cover his ears and throw tantrums on the floor. You can imagine what that looked like in the middle of a supermarket."

"It sounds like it's been difficult for you," says Doctor Waterstone.

"Yes; for all of us, really. John just doesn't understand him. It's like he can't bond with him or something. And Hannah... well she idolises him, she really does, but sometimes she will shrink away from him, like she's frightened. It's heartbreaking to see, but you can't blame her. Did I say I caught him hurting her a couple of times?"

"Hurting her?"

"Sometimes, when she'd be crying and I couldn't reach her quick enough, he'd beat me to it. I'd go into her room and Matthew would be in there, screaming at her to stop crying and to be good... to be a 'good boy', actually." She makes a little laugh. "But sometimes... sometimes he wasn't just screaming; a couple of times I found him slapping her hand. It's just something we have done to him when he's been naughty - not in a bad way, you know, just a tap on the wrist..." Mum stops talking again, and I can see her taking a new tissue from the box and lifting it to her face. "I feel so awful for saying this. You must think we are the worst parents in the world?"

"Of course not," Doctor Waterstone says. "It's obviously just something that he has picked up and not understood the context."

"Well, we told him straight away. We said he's not to hit anyone, especially not his little sister. And we don't tap his wrist any more either, we don't want to confuse him."

"I think that's very sensible. It sounds to me like you're doing a fantastic job with him and are coping really well, but you don't need to do it on your own. If we can confirm a diagnosis for you then there's all sorts of help we can provide. Shall we carry on with the assessment for now? Are you okay?"

My mummy says, "Yes, I'm alright. Thank you, Doctor."

John Pickering
August 1995

A mate once told me that if I was ever lucky enough to have a daughter my heart would instantly melt and never quite fix itself back together again. I remember laughing hysterically at the time and telling him that he could no longer call himself a man after making a comment like that, but here I am, just a few years later, and I can almost feel my heart dripping down through my stomach as I watch my sleeping beauty. Not that anyone else will ever hear about that, of course. Hannah is the absolute spit of Susie, her beautiful mother, and it won't be too many years before she's melting the hearts of many other men as well, but none of them will ever love her quite as much as I do. Besides, she won't have a boyfriend until she is at least thirty-five so it's all moot for a while anyway.

Having a daughter is somehow a bit different from having a son. With Hannah, I feel an uncontrollable need to protect her from everything the world has to throw. With Matt, it's more like I want to teach him how to deal with the world for himself. That's why I am driven absolutely insane by Sue's constant pandering to him. He's the way he is because of her, I'm sure of it. If she'd just allow him to be a boy; to make mistakes, to fall down sometimes... She's taken him off to see some shrink again today; reckons there's something wrong with him. She drives me totally crackers with this. It's constant, and she refuses to listen to sense. Hopefully this doctor she's gone to see can make her realise it's all in her head. Perhaps book her in for a few sessions herself? That might sort her out a bit.

Don't get me wrong, I love Sue very much. It will be seven years in September that we've been married, and I couldn't have had a happier life with her. She's totally beautiful (way out of my league), and she's given me my two gorgeous babies, so I do hate arguing with her about this, but she needs to see things from my perspective a little bit more, and she needs to chill out.

I hear the front door opening and look at the fairy clock on Hannah's wall. An hour later than expected, but they must be back. I hear the faint sound of the Thomas the Tank theme tune hummed very out of tune, and know that they are. I brush Hannah's red hair back over her forehead and give her a little kiss before leaving her room, with the door slightly ajar, and heading downstairs.

"Alright, Champ?" I say, grinning at Matthew as he continues singing his little song while Sue struggles to pull his green fleece over his head. "Alright Babe?"

She sighs loudly as she finally gets the fleece over his chin. "Fine," she answers me, throwing the offending jumper onto the floor. Oh dear, this doesn't sound good so far.

I notice Matthew's hand, in which he is clutching what looks like a five-month-old empty packet of salt and vinegar crisps. The things that boy picks up to play with – correction - the things Sue lets that boy pick up to play with, are just foul. The minute he can understand me I am going to teach him all about those little things called 'germs'. See if I can stop him constantly bringing them into my house. He is lost in the world of crisp packets now, waving the faded blue foil in front of his face, and seems to have forgotten all about singing to Thomas.

Sue finishes pulling Matthew's shoes off his feet and looks up at me. "Well?" she says, as if I should telepathically know what she's on about.

"Well, what?"

"Aren't you going to ask how we got on?"

I *was* actually about to ask, but her tone irritates me. "I don't need to hear about some Quack's opinion on my own son." I grin at Matthew. "You're fine, aren't you, Kid?"

I reach out to take the dirty packet from him, but he turns away and starts hitting his other hand with it. Why can't he play with cars, or something, like most four year old boys?

"I knew you wouldn't care; you never care," is the next line that Sue throws at me. I don't know about time of the month, this woman seems to have constant PMT when she's around me.

"All right, what did the shrink say, then? Did she confirm for you that our boyo's got a screw loose?"

She flashes me a look I have seen more times than I'd like to admit, and throws her handbag onto the floor next to Matt's fleece. "Matty, go and play in the living room for a bit, Sweetheart. Mummy would like a little word with Daddy."

Great.

"A little word," Matthew says. This is ridiculous; he's almost five, yet doesn't seem to speak a word of sense.

Sue ushers him into the living room, shuts the door, and then marches into the kitchen. I assume I am supposed to be following.

As I walk into the room she is pulling off a square of kitchen roll and dabbing beneath her eyes with it. I think I need a beer. "Go on then," I say to her, in as nice a voice as I can muster, "enlighten me."

She reaches past me to close the kitchen door, presumably so Matthew can't hear. I don't know why she bothers; he wouldn't understand a word, even if he were stood right next to us. "The *psychologist*," she begins, saying the word slowly, as if I wouldn't have a clue what she was talking about if she spoke at normal human speed, "says that he's definitely got ... what we thought he had got."

'We,' she says. I can feel my temper rising. "What? Ignorant Kid Syndrome?" I reply. "Great, well I'm glad they cleared that one up for us. Not a waste of time at all, then."

Sue's eyes are wide, like she's about to grab a kitchen knife out of the block behind her at any second. Maybe I should take a couple of steps backwards. "No, you know the word I mean. And I don't remember you wasting any of your time coming along with us."

"Like I told you, I don't need someone I've never met to tell me my son's a hammer short of a toolbox. I can work that much out for myself. And yes, I do know the word you mean - autism - you've been banging on about it for long enough, you might as well say it."

She dabs her eyes again, but as far as I can see they're not even mildly wet. "I need you to start taking this seriously, John. I can't do it on my own any more."

I laugh at this, but the look on her face suggests it's probably not the best move. I straighten my face and take a deep breath. "Babe, you know I would support you to the death if it was something that I believed in, but 'autism'? It's a new fancy fad-word, made up to mean 'ignorant little sod'. I'm sorry, Babes, but it's a load of rubbish."

"It's a lot more common than you think, actually, and it's being diagnosed more and more these days."

"Of course it is, because it makes these so called doctors sound like they know what they're talking about, doesn't it? Don't fall for it, Suse."

She hits the kitchen work surface with her hand so hard that it makes me jump a little. I know this isn't what I should be thinking about right now, but the phrase about looking hot when angry really could have been written about my wife.

"Oh, you infuriate me, John, you really do." The apples of her cheeks are turning a shade of scarlet. "There is research; there is evidence to support it. It's not a 'fad word' as you like to call it."

I can't help but laugh this time. My wife, the scientist. "Go on, then, throw some research at me. Hit me with some facts."

"Oh," she says.

Oh. I smirk, and can see her face twisting up even more with anger. Anger at being caught out, presumably.

"Well, I don't know names and dates if that's what you mean?" She looks flustered. "Don't look at me like that. You think you're so clever. I *can* throw some facts at you, actually - like, autism is about four times more common in boys than in girls." She folds her arms, and gives me a look as if she's just proved me wrong about everything. And she says that I infuriate her; the feeling could not be more mutual.

"Well, I flaming well hope you're right about that, Sue, because I can't handle it if Hannah turns out like him too." I didn't mean to say that. I really didn't mean to say that, but I can't take it back now.

She looks at me as if I've just shot her, and makes that noise she always makes before the tears come pouring out. She covers her eyes with her hands and turns away from me.

"And on come the waterworks, right on cue."

I wait, but she doesn't say anything. Marvellous. She is so manipulative. And the worst thing about it is that it works. My head says to yell at her, and my heart says to put my arms around her and make it all okay. I take another deep breath and try to tone it down a bit. "Right, so say this autism baloney is true," (okay, I did just say a bit), "how do they plan on fixing it?"

After a moment she answers me in a voice I can barely hear. "You can't... you can't fix autism, John. It's a lifelong condition."

"Well, that's handy. I'm so glad you took him to that doctor, then."

She turns to scowl at me. "You are such a sarcastic sod."

Yep, I guess I deserved that.

"They can support us through it. They can support *him*."

I am getting fed up of this conversation. "Susan, he doesn't need a doctor, he just needs to man up a bit. And you could stop mothering him so much - 'Oooh, give me a cuddle, Matty,' - 'Oooh, give Mummy a hug, Darling.' He's a boy, for crying out loud. You'll have plenty of time for cuddles with Hannah."

"Oh, what? So, because he's a boy he doesn't need a mother's love?"

"He doesn't need smothering. Let him stand on his own two feet a bit."

"It's all my fault our son's got autism then, is it? It's because I mother him too much. Is that what you're saying?"

"No, because he hasn't got autism, or any other made up disorder. He just needs to learn some manners, that's all."

I actually think she might reach for that knife now.

"You are so wrong!" So much for sending Matthew into the living room, the old lady four doors up could probably hear her shouting now. "What's the matter with you? All I'm asking for is a bit of support from my husband. For him to love and care for his son."

That was too far. The lady up the road is about to hear a lot more from me too. "Don't you dare say I don't care! You, Matthew, and Hannah are everything to me, and I'd do anything for any of you, you know that."

"Then *support* us."

"I *am* doing." I turn away from her and try to calm myself. My temper is never good to me, and I need to chill it before I do something stupid. I take in a very deep breath, and slowly turn back to face her. I reach my hand out and place it on her left arm. "Can't you see, Baby? I'm doing the best I can. Have you never heard of tough love? I just don't want you to get drawn in by some crazy Quacks who think they know it all. Look at me. Who do you think, honestly now, who do you think knows our son better, his father, or some random doctors he's seen three times in his life?"

"You do, but - "

"Then trust me. My son does not have 'autism'; he's just a strange, rude little boy who needs to grow up a bit."

She brushes my hand away from her arm. "Oh, I'm sorry," she says, "I forgot about your psychology degree."

Now who's the sarcastic one?

"I don't need a degree to know my son. Seriously, we just need to get tougher with him. When you're in the town centre on a busy Saturday and he starts screaming and throwing himself onto the floor, what do you reckon people think? I'll tell you, they think, 'What an insolent little boy, with a mother who can't control him'. What about when he's twenty-five and still doing the same thing? Do you reckon they'll still just roll their eyes at him? No, he'll get beaten to a pulp. Trust me, the sooner we knock this thing out of him, the better. And we don't need any doctors to tell us how to do that."

She opens her mouth and holds up her finger at me, as if she is about to say something very profound. Then she closes it again, puts her hand back to her side, and walks out of the room.

Now I definitely need a beer.

Susan Pickering
September 1996

He moves his hands away from my face and down to my hips. I open my eyes.

"Surprise," he says.

I blink.

"Do you like it?"

I never really know what to say when someone spells out, 'I love you,' in salt across my kitchen floor. "You know, the old favourite anniversary presents are still good; necklaces, eternity rings, that sort of thing." I turn my head, and plant a kiss on his stubbly cheek.

"You're supposed to give salt as an eight year anniversary gift. Didn't you know that?"

I laugh. Last year he bought me a woolly jumper; the year before that a sugar bowl. He's clearly a man of traditions. "And you didn't think to get me a salt shaker, or something? Rather than pouring my existing salt all over the floor for me to clean."

He looks upset, so I kiss him again.

"Sweetheart, I'm joking. It's a lovely sentiment. Maybe I'll take that watch back to the shop, and write you a message out in porridge oats, instead."

He lets go of me.

"I'm kidding. It's really nice, honestly. And I love you, too." I turn to face him and place his arms around my waist. How did I ever manage to catch myself a man this hot? Sure, he's not in his seventeen year old prime, when I met and fell in love with the neighbourhood bad boy as he rode around our estate on his burgundy Harley, head to toe in black leather, with the sort of smile (and body...) that could break a thousand hearts in a single second, but he's certainly not spoiled. If anything, the shoots of grey appearing behind his temples only seem to add definition and culture to his face. The shoots of grey in my tangled mop, on the other hand...

"Well, I'm sorry about the cleaning," he says sulkily. "I'd better get to work."

"You're sure you have to work today?" I pull him towards me by his tie, kissing him gently on the lips. I breathe him in. Mmmm. There's something about the juxtaposed shirt and tie and the unexplainable 'factory man' smell he has that is somehow magnetic. John does well for us. He is one of the managers at the local printing factory and, although the wages aren't amazing, they are enough to allow me to be at home full time with the kids - and the washing - and the ironing - and the clearing up salt from the floor – so that's all I can ask for, really.

"I'm sorry, Gorgeous," he says through kisses. "I'll make it up to you, I promise." He pulls away from me, prises my hands from his tie and reaches for his jacket from the hook by the door.

"Whatever." I cross my arms in mock annoyance.

"Susie."

"What?"

"I love you."

"Hmmm."

He grins, pulls his jacket on, and gives me one last kiss before heading for the door. "Oh," he says as an afterthought as he pulls it open, "be sure to get that dustpan and brush out as soon as possible; we don't want the kids slipping on all that salt."

"Pig!" I shout as he closes the door behind him. I make my way back into the kitchen and smile. His message really is quite sweet, in a juvenile kind of way. I kneel down, pinch some of the salt between my thumb and forefinger, and throw it over my left shoulder; I could do without seven years of bad luck, thank you very much.

Throwing open the doors to the cleaning cupboard, I stare. Taped to the navy dustpan is a small note. I peel it off and read it.

To my gorgeous girl,
Eight years together is not enough.
Neither would eighteen be.
Not even eighty will do.
How about an eternity?
Take a look in the salt pot.
And then get dressed up for tonight – I'm
taking you out.
I love you with all my heart.
Your John x

I hug it to my chest. My John.

'Take a look in the salt pot'? I make my way to the condiments cupboard, open up the tub of salt (which now has absolutely no salt in; thanks John), and gasp. It's the one I saw in the window. It's the one I have been hinting at for months – or is it years? I instantly slip it over my finger, and it is a perfect fit.

My eternity ring: from *my* John.

Hannah Pickering
August 1997

Mummy and Daddy have been arguing again. It makes me very upset when Mummy and Daddy argue. Sometimes, when I can hear them arguing downstairs, I sneak into Matty's bedroom and climb into his bed. But I don't think Matty likes it when I do that because he always hides his head underneath his pillow and does not talk to me, so I don't go into his bedroom very much now.

Me and Matty are at Nana Brady's flat this weekend because Mummy and Daddy are going on a holiday. Nana said they are having a romantic weekend to make them forget their arguing. I don't know what a romantic weekend is, but I hope that they do forget to argue.

I do not like staying at Nana's flat very much, because me and Matty have to sleep in a tiny bedroom that is cold and full of boxes, and we have to share a bed. I do not like sharing a bed with Matty at my Nana's flat because he likes Nana's dog, Rose, to sleep on our feet, because he likes Rose a lot. I do not like Rose a lot; I think Rose is scary, and a bit smelly. Matty says that she smells of dog, and that it is a nice smell, but I think it is a horrible smell.

I want Matty to play with me today because I am very bored. It is a sunshiney day and me, Nana, Matthew, and Rose are in the little garden outside Nana's flat. Nana is doing some knitting, and Matty is holding a big stick and making Rose jump up to catch it with her mouth. That is a bit scary, and this is a small garden so Rose keeps nearly landing on me when she jumps.

"Lets play doctors, Matty," I say. "You pretend to break your leg and I will fix it."

Matty bends down and strokes Rose's back, and then he gives her a kiss and she licks all over his face.

I think that is disgusting.

"You can't be a doctor," he tells me.

"Why can't I be a doctor?" I want to be a doctor when I am a big lady. A doctor, or an ice-cream van driver.

"Because you are a girl. Girls can only be nurses."

I look at Nana because I want her to tell Matty that he is wrong. She carries on with her knitting, but she has got a smile on her face.

"Okay," I say in a cross voice, "I will be a nurse. You lie on the grass and I will fix your broken leg."

"I don't have a broken leg," he tells me.

"*Pretend* you have got a broken leg."

"But I haven't."

"It's a game; play with me."

He shakes his head. "I am playing with Rose; I don't want to play with you." He stands up again and throws Rose's stick across the garden for her to chase. She doesn't have far to run because it is a very small garden.

I feel sad. I want Matty to play with me.

"Ouch," says my nana, and I see her putting her knitting back in her bag when I turn around to look at her. "Oh, Nurse Hannah, I think I have broken my leg; can you come and fix it for me, please?"

I smile. "I am not Nurse Hannah, my name is Nurse Cinderella."

"Oh, sorry, Nurse Cinderella. Come quickly." She takes a ball of white wool out of her bag and gives it to me. "Here's a bandage, can you put it on my leg for me?"

"Yes, I can," I say, taking the bandage and starting to wrap it around her leg. "What is your name?"

"Oh, erm - "

"Your name is Ariel. Don't worry, Ariel, I will fix your broken leg."

When I am wrapping the bandage around Ariel's leg, something jumps onto my back and then starts to pull at the wool, and it is Rose.

"Rose, get away," shouts Nana.

Rose does not get away.

"Shoo," shouts Nana, and she pushes Rose away from me, but she does not go away.

Then I hear Matty say, "Come here, Rose. Heel."

Rose turns her head to look at him, and then she drops the wool out of her mouth and walks back to my big brother.

I am crying because I had a nasty surprise. My Nana picks me up, puts me on her knee, and gives me a big kiss and a cuddle. I love my Nana. I do *not* love Rose.

Matthew Pickering
May 1998

I am not asleep. I should be asleep because it is past my bedtime, but I am not because it is too noisy for me to be asleep. The ticking clock in my bedroom keeps me awake every night, even if I put my pillow over my head, and when I do put the pillow over my head my daddy always tells me to not be silly when he comes to check on me, and he puts it underneath me again. I have got to pretend that I am asleep when my daddy comes to check on me, because if I am not he gets cross with me and tells me that it was my bed time a long time ago and that I should be asleep now. If Mummy comes in to check on me when I am still awake she kisses me on my head and says, 'Come on now, Baby, it's very late; sleepy time now.' Mummy and Daddy both tell me that I have to go to sleep, but they don't take the ticking clock out of my bedroom, so I think that is it their fault that I cannot sleep.

Tonight it is definitely my mummy and daddy's fault that I can't sleep because they are doing some arguing downstairs. I cannot hear what Mummy is saying, but I can hear what my daddy is saying because he is shouting.

Daddy is saying, "Susan, would you just shut up about it? I know what's best for him."

Then there is a pause where I can hear a mumbly voice that I think is Mummy's.

"I don't want to hear it any more," Daddy carries on, "I am fed up with it. If you refuse to treat him like every other child, how can you expect him to grow up like every other child?"

More mumbling from Mummy.

"That flaming word again. There is *nothing* wrong with my son. How many times do I have to repeat myself? Nothing that some good old-fashioned discipline can't fix, anyway. I am fed up of hearing that the doctors say this, and a book you read says that. I don't care what they say. I know my son better than anyone. Better than you do, apparently."

Mummy's mumbling is very quiet this time.

"No, that's it now. I have had enough of this nonsense. I've put up with it from you for years, but not any more. I'm taking control of the situation now, and if you don't like it - well you know what you can do, don't you?"

Now I hear no mumbling.

"And the waterworks again. Brilliant. Every time I try to have a sensible conversation with you."

I hear the mumbling again.

"Yes, I do call it sensible, Sue. I call it living in the real world. That's what I call it. You seem to think that wrapping him up in cotton wool and letting him get his own way all the time is going to help him. Well I can tell you, it won't. That's a sure-fire way to a spoilt brat of a child, and a useless, hated adult."

Very quiet mumbling.

"I told you, I don't want to hear that word mentioned in my house again. You know I don't believe in that rubbish. When I acted up as a kid my dad gave me the slipper - the belt sometimes too, if I really deserved it - and I thank him for it because look at me now; a perfectly *normal* guy." Daddy shouts the word 'normal' the loudest of all.

I can hear that my mummy is crying, but it is not loud enough to hurt my ears.

"You seriously need to sort yourself out, Sue. Look at you; you are a mess. We have got a perfect little girl asleep upstairs so I know you are doing something right. Why can't you apply the same rules to Matthew?"

The mumbling is getting a little bit louder.

"You think I don't love him? You think I care about him any less than I care about Hannah? You are crazy. You are totally insane. My kids are my world; both of them. That's why I want to do the best for him, and I know what the best for him is, and it's not your little LaLa Land, dancing around him, doing anything to keep him happy way."

This time I can hear my mummy because she is shouting now, too. "I do not dance around him," she shouts.

"Oh, give me a break. You Tango him to school, and you Waltz him back home, and then you Foxtrot around him all evening until its time to Tango him off to school again. 'Yes, Matty. Of course, Matty. Anything you want, Matty.' This is why I won't even entertain that word you insist on using all the time, because I know what's causing his problems, and it is nothing more than *you*. You are the problem here. You."

There is a pause. It is silent for a few seconds, other than the ticking of my clock, and then the door from the living room beneath me clicks open and feet start to stamp up the stairs.

"How *dare* you?" Mummy is shouting these words as she stamps up the stairs. I think that they have forgotten that me and Hannah are trying to sleep upstairs because they are not being very quiet.

I pull my pillow over my head and hope that Daddy doesn't come into my bedroom and see it.

"Don't follow me," Mummy shouts. I can still hear what they are saying, even though my pillow is over my head.

"Of course I'm going to follow you," Daddy shouts, stamping up the stairs too. "Do you think I'm going to let you go to bed before we sort this out?"

"I'm not going to bed," Mummy shouts, but I can hear her walking into her bedroom so I wonder what she is doing in there if she is not going to bed. I hear her open her wardrobe door.

"Oh, I see," says Daddy loudly, "a bag; how mature. What a good way to solve this, Sue; running away."

"I don't want to solve it," Mummy says. "Not this time. I have had enough and I'm going. Seriously, I am going."

"Don't be ridiculous. Sue. Susan Pickering, you put that bag down. I'm telling you, put it down."

"You don't get to tell me what to do, John. I'm not one of your minions at the factory."

"No, you're not. You are my wife, and you can't just leave me."

"Of course I can."

I feel sad now, because I think that my mummy is going to leave this house, and then I won't live with my mummy any more. I make my train noise quietly, but it doesn't stop the shouting.

"No, you can't. Where will you go?"

"Where do you think?"

"Oh, I see. Running off to Mummy's again, are you? For what, the fifth time? Go then, and I wonder how long it will be before you are back this time. A week, maybe two? Oooh, you could even stretch it out to three; beat your record."

"I won't be back. Not this time."

"So you're abandoning your kids, then? Finally got too much for you, did they?"

"No they didn't, *you* did. And it won't be for long; just until I can get myself sorted with a place and then I will be back for them." There is a pause from the shouting, and now all I can hear is cupboards and drawers being opened and closed.

When Daddy speaks again he is a bit quieter. "Sue, come on, don't do this. Don't go."

Mummy is laughing. "What, scared of being left alone with the kids, are you? I would have thought you would be pleased; get rid of my bad influence for a bit and sort him out your way."

"Come on, Baby, you don't need to leave. We can make this work."

"Can we? How?"

There is a pause, and then Daddy says, "You just need to listen to me, and trust me a bit more with this Matthew thing. We can sort him out together, I know we can."

I hear Mummy make a loud grunting noise, and open another cupboard door. "That was it, John. Last chance - gone. No more, I am telling you now, no more. I will be back for the rest of my stuff tomorrow. And as soon as I'm sorted with a place I will be back for the kids. Tell them Mummy loves them. Tell them I will be back - for them, not you."

And then I can hear my mummy's feet running down the stairs. I can tell that they are Mummy's feet on the stairs because they sound different to Daddy's. Daddy's feet don't follow her.

I hear him say, "Leave us, then," and then he closes the bedroom door, and I hear his mattress wobble loudly so I think that he must have fallen onto his bed.

I can hear a little bit of banging about downstairs, and then I hear the front door open and close again. I hear a car door opening and closing next, and then an engine turning on. Then I hear the car driving away.

It is quiet in my house now, except for the ticking of my clock, and a very quiet crying noise coming from Hannah's bedroom.

* * *

It is very early when I get up the next morning. It is Saturday morning so I think that there might be some funny cartoons on the television. I go downstairs to turn them on. The sky outside is a little bit light, but still a little bit dark, so I know that it is early in the morning. I walk into the living room to turn on the television, and it looks different in here. The curtains are closed, and it smells funny. It smells like Daddy smells when he has been to the pub. I reach up as far as I can reach and turn the light on.

I can see that my Daddy is fast asleep on the settee, and he has got a little blanket on his body. There are lots of empty drink cans on the floor next to the settee. I wonder if my Daddy has drunk them all, because if he has I bet he will need to go to the toilet a lot. Daddy makes a funny noise and rolls over a bit when I turn the light on.

I pick up the television remote control and sit down on the soft, fluffy carpet, in the middle of the room. I press the number three on the remote control, because I know that there are usually some good cartoons on channel three on early Saturday mornings. The television is quiet for some seconds, and then it makes a kind of crackling noise, has a small flash of light come out of it, and the red light on the bottom of it turns green. Suddenly cartoons come on, and they are very loud. I don't like it when cartoons are very loud, so I cover my ears quickly with my hands. I can still hear the loud cartoon, and I can also hear a very loud grunting noise.

I turn to look at my Daddy, where the noise came from, and he is sitting up, looking at me with a very cross face on. His eyes are a pinky colour, and his hair is sticking up in lots of different directions. Daddy stands up, walks very quickly over to the television, and presses a big button on it that makes it turn off.

I say, "I was watching cartoons," in a cross voice, because I feel cross that Daddy turned the television off, even though I am a bit glad that the loud sound has gone away now.

"And I was sleeping, you ignorant little brat." Daddy is shouting at me now, and I don't like it. He walks quickly back over to the settee, and stands on an empty can, which makes a crunchy noise. Then he sits down and pulls the blanket over himself again. "Say sorry," he says to me.

I look at him.

"When people are cross with you, you have to say sorry, so say sorry."

"Sorry," I say, although I wonder why Daddy didn't say sorry to me for turning my cartoons off, because I was cross with him for doing that. "Where's Mummy?" I ask.

"Mind your own business," Daddy says, holding the front of his head with his hand and closing his eyes.

"Is she coming back?"

"Would you come back if you knew you were coming back to *you*?" he says.

I think he is asking me a question, but I don't understand what it means, so I just look at him.

He opens his eyes a little bit and looks at me too. "It's all your fault, you know?"

I do not understand. "What is all my fault?" I ask.

"Everything." He rubs the sides of his eyes with his pointing fingers.

I do not understand.

"It's your fault your mum's gone," he says. "Make you feel good about yourself, does it? That you drove your mummy away?"

I still do not understand. I start to bounce my right hand on the soft fluffy carpet, because it is a little bit bouncy. "She drove the car herself," I tell him. "I can't drive."

"Oh believe me, you can. You drive me up the wall, you drive your mummy away, and you drive everyone else around the bend."

I really don't know what my Daddy is talking about.

"Don't ever expect to have friends, Matthew. Not if you keep on driving like this."

I bounce my left hand in time with my right hand. I look at my Daddy, and he is stretching his legs back onto the settee again. He pulls the blanket over his legs and tucks it under his big feet. I think my Daddy is silly, because he should know that I can't drive. No one can drive until they are seventeen years old, by the legal law of England. In the United States of America people can drive when they are fifteen or sixteen years old, but in England you have to be seventeen years old to drive, and I am only seven.

"Matthew," my daddy says, "would you go away now, please? I need some sleep, and I don't want to look at you right now."

"Is Mummy coming back?" I ask him again, because he did not answer me the first time that I asked him. Daddy lays his head down on a settee cushion and looks at me through half closed eyes.

"In a bit," he says. "When she comes can you tell her something for me, please?"

I say, "Okay."

Daddy closes his eyes. "Tell her to take you with her. She can leave Hannah if she wants, but tell her to take you. Okay?"

"Okay," I say.

Susan Pickering
January 2000

I can't believe that I am a single parent at the wrong side of thirty-five, bringing up my children in a two-bedroomed flat with my mother. What did I do? What did I actually do to deserve this? My daughter whines non-stop that she wants her own bedroom, my son has barely got a relationship left with his father, and my mum - not that she moans - but she doesn't want to live like this.

I've been seeing this man, Ian, for a while now. He is a doctor, and could not be more lovely to me and the kids, which is more than I can say for that ex of mine. He watches hours of The Simpsons (the most recent obsession) with Matty, and takes him out for long walks with Mum's dog, Rose (another of Matt's great loves in life); never once complaining. I can't even *imagine* John doing that. And he spoils Hannah rotten with presents and things; and me, come to think of it, although he is stinking rich so I suppose it's not a massive deal to him. He is so much more considerate than John ever was, and he's just as handsome... if a little older... with a little less hair. I have been seeing him for around four months now, and things could not be better with him. He's wonderful.

I rarely even think about my husband... ex husband, these days. I don't even miss him any more. I suppose there are some things that I will always love about him to some extent, but I never really think about those things. He's in my past now. I only ever see him when I am dropping the kids off with him, or when he picks them up from Mum's. And we still have the odd argument over his treatment of his only son, but that never gets me anywhere. John is what he is, and that will never change. At least he is trying a little bit with Matthew. He fancies himself as a bit of a carpenter, and he's building some sort of wooden go-kart in his shed, which he lets Matty help him with - something that I'm not sure I'd dare do, but Matty raves about it whenever he comes home from a weekend with his dad, so I suppose he must enjoy it. John's always been quite handy when it comes to physical things. I suppose that's how he's got such a good body... No, Susan. Remember, he's still an arrogant idiot who hasn't got a clue when it comes to families. An arrogant, sharp-tongued, dominating, hot...stop it.

As I was saying, Ian is fabulous, and he is such a gentleman. He has taken me out to our favourite restaurant tonight for a romantic meal. I say 'our' favourite restaurant, I didn't actually know it existed until a couple of months ago, but I do quite like the chocolate and pistachio cheesecake they do for pudding, so I go along with it. And hey, if he's paying, what's not to like?

He's dressed up very smartly this evening. Perhaps even more smartly than usual. So much so that I might feel a little uncomfortable, but as I now know how to doll myself up for an evening here I don't feel too horrendously out of place... like I did the first time. Ian seems to be topping up his drink a lot tonight (if he's a closet alcoholic I'm going to freak out; John's borderline addiction was enough to last me a lifetime), and he seems to be taking ages looking at the menu, even though he's been here so many times he must know the entire thing by heart.

"Are you okay?" I ask, noticing a bead of sweat forming above his eyebrow.

He peers over the menu, with an expression that would suggest he was surprised to see me there. "What? Oh, yes, I'm fine."

Dating Ian is very different to being with John. Ian is safe. He doesn't muck around like other men, and he is relatively baggage free... although you would expect there to be a little in the background of a man of fifty-two. He does have a sort of step-daughter from a previous relationship, but I don't think he has a massive amount to do with her anymore. She lives with her grandmother since her mum, Ian's ex, died in some accident. I don't really know much more about her except that she has a really odd name - something like 'Sunshine' or 'Rainy'... he doesn't talk about her very much.

"Something scary on the menu?" I ask, wondering why his hands are now shaking.

He looks confused. "Scary? No. I don't understand."

"Never mind." I wouldn't call Ian boring. No, definitely not boring. He's not quite as interesting as John was, but look where interesting got me. No, Ian is safe, and that is just what I need at this time in my life; safety and security.

My thoughts are interrupted by the waiter, who appears behind me. "Your champagne, Madam." He places an empty glass in front of me and holds an open bottle beside it.

"I have my drink already," I say apologetically, "you must have the wrong table." I smile up at him, but he is looking at Ian.

"I... I wanted this to be special," Ian says, placing his menu down on the table. His hands are visibly trembling in front of me.

"I don't need champagne to make our evening special," I reassure him. He should know by now that I actually really don't like the stuff.

He reaches forwards and takes my left hand in his right. "You deserve it, though. Is your glass clean enough?" I think he may have lost it slightly.

I feel a little embarrassed at his suggestion, and flash the waiter another apologetic smile.

He grins back at me.

"I'm sure everything is very clean."

"Just take a look."

I raise my eyebrows slightly, but co-operate, and take a fleeting glance towards the glass. "It's fine..." I notice something. Something is sparkling at the bottom of the glass. I blink, but when I re-open my eyes the massive diamond is still there, perched on the bright golden ring. "Oh."

"You see it?"

"Er... yeah." I am not sure what to say or do. It feels like the whole room is silent, although I am sure everyone else has enough of their own worries to care about my dilemma.

I am reminded of the day John proposed to me; not that he even had a ring to offer. He took me out for a ride on his Harley, and as we stopped at traffic lights he shouted back to me, 'Are you going to marry me, or what?' It was the least, yet the most romantic moment of my life, and there wasn't even a second of hesitation before I answered with the loudest, 'Yes,' I could muster. Now I am struggling to find any words to say.

"Do you like it? Try it on."

I am not sure I want to try it on, but I can feel his eyes boring into me. I tip the ring into my open hand and try it on the ring finger of my right hand.

"No, it's not… it's not really for that hand."

I feel like arguing that if he buys me a gift it should be my decision how I choose to wear it. He reaches over, takes my right hand, and gently removes the ring. Then he moves it across to my other hand and pushes it onto my recently empty wedding ring finger.

"Thanks," I mumble, "it's beautiful."

"Just like you are."

I feel a little bit sick.

"What do you say?"

I really don't know what to say. I feel very hot. "I think I just need some air." I stand up quickly, lifting my clutch bag from beside me, and walk determinedly to the door. I don't look back, and he doesn't call after me.

* * *

I have been sitting in the back of this taxi for an hour and a half, and I think the driver is getting more than a little miffed with me. First, I made him drive me back to Mum's, but then I realised what a complete cow I was being and asked him to take me back to the restaurant. However, as we were pulling up outside I knew I couldn't face it. I couldn't face him.

All of the drive back to Mum's I knew where I was eventually going to send the poor guy, but I put off the inevitable for as long as possible. When we were within a mile of home I gave him the address I really wanted him to take me to. This is where I have got to go. John will always be the love of my life; I don't think that will ever go away. And right now he is the only person in the world that I want to see.

My tummy is flipping over as we turn the last corner and the taxi starts to slow down. This is exactly where I need to be, this is my home. John is my home. I feel like I am finally seeing the world clearly again. Who cares about the differences we have? They're what make us what we are. I'm not sure that I even feel nervous now, just excited. I throw a wad of notes at the driver as he pulls up outside the house, and I hurriedly open the door.

I can hear laughter behind me, and turn to look. In shock, I slam the door shut again, craning my neck to watch through the window.

It is John. John, and a very young, very blonde girl, who is almost smothered under the weight of his heavy shoulder. They don't appear to have noticed the car, even though it is parked directly outside his house. They stop just yards from where I am sitting, and my heart seems to disappear as they entangle one another in a heavy embrace.

"Are you getting out, Lady?" the driver asks.

I cannot answer him. I am frozen. I watch as John begins to pull the girl into the house by her faux leather jacket.

* * *

It is only the second ring and he answers. "Susan?"

"Yes, it's me."

"What happened to you last night? I went back to Nora's but she said she hadn't seen you. I'm really sorry if I upset you. I know I was trying to move things too fast. I'm so sorry."

"Shush," I tell him. "Just to clarify, were you asking me to marry you last night?"

"Well of course I was, but - "

"Yes," I interrupt him. "I would love to be your wife."

Matthew Pickering
July 2000

Today my mum got married. But she did not get married to my dad, because she already got unmarried to him when I was eight years old. Today my mum got married to a man called Ian Hobson. He used to be called Doctor Hobson because he was one of my doctors when I was little, but now he is married to my mum, so I call him Ian Hobson instead.

My mum has got a different name now, too. She used to be called Susan Jane Pickering, but today her name has become Susan Jane Hobson. I am a little bit sad about that because I liked it when me, and my sister, Hannah, and my mum and my dad all used to have the same last name of 'Pickering'.

My mum's wedding this morning was a bit boring because there was lots of talking that I had to listen to. It made me tired and I yawned in a loud voice, but then lots of people looked at me, and I don't know why. My sister, Hannah, looked at me and said, "Shush," in a whispery voice, and then she looked to the front of the room again, where Mum and Ian Hobson were standing and holding hands.

My little sister looks funny today because she is wearing a long, purple dress, and she never wears dresses, even though she is a girl. It is because she is a bridesmaid, which means that she has got to wear a dress and carry some flowers. I think she looks a bit silly because the dress is too long and it hits the floor, and she keeps tripping over it when she walks. She has made a rip in the bottom of her dress, but I am not supposed to tell Mum that because Hannah might get into trouble.

I look very smart today. I am wearing a black suit, and a white shirt, and a little jacket without arms, called a waistcoat, and a funny thing that is like a tie, but is not a tie, called a 'cravat'. My cravat is the same purple colour as Hannah's dress, which I think is a bit funny.

My Mum looks very pretty today because she has got a long white dress on that is called a wedding dress, and Nana said to me that she looks very pretty and 'stunning', but I don't know what that means. Hannah said that Mum looks like a princess, and I think that she is right because Mum has got a crown on her head like princesses wear. Also, my mum and Ian Hobson got married in a big room inside a castle, which is like where princes and princesses get married.

I like Ian Hobson. I think that he is a nice man, and he is very kind to me. Ian Hobson has got lots of money because he is a doctor, and so I like him a lot because he buys me lots of nice things, like a big model of the Statue of Liberty. The Statue of Liberty is a big statue that lives in New York, in the United States of America, and I like it a lot because I really like the United States of America, even though I have never been there. Next week, Ian Hobson is going to take me, and Hannah and Mum to Florida, in the United States of America for something called a Honeymoon. I am very excited about going there for our honeymoon, but I wish that we were going to visit all of the fifty states and not just Florida. I asked Ian

Hobson if we can visit all of the states when we are there, but he told me that we can't, which I am sad about.

I also like Ian Hobson very much because he said yes when Mum asked if Rose, my nana's greyhound dog, could move into his house with us because Nana is too frail to look after her. I love living with Rose so much because she is my best friend, and it makes me very, very happy. Rose sleeps on my bed with me every night in Ian Hobson's big house, and that is a very good thing. I am very upset that Rose was not allowed to come to this wedding, because Mum said that this is a wedding for family and friends to come to and Rose is both of these; because she is in our family and she is my best friend too. I think it is very horrible that she was not allowed to come to this wedding today, and I will miss her a lot tonight because she will not be sleeping on the bottom of my bed like she usually does, because I am not sleeping in my bedroom tonight.

Ian Hobson also bought me a computer for my new bedroom so that I can play computer games and learn things on the Internet. I am very clever on my computer, and it means that I can learn lots of facts about my favourite things, like the United States of America, and The Simpsons television show and rivers. I like rivers a lot because they make me feel calm, because they are nice to watch and listen to. I know lots about rivers, and The Simpsons, and the United States of America and computers, because I like to learn things, and I like to know how things work.

There are some things that I don't like about Ian Hobson, though. I do not like that he is making my mum have a different name to me, because I like it when my mum has the same name as me because that is how it is supposed to be. I also don't like that

Ian Hobson has made my dad very sad. My dad says that Ian Hobson is an 'idiot wife stealer', but I think that that is a little bit silly because my mum was not my dad's wife any more when she was boyfriend and girlfriend with Ian Hobson, so I do not think that he is a wife stealer. I think that my dad is very sad that my Mum has got married to Ian Hobson because he told me that he did not want her to marry him. He said that he would stop the wedding and that she would not get married to him, but I think that he was lying because he did not stop the wedding, and my mum did get married to Ian Hobson this morning.

* * *

Now, it is the wedding party. There is lots of loud music at this party, and lots of people are singing and dancing in the big castle room where we have been all day. There are flashing lights and the room smells like cigarettes, which I do not like. Some people are shouting loudly, and I think that they have been drinking lots of wine because I know that drinking wine makes people shout loudly. Hannah is holding hands with my mum and my Uncle Henry's stepdaughter, Louise, who is also a bridesmaid, and they are dancing too.

My nana has gone upstairs to stay in a bed in the castle, which I think is very funny. I am going to stay in a bed in the castle tonight too, and I am very excited about it because I have never stayed in a bed in a castle before. Ian Hobson is sitting at a big table with his brother, Robbie Hobson, who is his best man, and lots of other men, who I think are Ian Hobson's friends.

I do not like it in this room because it is too loud and too smelly, and I do not like the lights. It is raining outside, and usually I do not like the rain, but I don't mind this rain because it is quite warm because it is the month of July. It is still light outside too. I think that there are not many people out there because they don't want to get wet, so I decide to go outside, because I think that it will be nice and quiet out there.

I walk out of the big castle doors onto a large bit of grass in the middle of the castle. I was right when I thought that it would be a lot quieter outside than inside, because it is, and I think that this is good. I like it outside. I can hear some birds chirping, but it is a quiet sound, and it is a bit of a nice sound. I can also hear the rain dripping, but it is only soft rain and so it does not hurt my ears. I do not like rain that it is hard because it is loud, and it is scary, and it hurts my ears. I especially don't like rain when it is a rainstorm and there is thunder and lightening with it, because those things are very, very scary. I also don't like getting wet from the rain.

I am getting a little bit wet now. I can see a small shed on the other side of the garden and its door is a little bit open. I think that it must be quiet and dry in that shed, so I walk over to it because I want to go inside. When I reach the shed I open the door a little bit wider. It is quite dark inside and it has got a funny 'shed' smell. I know that it is a shed smell, because it smells like the shed in my dad's garden, and it smells like the shed in my garden at Ian Hobson's house. It has got lots of gardening tools inside it, and they are hung up on the walls.

"Do you mind?" a voice says.

I look down to the dirty floor, and I see a girl sitting there. My dad taught me that dirty things have got lots of germs on them, so I think there must be lots of germs on the floor. Maybe she should not be sitting on it. The girl has got long, straight, yellow hair that is covering most of her face, and she has got her knees pulled up to her chin.

I don't mind that she is there, so I say, "No."

She looks up at me, and I can see her face in the little bit of light that is coming through the door. She looks like she is a bit older than me, but not a lot older. I think that maybe she is in senior school. I wonder why she is sitting on the floor in this shed.

"I want to be alone," she says to me.

"So do I," I tell her. "People are very noisy at the wedding party."

"I'm Hinting," she says, making a funny face at me. Her face looks a bit ugly when she does that, because she scrunches it up and it goes all wrinkly.

"I'm Matthew," I tell her. "You have a funny name."

She makes one of her eyebrows lift up. "How do you know my name?"

I think she is a bit silly, because she just told me her name.

Now she scrunches her face up again.

"Because you told me," I answer.

"No I didn't."

I think this girl is silly.

"Rain."

"Yes," I say, walking into the shed a bit more so that I don't get wet, "but it's soft rain, and it isn't too loud or too scary."

"No. Raine is my name," she tells me. "R-a-i-n-e."

I am confused. "You said your name is Hinting?"

She puts her hands over her face and makes a moaning noise. "Could you leave me alone, please?"

"But I want to stay in here too," I tell her. "It is too noisy in the castle, and too wet outside."

She doesn't say anything for a second, but then she takes her hands away from her face and looks at me. "Fine," she says, "sit down. But can you be quiet?"

I look at the dirty floor. I am not sure I want to sit down on it in case I get germs, but my legs are getting tired. "Yes," I say, because I can be quiet. I like being quiet. I sit down on the floor and I cross my legs, but I make sure I don't touch it with my hands. I am a little bit worried that my new suit is going to get dusty from this floor and that Mum will be cross.

Me and the girl whose name I do not understand are sitting quietly. She is resting her head on her knees, and she is looking at the floor. I am looking at her. She is wearing jeans trousers, and a top that looks like it is a lot too big for her. It is coloured in lots of different colours, and has got some funny patterns on it.

After some minutes, she looks up. "Would you stop looking at me?" she asks.

"Sorry," I say, because she seems to be cross with me. I look at the floor and count how many floorboards I can see. There are twelve. The shed is quiet again.

Then the girl speaks. "So who are you, anyway? Susan's son, or something?"

"Yes, I am Susan's son, because Susan is my mum."

"And you're called Matthew?"

"Yes." I wonder if I am allowed to look at her yet.

"I'm Raine," she tells me. "Raine Bishop."

"Oh," I say. "I think that Raine is a silly name."

I hear her laugh a little bit, so I decide to look up at her. She is not smiling, but I did hear her laugh. She is not looking at me; she is looking at the floor. "So do I," she says. "My mum was a bit of a hippy, you know?"

I do not know what she means. "What is a hippy?"

"A bit like this," she says, sitting up and waving her big, colourful top about.

That does not really answer my question.

"I guess I got it from her."

"Your mum gave you that top?"

"Not the top. My hippyness." She looks at me like she is waiting for me to understand, but I don't. "Never mind," she says eventually, and she looks at the floor again.

"Is your mum at this wedding party?" I ask her. I think that I would like to meet Raine's mum so that I could learn about what a hippy is, because I like to learn things.

"My mum's dead," she tells me. "She died when I was five."

"Oh," I say.

Raine doesn't look sad or happy. She just keeps staring at the floor.

"My mum's still alive," I tell her.

Now she looks at me, but she is quiet for a few seconds. "You're strange," she says after a pause. "Has anyone ever told you that you're strange?"

"Yes," I say, because lots of people have told me that I am strange.

She looks at the floor again.

Then I think of a question that I want to ask her. "How do you know my mum?" I ask.

"Susan?" she says. "I don't. I know Ian. He was my... well, him and my mum were very close, before..." she stops.

"Before what?" I ask.

"Before she died." She is still not looking at me. "It was six years ago now, so I don't blame him for finding someone new. I just never really had a dad, so I thought... you know."

I don't know what she means, and I don't know how she never had a dad, because everyone has a dad. My dad lives in a different house to my mum; but I still have a dad. "You must have a dad," I tell her.

Now she looks at me, and she smiles. "You've clearly had a nice life up on Walton's mountain."

I don't know what she means.

"Let me guess - your dad is this perfect man, who always gives your mum money to look after you, and always plays football with you, and takes you out to the seaside?"

"I don't like football," I say.

"Yeah, well, my dad didn't stick around long enough to even see me be born. That's how much he cared about me. I've never seen him; not once in my life."

"Are you an orphan?" I ask, because I know that people who don't have a mum or a dad are called orphans.

"Kind of," she answers.

"Do you live in an orphanage?"

She laughs a bit, and stretches her legs out in front of her. Her feet are nearly touching my knees. "I live with my grandma: my mum's mum."

I am surprised. "So did I," I say, "but now I live in Ian Hobson's house."

"So did I," she says in a quiet voice.

I am looking at her shoes now. They are pink, and the bottom of them is quite thin at the front, and very thick at the back. There are pink feathers stuck to the straps on her shoes.

"Anyway," she says. "Why did you want to get away from the party?"

"I don't like parties," I tell her. "They are too noisy."

"I don't like parties, either," she says. "There are too many people there."

"Don't you like people?"

"Not really," she tells me. "People ask too many questions. People expect you to be cool and interesting all the time. People will never let you just be you, you know what I mean?"

I do not know what she means.

"Sometimes I wish people just didn't care about me. I wish people would just leave me to it. Like you, you don't care about me, do you?"

"No," I say, because I do not really care about this girl.

"See, that's good. Now I don't have to put on a nice person act around you. I can just be me, because you don't care about me, right?"

I look at her, and she does not look sad or happy, she just has a straight-line mouth.

"See, you don't even care enough to answer. That's good, that's what I like. That's what I'm used to. The only person in the world who ever cared about me was my mum, and look what happened there. I suppose my grandma cares about me on some level, but I don't care about her. I don't want to, because the minute you love someone you put yourself in danger, you know what I mean?"

"No," I answer.

She is quiet for a second. "Are you, I don't know... different, or something?" she asks me.

"Yes, I am different. My dad tells me that I am different. He says that I am naughtier than most boys. He thinks I should be more good."

Raine's eyes go a bit wider and she smiles a little bit. "What do you do that's so naughty?" She looks like she is excited that my dad thinks I am naughty.

"I don't know," I answer, because I do not know what I do that is so naughty. "My mum says that I am a good man."

"Well, your mum would. That's what mums say. Even murderers' mums probably say that their kids are good, deep down. Your mum doesn't count. So, have you got special needs or something?"

"I don't know."

"You seem like you have. Don't think I'm a cow or anything, but you do seem like you have."

I think she is silly, because I do not think she is a cow, because she is a human. "I don't think you are a cow," I tell her.

"Good. Not that I care what you think. I'd prefer it if you didn't like me, to be honest. Most people don't."

"Most people don't like me," I tell her.

"I can believe that." She picks up a small plant pot from the floor next to her and puts it over her left hand. She makes it spin around. "But you shouldn't care what other people think about you. Trust me, I know these things. I've learned these things. I bet I'm older than you; I have more life experience. How old are you, anyway?"

"I'm almost ten years of age," I tell her.

"Oh, I was right. I'm twelve; well, I'm nearly twelve. Close enough. So what school do you go to? A normal one or a special needs one?"

"I go to Harleyfield Junior School," I tell her.

She spins the plant pot again. "Oh, right. A normal one, then. So you'll probably come to Harleyfield High in a couple of years?"

"Yes," I say, because I think that I will go to Harleyfield High School when I'm older.

"That's my school. I'm in year seven."

I look at her, but I don't say anything.

"Are you going into year five?"

"Yes," I tell her, because she is right.

She puts the plant pot down and stares at my face. "Don't get me wrong," she says, "but you don't say a lot, do you?"

"You asked me to be quiet," I remind her.

"Well, it's freaking me out. Talk to me. Tell me something."

"What should I tell you?"

"I don't know... tell me what you want to be when you grow up."

"An actor," I tell her, because I would like to be an actor when I grow up.

"Really, why?"

"I want to go to Hollywood, in the United States of America, and I want to be an actor in movies, because I like movies, and I like the United States of America."

Raine's eyebrow goes up high again. "You know that will probably never happen, don't you? I bet you wouldn't be a very good actor, especially because you have got special needs or something. Anyway, it would be really hard, even if you were a good actor."

"Oh," I say. I feel a bit sad.

"So, ask me what I want to be when I grow up."

"What do you want to be when you grow up?"

"A conservationist."

I don't know what that is. "What's that?"

"I'm not sure, but it's what my mum did. It's about saving trees and animals, I think."

"I like animals," I tell her.

"Oh. Have you got any?"

"I've got my nana's old dog, and she is called Rose."

"Oh." She looks at my face. "Do you like me yet, Matthew?"

"Not really," I tell her.

"Good." She looks at the floor again, and I watch a daddy long legs walking up the wall behind her. "So, ask me why I'm in the shed," she says.

"Why are you in the shed?"

"Because I don't know anyone at the wedding; only Ian and my grandma, but she's busy talking to the old people, and he's busy talking to drunk men. I can't wait till I'm older and I can get drunk."

"I don't like drunk people," I tell her.

"I don't care," she says, "it doesn't matter if you don't like me. Anyway, I wanted to get away from everyone so I came and hid in here, but then you followed me." She is looking at the floor and she is looking cross.

"Sorry," I tell her.

"It's okay. You are all right to talk to, I suppose."

Suddenly, I hear somebody shouting my name, but it is not my mum, or Ian Hobson, or my sister or my nana. It is somebody that should not be here: it is my dad. I think he is outside in the garden, and he is shouting my name.

"That's my dad," I tell Raine.

"I haven't got a dad," she tells me.

I stand up, and I walk to the door, because I am wondering why my dad is at Mum and Ian Hobson's wedding, and why he is shouting for me. It is not raining any more, so I walk outside.

I turn around and say, "Bye," to Raine, but she isn't looking at me.

She does not answer.

I close the door a little bit, and I can see that Dad has seen me.

"Matt, my boy." He is running towards me now, and his arms are open wide.

I stand still, and watch as he gets closer to me.

Then he wraps his arms around me and squeezes tight. It feels nice on my arms. "Haven't you got anything to say to your old dad?" he says. He smells like he has been at the pub, and he is talking like he has been at the pub, too. I think he is drunk, and I don't like it when my dad is drunk because I don't like drunk people.

"Why are you at this wedding?" I ask him, because I am wondering why he is here.

"Why am I... well, of all the welcomes. Where's your sister?"

"I don't know," I answer. "She was dancing with Mum before I came outside."

"Inside? No, I can't go inside. Be a good boy and get her for me, will you?"

"Why do you want me to go and get Hannah, Dad?"

"Son, I let my wife go to this loser, do you really think I'm going to let my kiddies go, too? Do you think I'm going to let you start calling him 'Dad' instead of me? That's crazy. Go and get Hannah."

I do not understand what he means, but I know that he wants me to go and get Hannah. "Okay," I say. I walk across the garden towards the castle, and I try to ignore all the loud sounds from the party.

Luckily, Hannah and Mum are very close to the doors because they are not dancing any more, so I do not have to go into the very loud part of the room to find her.

I walk up to them.

"Hi, Sweetheart," my mum says. "Where were you?"

"In the shed," I tell her.

She puts a worried face on, and bends her body towards the door so that she can see out to the shed. I don't think she can really see outside from where she is, though. "The shed?"

"Hannah, you have to come outside. Dad wants you."

Hannah stands up and says, "Okay."

Mum looks at me. "What?" she says. "Who wants her?"

"Dad," I answer.

"Your dad isn't here, Matty."

"Yes he is; he's outside. Come on, Hannah." I take Hannah's arm, and I lead her towards the door.

I am surprised to see that my mum has stood up, and she is walking towards the door with us. When we get to the door we can see my dad, and Mum starts to walk faster towards him. "John!" she shouts.

My dad sees her, puts both of his hands on the back of his neck, and spins around once.

I can see Raine's head poking through the door of the shed and looking at my mum.

"What the... John?"

My dad makes his mouth open a little bit, and he says, "Susie. Wow, you look... wow."

"How did you get in here?"

Dad looks at an open door on the other side of the garden. "More than one way into a castle," he says, and he laughs.

"You are not invited. What are you doing here?"

"Relax. Chill. This is your special day; enjoy it."

"I can *not* enjoy it with *you* here."

"Hey, Susie, back off. I've just come to take the kids off your hands for a bit."

"Don't call me that. And back off, yourself. The kids are fine."

"You think Matty's fine? He was sitting in a shed, for crying out loud."

My mum is now standing right in front of my dad. She is not shouting any more; she is talking in a very cross whisper, but there are still some people outside that are watching. "Get *away* from my wedding."

"Susie, relax. Anyone would think you're angry that you married that idiot. Anyone would think you were missing me, or something."

My mum takes a step back, and she looks like she is breathing in a big breath because her chest goes big and then small again.

Hannah grabs onto my arm.

"Okay," Mum says, "you have to leave now. This is *my* wedding day, and I will *not* let you ruin it for me. Thank you for popping in, but goodbye."

"Okay, bye." Dad smiles, and he holds out his hands to me and Hannah. "Come on, Kids," he says.

We walk towards him, but Mum stands in front of us. "Oh, *no* you don't. Where has this come from all of a sudden? You were fine with them living with me and Ian. It was *you* that asked me to take them from you in the first place."

Hannah looks at me with a sad face.

"Not forever. Not into the arms of some other 'dad'." Dad suddenly has a sad face on, too. "Why did you do it, Susie? Why did you marry that... that... him? I thought you'd come back to me. I always thought you'd come back to me." He is looking at my mum's face, and he looks very sad now. "Why didn't you come back to me?"

Mum does not look cross any more, but she is still standing between my dad and me and my sister. "John, listen to me," she says. "Go home, and sober up. I will call you when we get back from Honeymoon. You can see the kids all you like then, and we can chat, but I will *not* talk to you now. Not while you are like this."

I look at the shed where Raine is standing, and she has got a big smile on her face like she is finding this funny. But I am not finding this funny. I am finding it sad, because I don't like it when my mum and dad are arguing.

"Susie," Dad says, "I love you."

"Too late."

"But I do."

"Too late. I'm married."

"But I love you."

"Tough, I don't love you. I love Ian. Now will you leave us? Go and sober up."

Dad makes a loud roaring noise, a bit like a lion, and I don't like it.

"Shall I call you a taxi?" Mum asks him.

"No, I'm fine," Dad answers, and he turns around and walks towards the open door at the other side of the garden. As he walks away he pulls his car keys out of his trouser pocket.

Hannah Pickering
October 2001

"Come on, Hannah; we want to practice our Destiny's Child dance. Chloe and Sarah say they have made a really good one up for 'Survivor', and we have to beat them."

"I don't want to. Leave me alone." I lift my feet up from the wet floor, and push them up against the toilet door so Lucy can't get in. I notice a bit of damp toilet tissue is stuck to my shoe.

"Is it because those naughty bigger boys called you a carrot top?"

I don't answer her.

"Or because they called you a ginger nut?"

I have emptied the contents of my purse onto my lap, and am counting the pocket money I have saved up. I've got seventy-eight pence all together. I wonder how much hair dye costs? I don't think my mum would be too cross if I dyed my hair, because she dyes hers all the time to make it brown instead of red.

"Hannah? Are you crying?"

"No," I say, but I am crying a little bit. I don't want to go outside this dinnertime, because those horrible boys will be out there. I thought that I would really like coming to my new big school, but I have been here for four weeks and I think it is horrible. There are three bigger boys who are in Matthew's class, called Billy, Anthony and Jamie, and they are really naughty, and very nasty to me. Every playtime they come and find me, and they call me lots of names, and they make me cry. This morning, at playtime, they said that my dad must be a carrot and my mum must be an orange. I don't want to go outside.

Lucy makes a cross groaning noise outside the door. "Come on, Han," she says, "I've got a really good idea for a move we can do on the chorus. It's where you hold your hands together, lift your elbows up one at a time, and then spin around. I think it would look really cool - " Then she stops talking.

"Lucy Barlow, what are you doing in here? You should be outside with the other children." That is our teacher, Mrs Evans' voice. I thought she would be in the staff room right now, because that's where the teachers eat their dinner.

"Sorry, Miss, but Hannah won't come out of the toilet."

"Hannah Pickering? Why not? Hannah, this is Mrs Evans, will you open the door, please?"

I do not want to get into trouble, so I put my feet down on the floor again, stand up, and open the door.

Mrs Evans is standing behind Lucy, and she has got her hands on the top of her hips. She is looking under her glasses at me. "Well?" she says.

"I'm sorry," I tell her, and I look down at the tiles on the floor.

"Are you going to tell me why you locked yourself in the toilet? You look like you've been crying. What's the matter?"

I think I should tell her, but my mouth feels like it won't open, and my throat hurts like it has closed up. I always find it hard to talk when I want to cry.

"Are you going to answer me?"

I nod my head, but still no words come out.

"It's because Billy Robin and his friends called her a carrot top and a ginger nut," Lucy says.

Suddenly I see Mrs Evans bending down, and her face is near to mine now. She is holding up the bottom of her black skirt so it doesn't go into the water on the floor. "Is that right, Hannah? Are you being picked on by some of the older children?"

I nod my head again.

She puts one of her hands onto my shoulder. "Oh, you silly girl. Why didn't you come and tell me? What exactly are they doing? Are they making fun of your hair?"

I nod again.

"Anything else?"

I pause, and then shake my head.

She sighs quite loudly, and then stands up. "Well, it isn't exactly bullying, is it? Just ignore them and they will stop. You're only interesting to them because you are reacting like this. Go and play outside with Lucy, and if they do anything nasty to you just come and let me know, okay?" Before I have time to nod my head, she has taken my coat down from its peg, put it into my arms, and is pushing me out of the door.

* * *

There are lots of children on the playground when we get there. Me and Lucy walk towards our friends, Maria and Stacey. They are next to each other, putting their hands up in the air and then onto their hips, and jumping forwards and then backwards. As we get closer I can hear them singing the Destiny's Child song, 'Survivor'.

Behind them, I see something, and I stop walking.

Lucy is looking at me.

Standing against the fence at the back of the playground are Billy, Anthony and Jamie. They are not facing me, but I can recognise them by their coats. They are all crowded together, and I can see some brown hair sticking up behind them. They must be bullying somebody else. I feel a bit scared and sorry for that person, but I'm glad that it's not me this time. It doesn't look like they are hitting the brown haired boy, but I think they will be saying mean things to him.

"What are you looking at?" Lucy asks me.

"It doesn't matter," I tell her, and I try not to think about the poor person who is being picked on, but then Jamie moves to the side a little bit, and I can see that the person they are surrounding is my big brother.

"Where are you going? Hannah?" Lucy is shouting me, but I don't care.

I have got to go and help Matty. I am walking very, very fast towards them, and I don't feel scared anymore. As I get closer I can see that Matthew has got his hands over his ears, and his eyes are closed. His mouth looks like he is making the funny noise that he makes when he is upset. I can hear that the boys are singing something, but I can't tell what it is.

When I get really close, Anthony spots me. "Hey, it's Carrot Top," he says, and they all turn around.

"What do you want? Come for a grating, Cheese Hair?" Billy says, and they all start laughing loudly.

Matty opens his eyes and looks at me. I think he looks a bit relieved to see me, and he stops his funny noise.

"What are you doing to my brother?" I say, making my voice as loud as I can.

They start to laugh even harder, and then Jamie says, "He's your brother? Wow, your mum and dad must be pretty spazzy oranges and carrots then."

"What?" I ask crossly, walking through them and putting my arm around my brother.

They don't answer me, so I look at Matty and gently pull his hands away from his ears. "What did they do to you?" I ask him.

"We were just singing," says Billy. "We were singing him the tune to The Simpsons; it's your favourite, isn't it, Pickers?"

"You were singing it wrong," Matthew shouts, hitting himself in the head with his hand.

I take hold of his hand in my own.

"We thought you'd like it; you are always talking about The Simpsons."

"You were singing it wrong."

"We can't help it if we're not great singers," says Anthony, with a silly smile on his face.

"You were doing it on purpose," Matty is shouting. "You were laughing. You made it sound like The Flintstones, and you were doing it on purpose."

I was so busy looking at Matty that I didn't notice that the dinner lady has come up behind the boys. "What's all this about?" she asks.

Good, I'm glad she's here. "Miss, they were picking on my brother, and being naughty and horrible."

She looks at them, and they have got cross faces on.

"No, we weren't. We were just singing him a song that he likes."

The dinner lady looks confused.

"Yes, but they were singing it wrong," I tell her.

"Okay..." she still looks confused. "So how exactly is that picking on him?"

"They were doing it on purpose. They knew it would upset him."

I watch her open her mouth, and then close it. Then she opens it again and looks at Billy. "*Were* you trying to upset him?"

"No, we were trying to be nice to him." He smiles at her, and her face goes into a tiny little smile too.

Then she frowns again, and looks at me and Matty. "Stop being silly, you two. And stop making nonsense out of nothing. There's no crime against singing." She turns and walks away from us.

"You heard her," says Anthony to Matthew in a quiet voice. "Stop being silly, you spaz."

I feel very angry all of a sudden. "What did you call him?" I step a bit closer to Anthony, and I can feel my face going hot and red.

"Just what he is; a spaz." He starts to laugh very loudly, and so do the other boys.

I am shaking right up and down my arms, and then I can't help it, and I don't know I am doing it, but I can feel my hand slapping him hard across his face.

"Young lady!" The dinner lady has turned around again, and she is looking at me very crossly. "You naughty little... get to the head teacher's office, now. I have never seen so much insolence from such a new starter. Get out of my sight."

Suddenly I can see Lucy, Maria and Stacey standing behind the dinner lady, and they look shocked, but they are smirking a bit, too.

"Yeah," Billy says very quietly, "you go, and leave the spaz with us; we'll look after him."

My body starts to shake again, but I stop myself from hitting him too, because the dinner lady is watching me. Instead, I hold my brother's hand and make him walk with me, away from the boys.

"Please can he come with me?" I ask the dinner lady, in a calm voice.

"By all means. It seems to be him that started all of this in the first place. You know where Mr Biggs' office is, don't you? Go and tell him everything you've done, and don't let me ever see behaviour like that from you in the future."

John Pickering
February 2002

Everything is a little bit blurry. Me and the lads came out to the Bull for a quick one, about... ooh, three hours ago. We have already drunk Kenno under the table, and his wife's on her way to pick him up right now. Well, it is Friday night. And it has been a flaming long week. I deserve a pint or two. Or three. Or - well, I deserve a good night. With Kenno down and out it's up to me and Barry Baldie to hold the fort for men everywhere...by continuing to get as blotto as we can.

There is a good reason our quick pint seems to have turned into slightly more than that; the new barmaid. We have been coming to the Black Bull for as long as I can remember, and never has there been an inch of hotness behind that bar (not unless you include Big Bazookas Barbara – who was pretty much big all over), but the hiring committee has clearly upped it's game this time.

This may be the first time I have willingly offered to get the drinks in. In fact, I think I have bought more drinks tonight than I did in the whole of last year. I tell you, I could have sworn aloud when Pete, the manager, came to serve me the third time around, instead of the leggy lovely. That round cost me nearly nine pounds, too. I was not impressed.

As the bell for last orders has just gone, this is my final chance of the night. Barry is currently walking (more like carrying) Kenno to the car park, and the bar has almost cleared for the first time all night, so I decide that now is probably the time to make my move. I down the last dregs of my pint and walk, slightly wobbly, over to the bar.

"What can I get you?" she asks, pouting her big lips slightly at the end of her sentence.

I can think of a million ways to answer that question. I settle with one. "A date?" I ask, with what I hope is a sexy raise of the eyebrow.

I can see a bit of a twinkle in her eye. She flicks her long, blonde hair back over her left shoulder. "We don't serve fruit." She's trying to frown, but I can see a smile hidden behind it. The Pickering charm never fails.

"You know what I meant. What are you doing when you finish?"

"Going home to sleep," she answers me, but her body language is telling me a totally different thing. I'm no expert, but when a girl chews seductively on her finger, and flutters her long, fake eyelashes in your direction, it doesn't usually mean, 'go away and leave me alone.'

"That's cool," I reply, standing up straighter. "Can I come?"

"You want to sleep at my flat?"

"Not exactly."

She turns away slightly. "Ugh, you men disgust me." She doesn't look all that disgusted. "You don't even know my name yet."

"I'd rather know your number."

That was definitely a smile. Definitely. She flicks her hair again. "Like that would happen. You're old enough to be my dad."

"I like to call it experienced. And you have to admit, I have something of the George Clooney about me."

She laughs a little bit. "You haven't asked if I have a boyfriend."

"Have you?"

"I might have."

"Is he as charming as me?"

"Snails are as charming as you." Ouch. I'd take her more seriously if she weren't practically salivating as we speak.

"I happen to think snails have a bit of that je ne sais quoi. They're pretty cool little fellas, with their shells, and - "

"Jenny," she says.

"What?"

"My name's Jenny. I don't have a boyfriend, and I'm free tomorrow night."

I stare at her.

Her blonde head waves a little. Is that normal? Actually, the whole room seems to be waving a bit.

"Oh. Right." I stare a bit more. "I'm John, and I'll pick you up here at eight?"

"Sure," she says, and then she turns away from me and walks to the other end of the bar. "Yes, Sir, what can I get for you?" I hear her ask.

Matthew Pickering
May 2002

I am finding my work very hard today. We are learning about rivers - and I like learning about rivers because I find them very interesting, and I already know lots of facts about them (for example, I know that rivers are often called different things: like streams, and creeks and brooks), but Mrs Smith is asking me to do lots of writing and that is very, very hard. We have got to write about how a river gets from the top of a mountain to the sea, and I know what I have got to say, but I am finding it very hard to write down the words. Writing is not an easy thing to do.

I write on the first line in my page, 'Rivers'. I underline it with my ruler, because this is the title of my work. I miss a line, and then on the third line down I put my pen to the paper.

'Rivers are - '

No.

'When a river - '

No. I do not know what to write, and I am getting cross. I make a noise, which is a bit like a long 'r' sound.

"What is it, Matthew?" my teacher, Mrs Smith, says.

I cannot see her because I am looking at my geography exercise book, but I know that she is talking to me because she said my name. "I can't write anything," I tell her.

The three other children who are sitting at my table start to laugh, but I don't know why.

"Don't be silly, you learned how to write years ago."

"I don't know what to write," I say.

Mrs Smith makes a groany noise. "Write whatever comes into your head. I'm far past hoping for a piece of work from you that actually makes sense, so anything will do." Then I hear her say, in a quieter voice, "Yes, Jessica? Well done, you're such a quick worker. Let me read it for you." I don't think she is talking to me anymore, because I think that she is talking to the girl in my class that is called Jessica.

I look at my pen, which is still resting on the third line of my page. Mrs Smith says to write whatever comes into my head. 'Rivers are very long and windy,' I write. I look at the words. I do not like them. I mark a line through them with my ruler, but I can still see the sentence. I mark another line through, but it does not make it disappear. I throw my ruler onto the floor, and I scribble the words out with my pen. I scribble them very, very hard. I keep scribbling, but I can still see the words.

I can hear that somebody is talking to me, but I can't really hear what they are saying. I want to get rid of these words. I scribble, and I scribble, and the page rips under my pen. I keep scribbling. The voice is still talking to me, and I can see that somebody is standing behind me, but I don't know who it is or what they are telling me. I scribble a bit more, but then suddenly I can't scribble any more.

Somebody has pulled the pen out of my hand from behind me. I turn around very quickly to see who it was, and I can see Mrs Smith. She has got a cross face on. "Matthew Pickering," she says, "what are you doing to your lovely new book?"

I blink my eyes. I don't really remember what I was doing to my book. I turn around again and look at it. It is covered in black ink, and the page has got a big black hole in the middle of it. "I don't know," I say.

The girls on my table are laughing at me.

"I don't want you in my classroom right now, Matthew. Go into the cloakroom and calm down."

I feel calmer now. "I am calm," I tell her.

"You think *this* is calm?" she asks me, reaching for my exercise book and holding it in front of my face.

I think that is a very silly question for her to ask, because a book cannot be calm, because books do not have feelings. "No," I say, "books do not have feelings."

Mrs Smith's face turns a little bit red. "Get out!" she shouts, and she is pointing towards the door into the cloakroom and toilets. I can tell that she is very cross with me, but I don't know why.

"Sorry," I say.

"Answering back like that. Of all the rude - go on, get out."

I don't know why, but she is telling me to get out of the classroom and go into the cloakroom, so I stand up and walk to the door.

As I am walking I hear Billy Robin say, "Miss, I need the toilet."

"Fine, go," she says to him, "but leave Matthew alone; he's in there to think."

I walk to the door into the cloakroom and toilets, and I open it. I walk through, and go and sit on one of the benches under the coat hangers. The boys' toilets are on the right side of me, and the girls' toilets are on the left side of me. I rest my head back against one of the coats. It is soft. There is a strong smell in this cloakroom, and I think that it is the smell of wet paper towels. I have learned what this smell is because I sit in here two, or three, or sometimes four times every day, and when the bin is full of wet paper towels the smell is stronger, and when it is empty there is not as much of a smell. Today the bins are very full of wet, green paper towels, and so it smells very strongly. I do not like this smell because it reminds me of being in trouble, and I do not like to be in trouble.

The door into the cloakroom swings open just after I have sat down, and it is Billy Robin that walks through it. I think that he has come in to go to the toilet, because he told Mrs Smith that he needs the toilet. He stands looking at the door until it closes completely. There is a window in the door, but nobody is looking through it because most people are doing their work at the other side of the classroom. I cannot see Mrs Smith through the window.

"Hi, Pickers," Billy says. Billy always calls me 'Pickers', and I think it is a shorter way of saying my surname, but I don't know why he doesn't just call me Matt, because that is even shorter. He is smiling at me, but I don't know why he is smiling because he is not usually very nice to me. He sits very, very close to me on the bench, and the side of his leg is touching the side of my leg. "Are you alright, Mate?" he says.

I am happy that he is being nice to me today, and that he called me, 'Mate', which means that he is my friend. "Yes, I am alright," I say. I smile at him a little bit. "Are you my friend today?"

Billy puts one of his arms around my shoulder and says, "I'm always your friend, aren't I?"

I am not sure if he is always my friend because usually he is not very nice to me, so I do not answer him.

He pulls his arm tighter around me. "You and me, we're like best mates, aren't we?"

I did not know that we were like best mates.

Then he says, "Hey, is this your bag?" He reaches his arm up to the peg that has got my name on, and lifts my rucksack from it. He puts it into his other hand, and then pulls it away from me. He has not got his arm around me anymore, because both of his hands are opening my bag.

"Hey, that's mine," I tell him.

"Don't worry," he says. "I'm your friend, remember?"

Then I remember that he is my friend today, so I think that it is okay for him to look in my bag.

He pulls out one of my books and says, "'A history of the USA,' not interested in that." He throws it onto the floor.

The floor is a bit wet, and so my book is getting a bit wet too. I get down to pick it up, but I hope I do not get any germs from this floor.

"An apple? I don't think so." He takes my apple out of my bag and throws it to the bin. It lands on the big pile of wet paper towels that is overflowing from it, and it rolls off, onto the wet, muddy floor.

I crawl over to it, as quickly as I can, and I can feel that my trousers are getting wet on the floor. I don't think Billy Robin is treating me like a friend should treat me. "Stop throwing my things, please. I don't like it."

I can see that Billy Robin is still looking through my bag, and then he smiles. "Aha," he says, "that will do." He pulls a chocolate bar out of my bag, and puts it into his pocket.

"That's mine," I tell him.

He stands up, with my bag in his hands. "Here you go, these are all yours too," he says, and he turns my bag upside down and makes everything fall out onto the floor. Then he drops my bag onto the floor as well.

"Oy!" I shout, and I throw my whole body onto the floor and pull as many of my things towards me as I can. My head is screaming.

I can hear Billy Robin laughing as he walks towards me.

I am lying on my tummy in front of the door to the classroom, and I am resting my face into my bag. I feel a foot on the bottom part of my back and I scream. It is a heavy foot. Then the foot comes off my back.

Billy is still laughing. "I was only joking, don't cry," he says.

I am not crying. I hear some chairs scraping across the floor in the classroom, and I can feel the vibrations through the cold, wet tiles that I am lying on.

Billy says, "You are such a loser," to me, and then he pulls the door open.

Even though I cannot see him because my face is in my bag, I know that Billy Robin has done this because I am in front of the door and he has pulled it into me. It is pressing into my side, and it is hurting me. I scream again as I am pushed a little way across the floor. I can feel his footsteps climbing over me, and I can hear and feel more footsteps running closer to me, and more chairs scraping. I scream because my head is screaming. I kick my feet hard against the floor tiles, as fast as I can.

"Look what he's done, Mrs Smith," I hear Billy Robin say. "I was just in the toilet and I heard him go mental. He threw all his stuff on the floor, and then he started rolling around, screaming."

I can hear some children making loud breathing in noises, and I can hear some other children laughing.

I scream once more. I am still kicking my legs up and down, and I am gripping my bag very tightly with my hands.

"Children, sit down," I hear Mrs Smith say, but I can't hear any footsteps moving away from me. "Thank you, Billy. You can sit down now."

I feel very cross because Billy Robin said that I threw my things onto the floor, but that is a lie because it was him that did it.

"Oh," I hear him say, "and he hit me too." He is lying.

I scream, as loudly as I can.

"He hit you? Where? Are you okay? Go to the nurse. Children, get away from him; you don't know what he will do. Go and sit down, please."

I scream. It is only helping a little bit, and not a lot. I still do not hear any footsteps walking away from me.

"Jessica," I hear Mrs Smith say, "go to Mrs Evans' class and ask if we can borrow Hannah Pickering for a few moments, please. Tell her it's about the 'M-problem'."

"Okay," I hear a girl's voice say, and I think it is Jessica's voice.

"What's the 'M-problem'?" somebody asks. "Does it mean the Matthew problem?"

I scream.

"Never you mind what it means. And if you are not in your seats in ten seconds, I will keep you all in over playtime."

This time I hear lots of footsteps walking away from me, and I hear chairs scraping against the floor again. I feel it too.

"But I need the toilet, Miss," another voice says.

"You will have to wait. Go and sit down." There is quiet for a few seconds, and then I can hear Mrs Smith saying in a quiet voice, "Why do I always get them? Every year, I get them. Do I look like I like crazy kids, or something? Every year. 'Hey, are they difficult? Put them with Mrs Smith'." Then I can feel her moving a bit closer to me, and her voice talks again. I can tell that she has bent down near to my head because I can hear her voice a lot louder now. "Matthew," she says, "you need to stop being so silly now, and stop disrupting my classroom."

I am not silly. I am a good boy. I make a scream, but it is a bit quieter this time. Every scream I make sounds funny because it is going through my bag.

"Every day we end up like this, don't we? You need to stop it. *You* might never make anything out of your life, but I have got children in this class who could and you are disturbing them. Now, please stop being so silly, and stand up."

"I am not silly," I shout.

I can hear that Mrs Smith is standing up, because when she talks again she is getting quieter as she says her sentence, which is, "Suit yourself; catch pneumonia on that wet floor if you insist on it. Hannah, good; sort him out, please."

Then I can hear my sister's voice. I lie still, and I listen.

"Why's he on the floor?" I hear her ask.

Mrs Smith makes a loud groany noise. "Don't ask me, he's just being Matthew, as usual. I despair sometimes, I really do. He's hit one of his friends today, you know? I'll be telling your mum about that. And he's thrown his stuff all over the floor. Look at that. Get him up, will you? What if an inspector walked in right now and saw him lying there? No, he needs to get up and stop being silly. Get him to pick everything up, too. Can I leave you with him? I have a class to teach."

I can hear some footsteps walking away, and then I can feel somebody moving closer to me.

"Matt, it's Hannah," I hear a voice say, and I know that it is the voice of my sister.

I do not want to scream now that Hannah is here.

I feel her put her hand on my left arm, so I know that she must be sitting on the floor next to me. She doesn't say anything for lots of seconds. Finally, she says, "Why are you on the floor, Matty?"

I don't say anything, because I do not want to talk about it.

"Are you hurt?"

My side is hurting, but I don't want to talk about it, so I don't answer her.

"Okay, you don't have to talk to me." I can feel her squeeze my arm a bit tighter, and she stops talking.

I turn my head a bit to the left and open my eyes. The right side of my head is now resting on my bag.

Hannah is sitting on the floor next to me, and her legs are crossed. She is smiling at me. Behind her I can see lots of children sitting at their desks, looking at us. Hannah's orange hair is tied into two ponytails at the side of her head, and she is twisting one of these in one of her hands. "Hello," she says to me when I look at her.

I smile a little bit.

She takes her hand from her ponytail, and rubs some water from my face. I think it was one of my angry tears that came out when I was screaming. "What are you like?" she says, but she is still smiling.

"Is he getting up yet, Hannah?" I hear Mrs Smith shout.

"Yeah, 'cause I need a wee," a child says.

Hannah looks around at them, and I can see that she is shaking her head. "Matty, you know you will get very wet on that floor," she says when she turns back to face me.

I can feel that I am getting very wet.

"If you get very wet you might catch a cold. And there are lots of dirty germs on that floor, too. You don't like germs, do you? Will you sit up, please?"

I think, and then I nod my head, because I do not want to catch a cold or get germs.

Hannah uses her hands to help me sit up.

I am now sitting cross-legged, on the cloakroom floor, opposite Hannah.

"Do you want to talk to me yet?" she asks.

"Okay," I say, quietly.

"What happened?"

"Billy Robin threw my things, and he stood on my back, and he opened the door on me."

I touch my sore side as Hannah turns and looks at the table where Billy Robin sits.

He is still there, so I don't think that he went to the nurse. That is probably because I did not hit him.

Then she looks back at me with a cross face. "He stood on your back? Did he hurt you?"

"He hurt my side with the door," I say.

"Show me."

I lift up my jumper, and I look down too. My side looks a little bit red.

"He is horrible, isn't he?" Hannah says to me.

I nod my head, because I agree that he is horrible.

"I am going to tell Mrs Smith for you. But she wants us to pick everything up first. Is all of this stuff on the floor yours?"

I nod my head again.

"Right." She picks up my bag and stands up. Then she walks around the cloakroom, picking everything up from the floor and putting them back into it for me. "We will need to wipe everything when we get home, and I think we should put this apple in the bin."

She holds up the apple, and I nod my head. I am sad because I wanted to eat that apple, but she is right, because I do not want to eat germs from the floor.

"He took my chocolate bar, Hannah," I tell her.

She has got a cross face again, and she looks over to Billy Robin's table. "I will tell Mrs Smith that as well. We will get it back. Will you stand up now?"

I nod my head, because I think I am ready to stand up now.

Hannah zips up my bag as I stand up, and then she puts it back onto my hook. Then she makes her arm link up with mine, like a chain, and we start to walk together to the front of the classroom, where Mrs Smith is.

* * *

I am at my house, and me and Mum are sitting by the telephone in the living room because I am going to telephone my dad tonight. Rose is lying across my feet, keeping them nice and warm. I have not seen my dad in a very long time because he is always very busy seeing his new girlfriend, who is called Jennifer Cooper. I do not like Jennifer Cooper, because she is not very nice to me. I have heard her say not very nice things about me to my dad when she does not know that I can hear what she is saying, and that makes me sad.

Last weekend, Hannah went to stay with my dad at his house, but he said that Jennifer Cooper thought that it would be better if I didn't go that time, because she wanted to get to know Hannah very well. My sister does not like Jennifer Cooper either, because she says that she is too young for my dad, and that she is not a very nice person. Hannah told me that Jennifer Cooper wore a very short skirt and had orange skin on Saturday, and she thought that she looked very funny.

Mum dials the numbers of my dad's telephone number for me, because I do not know them, and then she hands the telephone to me. It is ringing.

The telephone rings three times, and then a lady voice answers and says, "Hello?"

My dad does not have a lady voice, so I do not know who it is that has answered his telephone. "Who is it?" I ask.

"Isn't that my line?" the lady voice says to me.

I don't know what line she means, so I don't say anything.

She says, "Hello?" again.

"Hello."

She pauses for a minute, and then she says, "It's Jenny. Do you have the wrong number?"

I suddenly realise that it is Jennifer Cooper who has answered my dad's telephone. "Jennifer Cooper, why have you answered my dad's telephone?" I ask.

"Oh, it's you, Matthew," she says. She must have recognised my voice. I can hear her whispering something, and I hear a quiet voice in the background. Then she says, "Your dad's not here right now, shall I tell him to call you back?"

I don't know why my dad isn't there, because that is where he lives. "I want to speak to my dad." I say.

"I know, Matthew, but he's not in. I will tell him to call you back."

I don't like it when I can't talk to my dad, so I start to make my train noise.

Mum tries to take the phone out of my hand but I keep hold of it tightly, because I want to speak to my dad.

I keep making my train noise, but I can still hear Jennifer Cooper talking.

She says, "He's making that stupid noise again; you're going to have to speak to him."

I hear another voice, but I can't hear what it says.

Then she says, "I'm not answering it every flipping time; I don't like talking to him any more than you do."

I don't know what Jennifer Cooper is talking about, and I don't like not knowing what people are talking about, so I keep making my noise.

Mum is looking at me and asking me what is wrong, in a whispery voice, but I do not answer her.

Then I hear Jennifer Cooper say, "Well, can I just hang up, then?"

I don't know what the other person says, but then I can just hear a beep, and I can't hear any more talking. I am confused because I don't know where the talking went, so I make my noise even louder. This makes me feel a bit better.

Mum takes the telephone from me, because I am not holding it as tightly anymore, and then she puts it to her ear. She shakes her head and puts it down again. "What happened?" she asks me.

I make twelve more train noises, and then I feel calm enough to answer her. "Dad's not in," I say quietly.

Mum's eyebrows get lower, and nearer to the top of her eyes. "Not in?" she says. "Well, that's impossible, I only spoke to him ten minutes... I was telling him about your stupid teach... And it was Jenny who answered the phone, was it?"

I nod my head

Mum picks up the telephone again, and dials some numbers. I don't know who she is calling. She holds the telephone up to her ear for a long time, and I think that no one is answering her because she does not say anything. She presses a button on the top of the telephone, and then she dials the numbers again, holds it up to her ear, and waits. She waits for a long time, so I still don't think that anybody is answering the telephone call. Then, finally, she says something.

"Hello, Jennifer," she says, "it's Sue Hobson, here. Could I speak with John, please? -

Sorry, I don't buy that. I spoke to him not ten minutes ago -

Well, I don't think that's any of your business, do you? -

We were discussing running off together and having a sordid affair, if you must know. We were talking about the kids, you daft bat. Put him on the phone, please -

Don't lie for him. I lived with the man for many years, remember. I know all of his games. Put him on the line, please -

Jennifer, I don't want us to fall out so early in our wonderful friendship. Please, just put him onto the phone -

Thank you." Mum looks up at the ceiling and is quiet for some seconds. "Oh, John," she says, "so you are in, after all? I thought you would be. I've got someone here that would like to speak to you, if you could spare a precious moment? -

Yes, your son -

No, you cannot be too busy for a five-minute conversation with your firstborn -

I don't care about your work, and to be quite honest, if your fancy piece is there I doubt very much that you were planning on doing any work tonight anyway. I'm putting Matthew on. Goodbye." Mum gives the telephone to me and she says, "Talk to your dad."

I put it up to my ear and say, "Hello, Dad."

There is a little pause, and I hear Dad making a loud breathing out noise, and then he says, "Hi, Matthew. How are you?"

"I'm okay."

"What are you up to?"

I think that he is asking me a silly question, because he knows what I am up to. "I am telephone calling you." I say.

"Hmmm. I would never have known. Anything else?"

"I am sitting on the settee in my mum and Ian Hobson's living room, and my mum is sitting next to me, and Rose is sitting on my feet," I tell him.

Dad says, "Good. I needed to know all that."

I don't know why Dad needed to know all that, but he did, so it is a good thing that I told him. I wonder what else he needs to know. "What else do you need to know, Dad?"

He makes another loud breathing out noise and says, "Oh, I don't know, what's the weather like there?"

I think this is a funny thing to ask, because Dad lives very near to Mum and Ian Hobson's house, and I think the weather will be the same where he is, but if he needs to know this then I will tell him. "It is a bit sunny, but a little bit rain - "

I can't finish my sentence because Dad makes another really loud noise, and says, "Oh, for crying out loud, Matthew, I don't really want to know about the weather."

He sounds cross, so I say, "Sorry," but I don't understand why he is cross. He said that he wanted to know about the weather, and then he got cross when I told him about it. That is confusing.

Dad pauses again, and then he says, "So, what are you doing after this, then?"

"We are going to watch something on the television."

"Oh, yeah? What are you going to watch?"

"I don't know."

"Oh. Well, have fun." He pauses again, but for a long time this time. Then he says, "So, what have you been up to?"

I have been up to lots, but he gets cross if I tell him everything, so I don't know what to say. "I don't know," I answer.

He pauses again, and then he says, "I went to see a football match, last week. United won."

I say, "Oh."

"It was good. Maybe you could come too, next time?"

"I don't like football."

"Well, what *do* you like, Matthew?"

"I like the United States of America."

"Yes, yes I know you do. Do you like anything else, other than America...or rivers, or The Simpsons?"

I say, "I love Rose."

I hear Dad saying a very quiet rude word, and then he says, "Oh yes, the dog. How could I forget? Put your mum back on, please." I wait, but Dad does not say anything else. After lots of seconds he says, "Matt? You're still there, aren't you?"

I say, "Yes".

He says, "Matthew, I... I do love you, you know."

I say, "Thanks."

Then he says, "Give the phone back to your mum, please."

So I do.

Susan Hobson
August 2002

"Can we talk?"

Everyone dreads that question; it never leads to anything good. I am washing up at the sink, watching Matt and Hannah playing with Rose in the garden. Actually, I'm watching Matt and Rose chasing each other around, having a whale of a time, and Hannah looking lonely in the corner. I can see she keeps trying to engage Matty in some sort of game with her, but he's not paying the slightest bit of attention. Although he can't be expected to be overly enthusiastic about playing 'girl band practice' with her. She managed to get five minutes out of him about an hour ago, and I had to laugh as she tried to teach him her dance moves to, 'Can't get you out of my head'. She had him singing, 'la la la,' and spinning around. Unfortunately for her, those were the only words and moves he picked up so it was slightly repetitive, and he ended up getting dizzy and falling over, at which point he decided to throw a stick for Rose rather than carry on being part of the world's next big girl group. Hannah's desperate for Lucy and the others to come back from their holidays, bless her. Matt doesn't exactly play ball when it comes to spending time with her.

I let out a lungful of air and dry my hands on the tea towel, turning to face Ian with what I'm sure is a pretty obvious look of irritation. "What?"

"Sit down."

"I'm washing up."

"Susan, I'm worried about you."

"Don't call me that, it irritates me when you call me that." It does. It makes me feel about seventy. "And what do you mean, you're worried about me?"

"Sit down, and we'll talk about it. I want to help." Even his voice is dull.

I throw the tea towel onto the side and pull up a chair, purposely placing it in the middle of the room in front of him, as if he's interviewing me. "There. Interrogate away."

He pulls another chair out from under the dining table, and sits it close to me. "I don't want to interrogate you, Sweetheart, but you haven't been yourself lately. Can you tell me what's wrong?"

He wants to know what's wrong? Where do I start? I'm married to Mr Snore Inducer, 2002, my ex is loved up with some young bimbo, I've got an autistic son starting a new school in September, where he is going to get ripped to pieces by the other kids, and a daughter who appears to be starting her teenage years early, and has moped around for the past two weeks, moaning that she is bored. Well, so am I, Hannah. It's called life.

"Nothing's wrong."

"Something's bothering you. Are you mad about me going to that conference next week?"

I really could not care less. In fact, I'm looking forward to a few days apart from him. I only wish the conference was longer. I pause. "Yep. That's it."

He reaches his hand out and puts it on mine. "I understand, but it's only a few days, Darling. And it's for work. It's not like I'm going down there to seduce lots of women."

Like he could.

"I will phone you every day, and I'll be back before you know it."

I'm sure he will.

The doorbell interrupts his spiel of explanations. I stand up immediately, ignoring his offer to 'sit down and rest while he gets the door'. So caring of him.

When I pull open the door I am unsurprised to see Ian's step-daughter, Raine, standing there. She has been here most days of the summer holiday. Anyone would think living alone with her grandmother was dull for her. Try living with Ian. Oh wait, she has.

"Hi, Raine," I smile. I do genuinely like the girl. She's a nutcase, granted, but she's the only friend Matty's ever had, barring the dog, and she's been really good for him. That is the one thing that I can say is a positive about him going up to his new school; Raine will be there with him.

"Is Matt in, Suse?" She asks me this as she is pushing the door wider, walking in, and removing her shoes.

I smile to myself.

She is wearing something a little more conventional than usual today; flared jeans, and a fairly normal t-shirt…albeit tie-dyed. Her hair is tied into two plaits. She is really a very pretty girl, and a very nice one - issues aside.

"He's in the garden. You might as well keep your shoes on."

She doesn't even look at me as she slips her sandals back on and begins to walk through to the back of the house. "Cheers. Hi Doc," I hear her say as she passes Ian on her way to the back door, "Wassup?"

"Good afternoon, Raine." He even bores me from another room. That's impressive; his dullness now radiates.

I close the door, sigh, and head back to the interview room.

Matthew Pickering
September 2002

Something hits the back of my head. It does not hurt, but I can feel it. I hear some laughing voices, and I turn around to see who the voices are coming from.

Jamie Bates is standing up from his seat on the back of the school bus, and his right hand is lifted in the air. He is holding a screwed up piece of paper, and he looks like he is about to throw it at me.

I wonder if that was what just hit me on the head. I look on the floor of the bus and can see another screwed up bit of paper, and I think that I am right. When I look at him he puts his hand by his side, looks at the floor, and starts to whistle. I am not sure why.

Billy Robin, who is sitting next to him, starts to laugh very hard, and so does Anthony Richards, who is next to Billy Robin.

I say, "Please don't throw paper at me," and then I turn to look to the front of the bus again.

Now a lot of children on the bus start to laugh, and I feel another ball of paper hit the back of my head.

I make a very quiet train noise, because I do not want to get angry on my first day at my new school. People are still laughing a lot, but my train noise is helping to make them disappear.

I do not know everyone that is on this school bus, because today is my first day at senior school, and there are children from other junior schools as well as Harleyfield Junior School who are here today. I hope that there are some nice people at my new school, because there were not very many nice people at my old school, apart from my sister, Hannah.

I will miss my sister very much when I am at my new school, because Hannah is only in year five and so she is still going to the junior school, but I am in year seven so I am going to a different school to her. I will miss her a lot, because Hannah is very good at looking after me when I am being treated horribly and when I am upset or angry. Hannah is good at making me feel better.

But I know that there is one nice person at my new school, because she is my best friend, called Raine. Raine is in year nine at Harleyfield High School, and that means that she will not be in the same class as me, which is sad, but I will get to see her at dinner times, which is good. Raine does not have any other friends at school, so it will be nice for her if I join her there because I am her best friend. I know Raine because her mum used to be boyfriend and girlfriend with Ian Hobson, but then Raine's mum died because she fell out of a tree that she didn't want people to cut down and she broke her neck. Raine says that she doesn't care that her mum died, and that she isn't sad about it, but I think that she is lying because every time I ask her about it her eyes go red, and sometimes tears come out of them. Tears mean that someone is sad.

Raine lives with her grandma, who lives three miles away from me, Hannah, Mum and Ian Hobson. She comes over to see me at my house sometimes, and sometimes I go to see her at her grandma's house. We like to watch movies together, and we like to teach each other things. I like to teach Raine all about the different states of America, and Raine likes to teach me about animals and plants. I like learning about animals because I like animals a lot. I especially like my dog, Rose, because she is my best friend, other than Raine. I do not like to learn about plants very much, because I do not find plants that interesting.

"Yo, Pickers," I hear somebody shout.

I wonder if they are talking to me, because some people call me Pickers because it is short for Pickering, which is my last name. I turn my head around, and I can see a boy that I have never met before waving his hand at me. He is sitting on the back seat of the bus with Anthony Richards, Billy Robin and Jamie Bates. I stop my train noise and say, "Yes?"

He puts his right hand up to his forehead and stretches out his thumb and his finger. He shouts, "Loser."

Lots of people on the bus start to laugh. I think that this boy might be a bully too, and I do not like him. I wonder why he is bullying me when he has never met me before. Lots of people on the bus look at me, and lots of people laugh, which I don't think is very nice.

I turn around to face the front again, and then I close my eyes and put my head down. I put my hands over my ears and make my train noise again to cover up the laughing.

The bus is a bit bumpy. I do not like it when it goes around a corner, because my eyes are closed so I cannot see the corner coming and I fall over in my chair. My hands are covering my ears so I cannot hold on, so I fall onto my side across the bus seat. It is a good job that nobody is sitting next to me. When this happens I can hear very loud laughing, even though my ears are covered. I decide that I do not want to sit up, because I know that I will fall over again when the bus goes around another corner, so I stay lying down sideways on the seat, the way that I fell.

I can feel the bus slowing down a little bit, but it is still bumping up and down. I am not very comfortable. Even though my eyes and my ears are closed, and I am making my train noise, I can still feel people poking my head, and I can feel another ball of paper hit my face, and then I can feel somebody putting something hard and round down the back of my school jumper. I make a quiet scream, but I do not move or open my eyes. The bus is stopping now.

I can still hear laughing, but now the poking on my head has stopped, which I am very glad about. I lie still, and I feel the bus start to move again. Then I can feel something else. Somebody is pulling at my left hand, which is pressed hard on my left ear, which is the side of me that is facing up. They are trying to pull my hand away from my ear, so I hold it on tighter. They give up and let go. Then I feel a hand cover up my mouth and pinch my nostrils together so I cannot make my train noise, and I cannot breathe. Somebody is trying to make me die.

I quickly put my hands onto theirs to pull them away from my face, and it works.

I hear them laughing, and then their voice says, "I knew that would work. Now you can hear me, shift up, will you?"

I know who that voice belongs to. I open my eyes up, and I can see Raine bending down next to my face.

She smiles at me, and says, "Sit up, then." I think that Raine must have got on the bus when it stopped the last time, because the bus is driving very near to her house now.

I sit up, because Raine told me to, and she sits down on the seat next to me. As I sit up, something cold and hard rolls down my back. I take it from the bottom of my jumper, and I can see that it is an apple. I wonder why somebody put an apple down my jumper. I look at Raine, and I give her the apple.

"Idiots," she says, and she throws it at some people in front of us who are looking at me and laughing.

They scream and duck down in their seats. Then they sit up again and laugh a bit more.

Raine looks at me. "Ignore them," she says.

So I do.

"Aren't you going to say hello?" she asks me.

"Yes," I say, "hello, Raine."

"Hello, yourself. So, do you like your new school yet?"

"I'm not there yet," I tell her.

She smiles at me. Then she looks to the front of the bus, and doesn't say anything else to me for the rest of the journey. I like that, because I don't have to think about what to say to her, and how to answer her questions.

I can still hear people laughing, but Raine told me to ignore them, so I am ignoring them.

* * *

I am in my new school now, and I am standing at the front of my new form room. A form room is the senior school word for a classroom, because a form is the senior school word for class.

My form teacher is called Mr Andrews, but I do not know what his first name is. I wonder if it is Andrew, because then his name would be Andrew Andrews, and that would be very funny. I am laughing when I think about this, because I have made a funny joke. I will tell my mum this joke when I get home. Mr

Andrews is very tall and thin, and I think he is quite old because his hair is a bit grey, like my dad's. He has got a big grey moustache, which is not like my dad, and he is wearing a bit of a cross face.

There are thirty-one people in my form, but I do not know many of them because some of them have come from different junior schools to me. Two people that I wish were not in my form but they are, are called Billy Robin and Anthony Richards. I do not like them at all because they are mean boys who are horrible to me. I am glad that Jamie Bates is not in my form though, because he has gone into another form. That is good.

I am standing at the front of the room, next to Mr Andrews' desk. All of the children in my form are standing here because we have not been told to sit down yet.

Mr Andrews is walking along the line of children, and he is looking at us all. When he comes close to me I can smell that he has been drinking coffee, because he smells a lot like coffee (unless he has got coffee smelling aftershave on, but I don't think that that exists). He walks to his desk, picks up a list, and then stands in front of everybody again and begins to talk. "As you all know, I am Mister Andrews," he says, "and don't forget the Mister - I don't tolerate rudeness, as you will learn. Now it's time for me to learn your names. In my hand I have a seating plan. You will be sitting in alphabetical order."

I hear lots of groany noises from the other people in my form, but I don't know why they are making groany noises.

"What did I say about rudeness?" he asks.

"You said that you don't tolerate rudeness," I answer.

He looks at me for some seconds, but he doesn't smile. Then he looks away. "Yes." He makes a little coughing noise. "Yes, that's right, I don't. So, when I call out your name I want you to take a seat where I point. Elizabeth Barry, over there." He points to the end seat of the first row on the left hand side of the room.

There are four seats on each row, and there are four rows on each side of the room, with a bit of an aisle in the middle. A girl, who I think is called Elizabeth Barry, walks over to the seat, puts her bag on the table, and sits down.

"Thank you," says Mr Andrews. "Next..." and he continues to name people and tell them where to sit. I have not heard my name yet.

* * *

The whole of the left side of the room has got its rows full of people now, and the first two rows on the right hand side are full too. A girl, who I think is called Claire O'Neal, has just sat down on the third row from the front.

Then Mr Andrews says, "Matthew Pickering," and he points to the seat next to Claire O'Neal.

I think that he wants me to sit there, so I walk to the seat, put my rucksack onto the table, and I sit down on the chair.

Claire O'Neal does not look at me.

"Anthony Richards," Mister Andrews says, and I realise that Anthony Richards is going to sit next to me. I am not happy about this, because he is not a very nice person.

I see him slap his forehead with his hand and pull a cross face, and then he walks to the seat next to me and puts his bag down very hard. He does not look at me, and when he sits down he pulls his chair away from me. I do not know why he does this.

"William Robin," Mr Andrews says.

I am surprised to see Billy Robin smile and run towards Anthony Richards, hitting his hand together with his before sitting down next to him. I wonder why Billy Robin came to sit there when his name is not William.

Mr Andrews watches them slap their hands together and he looks up at the ceiling for a second, then he looks to the front of the room again and names the last three people there.

They come and sit on the row behind me.

Then Mr Andrews looks at everybody again, and he says, "The first ten minutes is 'get to know each other' time, so I want you to turn to the person next to you and have a chat with them. Now."

I do not know which person to turn to, because Claire O'Neal is next to me on my right hand side, but Anthony Richards is next to me on the left hand side. Then I see that Anthony Richards is talking to Billy Robin, so I decide to talk to Claire O'Neal. I turn and look at her.

She is a small girl, and she has got straight black hair that is down to her shoulders. She has got green eyes, and some freckles, like me. "Hello," I think she says, "I'm Claire. Were you called Matthew?" I am finding it hard to understand what she is saying to me because she is talking to me in a very funny voice, but I think that she asked me if I was called Matthew.

"Yes," I tell her, "I still am called Matthew."

She pulls a funny face. "Ha Ha Ha," I think she says, but she is not laughing. "So what school are you from?"

"Harleyfield Junior School," I say.

"I'm from Saint Anne's." Claire really does have a funny voice. "Do you know anyone in this form?"

"Some people," I answer. "Why do you have a funny voice?"

She looks upset, but I was not being horrible, I am just wondering why she has a funny voice. "I don't," she tells me, but I can hear that she does. "I'm Irish."

Now I realise that her voice sounds funny because she is Irish, so she is speaking with an Irish voice that sounds different to Yorkshire voices. I am confused, because I don't understand how she is Irish but she is in England, because Irish people live in the country of Ireland.

"How are you Irish?" I ask her.

"What do you mean, how am I Irish?"

I think she is silly.

"I just am; I was born Irish."

I don't understand this. "But, how does it work?" I ask.

She just looks at me.

"Because Irish people don't belong in England," I explain.

I can see her mouth opening very wide. "You're being what my mam calls a racist," she says.

I do not know what she means, but I can see that she is cross so I say, "Sorry." Then I say, "I just want to know how it works. You're Irish, but in an English school; it doesn't make any sense."

"Well, you're a freak and in a mainstream school, which doesn't make any sense to me."

I am not a freak. I feel a bit cross and upset that Claire said that I am a freak. "I am not a freak," I tell her, "I'm just very special." That is what Mum tells me.

"You're that, alright," she says. "I'm going to talk to someone else now." I hear a heavy scrape on the floor as she turns her chair around to face the table behind us.

I am not sure if I like Claire O'Neal or not. I think that she is a bit silly. I am looking at her when I feel something nudge the top of my left arm. I turn around to see who it is, and Anthony Richards and Billy Robin are looking at me. I hope they will not be horrible to me.

"Alright, Pickers?" Billy Robin says. "We've got a question for you. Who was that fit bird you were with earlier?"

I am confused, because I was not with a bird earlier.

"That girl you were sitting next to on the bus."

I realise that he means my best friend, Raine. "That was my best friend," I tell him. "She is called Raine."

Both of the boys start to laugh at me.

Anthony Richards says, "She's called what?"

"Rain like the weather?" Billy Robin asks.

I think he is silly. "No, Raine with an 'e' at the end, and a capital letter at the start."

They look at each other, and then back at me.

"So, how did *you* end up being friends with *her* then?" He makes the 'you' and 'her' words sound louder than the other words.

"Well, Raine's mum was boyfriend and girlfriend with Ian Hobson - "

"Who on earth's Ian Hobson?"

"Ian Hobson is my mum's husband," I say.

Anthony puts his hands out towards me. "So, wait a minute," he says. "She is your mum's husband's girlfriend's daughter? That's twisted."

I do not know what he means when he says that it is twisted.

"Yeah," says Billy, "but why is she friends with *you*?"

"Because I met her in a shed at my mum and Ian Hobson's wedding, and then she was my friend."

They are looking at me, and then they start to laugh again.

"So," Billy Robin is still laughing while he is talking, "have you done it with her then, you dirty dog?"

I do not know what he means. "Have I done what with her?"

"It."

I don't know which 'it' he means, because I have done lots of things with her. "Which 'it'?"

Then Anthony Richards says, "Of course he hasn't. I bet he wouldn't even know how to. Will you give us her number, then?"

"What number?"

"Your friend's number. Her phone number. Her tel-eph-one number." He says the word 'telephone' very slowly, but I don't know why because I know what a telephone is.

"Okay," I say. Raine has a telephone number that I know off by heart, so I write the number on a piece of paper that Anthony has given to me with a pen from inside my bag. Then I give the paper back to him.

* * *

It is the end of my first day at senior school, and I am walking out of the gates with Raine. I met her outside my form room at the end of my last lesson so that we could catch the bus home together. I saw Billy Robin touching her bottom as he passed her, but she just smiled at him. I don't think that she should smile at him, because he is not a very nice person.

When we walk out of the gates I can see something that I did not expect to see. It is my dad's big red, four by four car, parked on the side of the road, and I can see that my little sister, Hannah, is sitting in the front passenger seat. She is looking at me and waving. I wave at her and walk over to the car. The window winds down.

"We came to pick you up, Matty," Hannah says. "Get in the car."

My dad smiles at me and nods his head. I walk to the back door and open it.

Raine walks up to the open front window. "Where are you going?" she asks my dad.

"Er, home. Sorry, who are you?"

"I'm Raine, Matt's friend."

"Oh, the famous Raine. Nice to meet you."

I climb into the back seat of the car and close the door.

I can still hear Raine talking through the open window. "You live in Wombsford, don't you?" She knows that because I have told her that. Raine lives with her grandma in Wombsford, too.

Dad nods his head, but he is not smiling any more.

"So do I. Could you drop me off?"

"Er...I guess."

"Cheers," Raine says, and then she opens the back door next to me and says, "shove over." She sits on the seat by the door as I move over to the other side.

Hannah turns her head to look at me, and then at Raine.

Dad coughs, then starts to drive. "I've heard a lot about you, Raine," he says. "Matt talks about you often."

"Right, yeah," she says.

"Are you in his form at school?"

"Nah." She takes a small mirror and some lipstick out of her bag, and she starts to put the lipstick on, looking in the mirror as she does.

"Didn't know kids wore that stuff," Dad says.

"I'm not a kid," Raine tells him, "and lads fancy you if you wear lipstick."

"Right. How old are you, if you don't mind me asking? Are you Matt's age?"

"No, I'm way older. I'm nearly fourteen."

"You seem older than that."

Raine smiles a little smile and puts the mirror and lipstick back into her bag. Then she takes out a comb, and starts to brush her long yellow hair back over the top of her head. "Yeah, it's 'cause I'm an orphan," she says. "I had to grow up fast."

"An orphan? I'm sorry, Love."

"No, it's fine. I'm not bothered."

I can see that Dad is looking at her in the mirror, and his eyebrows have moved lower and closer to his eyes.

Hannah interrupts, saying, "How was your first day, Matty? Did you get bullied?"

"Hannah," Dad says, loudly, "don't put silly words like that into his head."

"Yeah, I did," I say.

"It's not a silly word, Dad. He got bullied all the time at my school."

"It's a cowardly word. What do these so-called bullies do to you, anyway?" He is talking to me.

"They poked my head, and put an apple down my jumper, and threw paper at me," I say.

"Threw paper?" my dad says. "And you survived? Did you call the police?"

"No." I wonder if I should have called the police.

"For crying out loud, Matthew, it's paper. If they throw paper at you, you throw cardboard back at them. If they hit you with a bit of wood, you hit them back with a table. You know what I mean?"

I do not know what he means.

"I used to protect him, Dad," Hannah says, with a bit of a smile on her face.

"You? An eight-year-old girl? Matt, what do you think you are playing at, letting your little sister stand up for you? You're a big lad now, and you need to show them who's boss. What are you going to do now your baby sister isn't around to protect you?"

"I can look after him now," Raine says.

"Oh, great. Another little girl bodyguard for you."

"I'm not a little girl."

"Well, with respect, Love, you're not a six foot five man either, are you? What are you going to do to 'protect' him?"

Raine pushes her hair over the top of her head again. "I'll just make sure they are nice to him."

"And you'll do that how?"

"Any way I can," she answers. "I can usually get what I want."

Hannah looks around at me with a bit of a sad face on. She says, "Did you miss me at school today, Matty?"

I did miss Hannah at school today, so I say, "Yes, I missed you looking after me at school, but Raine can look after me now, so I don't mind a lot."

She says, "Oh," and turns to the front of the car again. She doesn't say anything else.

"I don't want to hear any more of this 'looking after' talk, Matthew," says Dad. "You're old enough to stand on your own two feet now. If someone hits you, you hit them back harder, okay?"

"But then I will get into trouble."

"I don't care. I won't have a weed for a son. It's about time you learned to stand up for yourself rather than letting little girls - sorry – *girls* take the rap for you all the time. It should be the other way around. Just promise me, if anyone starts to *bully* you, or upset you in any way, you clock them one, okay? You hit them."

"Okay," I say, but I do not want to do that. Then the rest of the journey is quiet.

Matthew Pickering
October 2002

Today is my birthday, and I am twelve years old. I am going to go to Pizza Hut tonight with my family and Raine, and I am going to get a pepperoni pizza, because my favourite food is pepperoni pizza. We are going to have cake and a drink at my house before we go out, and I am going to open my presents there, and then we will go to Pizza Hut at seven pm. I would like to dress up like a scary person for my birthday today because it is Halloween day, but my mum says that I should dress smartly because we are going for a nice meal. She said that I might scare my nana away if I dress up like a scary person, and so I decided that it is a good idea that I don't do that, because I do not want to scare Nana Brady away.

I am sitting on my living room floor and I am stroking Rose, who is lying over my knees. I am waiting for Nana Brady, and my dad and Jennifer Cooper to come to our house. They are coming at five pm, and Raine is coming at six thirty pm, because she is busy doing jobs with her grandma until then. I look very, very smart today. I have put some gel on my hair to make it spiky, and I am wearing my dark blue shirt with Bart Simpson on, because I love The Simpsons very much because it is very funny. I have got my best jeans on too. I hear the doorbell go, and me and Mum go to the door to see who it is while Ian Hobson puts some water in the kettle so that the grown ups can drink a cup of tea. Rose makes a whiney noise when I leave her, but I will be back to stroke her again in a minute.

It is my Nana Brady at the door, and she comes in and gives me cuddles, and kisses me on the side of my mouth. She says, "Happy birthday, Sweetie," and then she gives my mum a kiss on the cheek too, and Mum helps her to take off her coat.

Hannah is still in the living room because she is watching a television show, but she shouts, "Hi, Nana," through the door.

* * *

Hannah says that it is nearly half past five pm, and Dad and Jennifer Cooper are not here yet. They are both very late, and I don't like it when people are late because they are supposed to be on time.

Mum says, "Trust your dad; late for everything."

And Hannah says, "Jenny's probably still putting her slap on."

That didn't make any sense, so I look at Hannah with a funny face.

She laughs, but I don't know why.

It is lots of minutes later when the doorbell goes again. Me and Ian Hobson go to open the door, and it is Dad and Jennifer Cooper that rung the doorbell, so I say, "Hello, Dad. Hello, Jennifer Cooper."

Dad smiles at me. "Happy birthday, Son," he says.

Jennifer Cooper does not smile at me, but she says, "Hello, Matthew."

Dad turns to look at her, but I can't see what face he pulls. Then he looks at me again and gives me a hug. It is a bit of a funny hug because he only uses one arm, and he hits me on the back, which I don't like. He makes a coughing noise when he lets me go.

Jennifer Cooper does an, 'Ummm,' noise, and then says, "Happy birthday." She tries to kiss me on my cheek, but I don't think she is very good at it, because she misses. She is standing a long way away from me, and her lips don't touch my cheek as she tries to kiss it.

I laugh a bit, because I think it is funny that she is not very good at kissing. I wonder if she is good at kissing my dad, because she is his girlfriend.

Ian Hobson says, "Come in, we are all in the lounge."

Dad takes his shoes off and starts to walk into the living room.

Jennifer Cooper is wearing bright pink shoes with tall heels and very pointy toes. I didn't know that she has got pointy toes. I laugh again, because I find this funny. She does not take her shoes off, and I don't like that, so I start to make my train noise.

She looks at me funny.

Ian Hobson says, "Sorry, Matt likes everyone to take their shoes off; he doesn't like germs. Do you mind?"

Jennifer Cooper looks at me, and makes one of her eyebrows lift up really high. Then she says, "Yes, I do mind, actually. They go with the outfit."

I realise that she is not taking her shoes off and she is following my dad into the living room. I start to feel a bit hot and my head hurts a little bit. I blow air through my teeth even louder.

Ian Hobson says, "I really would prefer it if you could take them off."

Then my dad looks at us. "Oh come on, she said no. It's not as if her shoes are dirty; they're brand new aren't they, Babe? Matthew, don't be so silly. Come in here, shut up about it, and open your presents."

I don't like it when people tell me not to be silly, because I am not silly; I am a good boy. And I really don't like people telling me to shut up. I start to stamp my feet very fast and I make a very loud, fast train noise.

I can see Mum and Hannah standing up from their chairs in the living room, because the door is open.

Hannah shouts, "Dad!"

Mum says, "John."

Ian Hobson puts his hand on my arm. "Shhhh. It's okay, Matt. Calm down."

His voice makes me feel calmer, and I stop my train noise. I stop stamping my feet, too.

Mum says, "John, please remind your lady friend that your son has got autism and that he could do with a bit of respect for his needs."

"Are you going to let her talk about me like that?" says Jennifer Cooper.

Dad looks at me, and he looks at Mum and Hannah, who have got their hands on their hips, and he looks at Jennifer Cooper. Then he says, "Okay, fine. Come on, Babe, take them off if it will shut them all up."

Jennifer Cooper says quietly (but I can hear her), "I'm not putting my bare feet on *that* carpet. Who knows where his skanky feet have been."

I don't know what the word 'skanky' means, but I think it must be a bad word because she is pulling a face like it means something bad, and she is looking at my feet. I think that she is very rude and silly, and I want her to take her shoes off.

She stares at Dad, and he stares at her. Then she looks at everybody else, and they are all looking at her too. "Fine," she says, "whatever." She looks very cross as she takes one shoe off at a time, and then she places them very neatly on the floor. I am glad that she has taken her shoes off, and I am glad that she placed them neatly on the floor.

Dad says, "Thanks, Babe," and Mum and Hannah go into the living room again, with smiling faces.

I follow them.

Dad walks into the living room and sits on a chair. He pats the chair next to him and looks at Jennifer Cooper. I think he wants her to sit with him because he says, "Sit here with me, Babe."

She walks into the room on her tiptoes, but I don't know why. She looks at the chair next to my dad and makes her nose go all scrunchy. Then she sits on my dad's legs, and not on the chair next to him, but I don't know why she is doing that either. She watches me, as I sit back on the floor and Rose licks my face.

Rose always does that, because she is happy to see me. I don't really mind when Rose licks my face, because she is not a poorly dog, so I don't think that she has got any germs.

***

I am sitting in the living room with my family when my Nana Brady says, "Shall we do presents now?"

I say, "Yes," because I would like to open my presents.

She says, "You can open mine first," and she gives me a big present.

I am excited because I like big presents. I open it, and it is a big jumper that is orange, and it has got the number twelve on it in big red writing.

I can see Mum and Hannah laughing a little bit, but I don't know why because nobody said a joke.

Nana Brady says, "I knitted it myself. Try it on to see if it fits."

I try it on, and it fits me well. It is very warm.

Nana says, "Wear it tonight, Darling; you look so handsome."

"Okay."

Mum says, "No, Mum," (because my nana is my mum's mum), "I think he should wear the shirt he was in before; we don't want to confuse him. Take it off now, Sweetie."

"Okay." I take off the jumper.

Rose puts her paws onto the soft jumper, and lays down on it to go to sleep.

Mum gives me the present from her and Ian Hobson next, and she says, "Our present is in two parts. Here is the first bit."

I open it quickly, and I can see that it is a PlayStation game, but that is silly because I don't have a PlayStation. I say, "I don't have a PlayStation."

"I told you it was in two parts. Ian, give him the next bit of his present."

Ian Hobson reaches down the side of the settee and lifts up a big present, which makes me very excited. He hands it to me, and says, "Be careful, it's delicate."

I take it, and it is very heavy, so I drop it on the floor, but then I remember that it is delicate. I think that it is okay though, because I am sitting on the floor, so it didn't fall very far.

Mum says, "Can you guess what it is?"

I say, "No," because I can't guess what it is, because I haven't opened it yet. I open it very quickly. It is a very exciting present because it is a PlayStation, and I have always wanted a PlayStation. I think that it is very lucky that I got a PlayStation for my birthday, because now I can play my game. I say, "Thank you," because I really like my present.

I hear my dad say, "Show off," but I am not sure who he is talking to.

Then I turn to face him. "Can I have my present, please?" I ask, politely.

Dad pulls something out of his back pocket, which makes Jennifer Cooper wobble a little bit on his knee. That makes me laugh. He says, "Remember, I'm not a doctor like Ian, so I can't... just remember that I don't have as much money as your mum and Ian do."

I know that my dad is not a doctor, and that he doesn't have as much money as my mum and Ian Hobson. I don't know why he is telling me that.

He hands me a white envelope, but it isn't a card. It has been folded up in his pocket. I am disappointed, because Dad has not got me a present; he has only got me an envelope. "It's from me and Jenny, but really it's for you and me."

Mum says, "Typical; bought yourself something, as always."

I don't understand. When I look in the envelope, I feel a bit sad, because it is two tickets for a football match, and I don't like football. I say, "I don't like football."

Mum says, "Oh for goodness' sake, John. You didn't?"

Dad tells my mum to shut up, which I don't think is very nice, and then he says to me, "I know, Son, but you might enjoy it. We can spend some father-son time together. What do you think?"

I say, "I don't want to watch a football match," because I don't want to watch a football match.

Jennifer Cooper says, "Ungrateful little so-and-so," but she says it very quietly.

The room is quiet for a minute, and then Ian Hobson says, in a happy voice, "Well, if we are done with presents, shall I put a Simpsons DVD on?"

I say, "Okay."

***

The Simpsons has just finished, and I hear my doorbell ringing.

Rose wakes up and she starts to bark a little bit, like she always does when the doorbell rings.

Jennifer Cooper pulls a funny face.

I stroke Rose, and tell her that it is okay. She puts her head back down and goes back to sleep.

"I bet that's Raine, Matty," says Mum. "Go and answer the door."

I stand up from where I am sitting and go to answer the door, like Mum told me to.

When I walk past the chair that my dad and Jennifer Cooper are sitting on, I hear Jennifer Cooper whispering, "Raine? What sort of a messed up name is that?" to my dad.

I don't understand what she means.

Dad looks at her face and makes a little smile and a 'shhhh,' noise.

I walk to the front door and I open it up.

I thought it would be Raine at the door, and it is Raine. She is wearing some very little shorts made out of jeans, and an orange and red shirt that has got lots of its buttons undone. She has tied up the bottom bit of her shirt, which means that I can see her tummy. She is not wearing a jumper or a coat, and I think she must be very cold because it is nearly November, and it is very cold today. She is holding an envelope in her hand, and I think it must have got a birthday card in it for me, because it is my birthday today.

"Hello, Raine," I say.

"Happy birthday, Squirt," she says. Raine sometimes calls me 'Squirt' because it means that I am younger than her. But I am not that young, because I am twelve years old now. I don't mind it when Raine calls me Squirt, because she says that it is a nice name. She hands me the envelope and it says, 'Matt,' on the front. "I didn't get you a present," she says. "It's not like it's a special birthday."

I feel a bit sad that she didn't get me a present, but I take the card from her and I open it. It has got a picture of Bart Simpson riding a skateboard on the front, and it says, 'Happy Birthday, Dude!' on it, because Bart Simpson calls people, 'Dude.' I laugh, because I find it funny.

Inside the card it says, 'To Matt, Happy Birthday, from Raine x'. She put an x at the end of my card, and Mum says that an x on a card means a kiss. I wonder if Raine thinks that she wants to kiss me. Maybe she loves me a lot, and wants me to be her boyfriend.

I look at her. She is looking very pretty today, because I can see her legs, and I can see her tummy, and I can see the top part of her chest. She has got lots of nice make up on, and her hair is up in a bobble and looks quite nice.

Mum says, "Let her in then, Matty."

"Yeah, it's friggin' freezing out here."

"Okay." I move away from the door so that Raine can come in.

She does come in, and she takes her shoes off straight away, which I am very pleased about. Then she walks into my living room, in front of me.

"Hello, Raine Dear," I hear Mum say.

Jennifer Cooper makes a funny laughing, coughing sound.

"Hi, Love," says Ian Hobson. "Come in."

Then Raine says, "All right, Doc? Oh, hello, Mr Pickering. I didn't know you were coming tonight."

I walk into the living room behind Raine, and she is standing and talking to my dad.

Jennifer Cooper has got a cross face on. I don't know why she has got a cross face on, but I find it funny because I do not like her.

My dad makes a little coughing noise too, and then he says, "Er, hi. Jenny, this is Raine, Matthew's little friend. Raine, this is Jenny."

"His girlfriend," Jennifer Cooper says.

"Less of the 'little'," says Raine, smiling at my dad and not looking at Jennifer Cooper. She pulls her shoulders back and bends forwards a little bit, but I don't know why. "Nothing little about me."

Jennifer Cooper is looking at her. "Don't be so down on yourself, Rainbow; you're not that fat. How old are you, anyway? Eleven?"

I laugh, because Jennifer Cooper is very stupid because she got Raine's name wrong and called her 'Rainbow'. She is very stupid.

Now Raine is looking at Jennifer Cooper too. "Fourteen, actually," she says. "But I act much older than I am."

"Yes, I can see that. Are you going to a Halloween party after this, or something? Or did you just forget your clothes?"

My mum stands up right now, and she says, loudly, "Anybody for another drink before we head out? Tea? Coffee? Who wants what?"

"This is called style," Raine says to Jennifer Cooper. "Maybe you should look that word up."

"Anybody?" Mum says. "Tea? Coffee? Raine, Love, why don't you sit down over there?" She points to the window seat on the other side of the room, but I don't think Raine understands because she sits down on the empty chair next to my dad and Jennifer Cooper.

I sit on the floor, where I was sitting before.

"I'm fine here thanks, Suse," says Raine, and she is smiling.

"So," says Jennifer Cooper to Raine, and my dad makes a groany noise. "Raine - kind of an unfortunate name, isn't it? Were you born in a storm, or something?"

"No," says Raine, "were *you* born in a big pool of fake tan?"

My dad coughs loudly, and Hannah starts to laugh.

"I'll just make a teapot up, shall I?" says Mum. "Then whoever wants it can have it." She walks out of the living room and into the kitchen.

"Well, we don't all like to look like snowmen dressed in drag," says Jennifer Cooper to Raine. "Not that I'm saying that's what *you* look like, of course. I think you look lovely."

"What do you think, Mr Pickering?" Raine says, looking behind Jennifer Cooper at my dad's red face, and putting her hand on the part of his leg that Jennifer Cooper is not sitting on.

Jennifer moves her leg, and kicks Raine's hand away.

"Oh," says Dad, "I'm sure you look very nice. Although, when I say very nice, I mean..."

"Very nice for a *child*, he means," says Jennifer Cooper. "And I agree, you make a very sweet, cute child."

"How old are *you*, then, Jennifer?" says Raine, smiling at her.

"Twenty-One. Which is seven years older than you."

"And what, twenty years younger than your boyfriend?"

"Sixteen years, actually." She looks around at my Dad. "Oh, Babes, she thinks you look forty-one. Do you want me to knock her out for you?" Then she looks back at Raine, and says, "Because I could."

Ian Hobson stands up. "Actually, Raine, why don't you come and sit over here in my seat. You can't be comfortable on that kitchen chair. I'll sit there." He walks over to where Raine is sitting.

"But I was having a nice chat with the lovely Jenny, and her handsome hunk of a boyfriend."

"Yes, I know. I heard it all. Go and have a lovely chat with Nora now."

"All right." Then, I don't know why she does it, but Raine gives my dad a kiss on the cheek before she stands up. "Speak to you later, Sexy," she says. "Bye, Jen." Then she walks across the living room, smiling, and sits on the sofa next to Nana.

Ian sits next to my dad and Jennifer Cooper.

Jennifer Cooper has a very cross face on, and she turns around to look at my dad and wipes a red mark from the side of his face.

Matthew Pickering
November 2002

"But I don't like football," I say, again.

Dad doesn't answer me.

I think maybe he didn't hear me, so I say, "I don't like football," another time.

"So you keep telling me," he says.

We are driving in Dad's car, and we are going to see a football match played by the team called 'United.' We cannot park near the football stadium, so Dad says we are going to have to get out and walk soon.

"These tickets weren't cheap, you know," he says to me. "I'd be a little bit more grateful if I were you."

I feel hot. I reach to turn the temperature down on the car heater, but Dad slaps my hand away.

"Don't touch that."

"Sorry." Everything is quiet for a minute. Then I say, "I don't want to go and watch a football match. I want a different birthday present."

"You're a man. This is what men do. You can't be a man and not like football."

I say, "Yes you can," because I am a man and I do not like football.

"Have you ever even been to a match?"

"No."

"How can you know that you don't like it, then?"

I don't know how I can know that I don't like football, but I do know it.

Suddenly, a car drives out of a little road onto the road that we are driving on, and Dad has to slow the car down very fast. He presses his car horn for a long time and starts shouting rude words.

I cover my ears because it is too loud.

Dad looks at me, and uses his left hand to pull my right hand away from my ear. He says, "Don't be ridiculous," in a very loud voice, and I feel sad.

The road is getting busy, and there are lots and lots of people walking along the pavement, and lots of them are wearing football shirts. Some of them are shouting, and I can hear them loudly, even though my windows are up. I want to cover my ears again, but I think that it might make Dad cross if I do that, so I try not to. I want to make my train noise too, but I think that might make Dad cross as well, so I try not to do that either.

A group of people walk past our car, and they are wearing football shirts that are a different colour to my dad's football shirt, and to the football scarf that he made me wear. They look into our car, which is driving very slowly now because there are lots of cars on the road, and they walk right up to my window. They start banging on it and shouting lots of rude words. I do not know some of the words they shout, but I think they are bad words because they are shouting like they are very cross.

I shout, "Sorry," back at them to make them stop being cross, but Dad tells me off.

"Don't say you're sorry, you idiot."

I do not like being called an idiot, and I do not like being around football people when they are scary. I say, "I want to go home."

Dad doesn't answer me.

"I want to go home."

He still hasn't heard me, so I say very loudly, "I want to go home."

We are driving a tiny bit faster now, and we are driving past a little road on the left side of us. Dad suddenly swerves the car into the little road and starts driving really fast down it. He shouts, "Fine, we'll go home if that's what you want," and he starts driving even faster. I am a bit scared because Dad has only got one hand on the wheel, while his other hand is reaching into the back pocket of his jeans. He pulls out two football match tickets, and when we are on a straight bit of road he takes his other hand off the wheel too, and uses it to rip the tickets in half. Then he throws them onto me. He says, "There you go. Happy birthday."

I don't know why he is saying, 'Happy birthday,' because it is not my birthday today. I don't think that we are going to football anymore, because Dad has ripped up the tickets. I am glad about that, but I feel upset because I think that my dad is angry with me, and I feel scared because he is driving very, very fast.

We keep driving past signs that say the speed limit on this road is forty miles an hour, but I can see that Dad is driving more than eighty miles an hour, and I think that we are getting even faster. I am really scared now, and my head starts to scream, so I scream. I scream lots and lots, and I stamp my feet. I close my eyes, and I cover my ears. I am boiling hot, but Dad won't let me turn the heat down.

I don't know how long we are driving this fast and I am screaming for, but eventually I feel the car slowing down, very gradually. I feel safer now, so I stop screaming and I open my eyes. We are further along the same road, and there are not as many cars or people around us now. I stop stamping my feet. Dad is driving at forty miles an hour now, which is the right speed limit. I take my hands off my ears.

Dad does not say anything, but he doesn't look as angry any more.

I still feel hot, so I take off my scarf and my coat.

He looks at me.

"I'm sorry I made you cross," I tell him.

Dad is quiet for a minute, and then he says, "I'm sorry I got cross." He keeps looking forwards, out of the window. "And I'm sorry if I scared you."

I say, "That's okay," because that is what you are supposed to say when someone says that they are sorry.

Susan Hobson
July 2003

Happy third anniversary to me.

Ian had a 'wonderful surprise' planned for today. When he told me that all I needed were my walking boots and a Mac, I knew not to expect too much - and I was right. Myself, Ian *and* the kids, are currently eating a soggy picnic in an arbitrary piece of field, hoping desperately that the coats we are sitting on can protect us from the minefield of sheep faeces beneath us.

"See, I told you you would enjoy yourself," Ian says, handing me one of the tuna and cucumber sandwiches that he made himself – about a week ago, going by the texture of them.

Apparently my facial expression is suggesting that I am enjoying myself; that's clever of it. "Hmmm," I reply, wafting a humongous wasp away from my carton of orange juice, "you did."

"Ian, I'm bored," says Hannah, dramatically rolling her head into her hands like the premature teenager that she is. Can't fault the girl's sentiments, though.

"Well, you've finished your dinner. Why don't you go and sit with Matthew and Rose and watch the river?"

Her expression says everything.

"Okay, don't then. I never will understand you girls; I bring you to such a beautiful setting, and you both act like you'd rather be out shopping."

Hannah glances over at me, and I stifle a grin.

"Do you want some cake, Matthew?" I call, changing the subject rapidly.

He is lying on his stomach with his head hanging over the riverbank and his right arm curled over the lazy dog. I don't quite get his fascination with rivers. It's water, it's moving - not exactly the stuff of great action films. At the word cake, though, he rolls onto his back and sits up. "Yes, I do want some cake," he says, standing up quickly, and making his way over to us. He is, most definitely, my son.

Rose trots after him loyally.

"Me too, Mum," chirps in Hannah.

I hand them both a piece of my master chocolate cake.

"Did you know, Mathew, that there are around twenty major rivers in the United Kingdom?"

Hannah and me look at each other again.

"There are twenty-two, actually," replies Matt.

I feel a small glimmer of pride. There you go, Ian - there are twenty-two, actually.

"But there are lots more little rivers, aren't there, Ian Hobson? And we will never be able to count how many there actually are, will we"

"Well, yes, you're right. Now, do you know which is the longest river in the UK?"

Oh, give me strength - a battle of the river geeks.

"Yes, it is the river Severn, because that is two-hundred and twenty miles long. Although, I think it should be seven miles long because of its name." He begins to laugh, almost hysterically. "But," he continues, having composed himself, "the longest river in the world is the river Nile, because that is over four-thousand miles long."

This boy's photographic memory astounds me.

"What is the longest river in the United States of America, Ian Hobson? Is it the river Mississippi? Because that is a very long river."

"I'm not sure. Perhaps it is - but it may blend with the Missouri river, which may mean that it doesn't count."

"Can we please go home now?"

"Hannah, don't be rude," I reprimand, internally agreeing with her. "Although, it is looking rather cloudy over there, Ian - we don't want to get caught in a rainstorm." I look pointedly at Matthew.

Ian follows the point of my finger, and cannot deny the denseness of the cloud up ahead.

"I don't want to get caught in a rainstorm," Matthew announces. Good boy.

"Well, I think we have a good hour or so before that reaches us, Son."

"I don't want to be caught in a rainstorm. I want to go home."

"But we are having such a good time, watching the river, and - "

"I want to go home."

Ian looks at me and I shrug my shoulders. "Probably not worth the risk," I say, with faux regret.

He ponders for a moment. "Alright," he says eventually, "let's get all of this packed up."

"Probably best," I say, and, as Ian busies himself with his rucksack, I give Hannah an inconspicuous high-five.

Matthew Pickering
May 2004

Dad is walking up and down his living room while we watch the movie, and he keeps looking at his watch. I think he keeps forgetting what the time is. He must have got a bad memory.

I wish he would sit down, because it is very hard to concentrate on the Inspector Gadget movie when he is walking in front of the television. Suddenly, I hear the front door opening, and Dad walks out of the room. I can hear him say, "Finally. Thanks so much, Babe. I've got to go. He's in the front room." Then he shouts, "Bye, Matt," and I hear the door closing again. I think my dad must have gone out because he said, 'Bye, Matt,' and then the door closed. I wonder where he can have gone, because we are supposed to be having a father-son day today; watching movies and building a wooden kennel for my dog, Rose.

I can hear someone stamping around the house, but I don't know who it is. The stamping is very loud so I turn the volume on my movie up a little bit. Lots of minutes later, the door of the living room opens and Jennifer Cooper looks in. "You okay?" she asks me.

I say, "Yes. Where did my dad go?"

"Work. Urgent call, apparently. Don't look at me like that, this isn't how I'd choose to be spending my

Saturday either; I had a day of pampering planned. I don't know why he couldn't have sent you home instead. Where's your sister?"

"I can't go home because Ian Hobson is at work, and Mum is looking after Nana because she has caught a nasty bug called leukemia, and Hannah is at Lucy's house because she had a sleepover."

Jennifer Cooper is looking at the television and not at me. "Whatever," she says. "Do you need anything?"

I say, "No, thank you," because it is good to be polite.

Jennifer Cooper says, "Good." Then she comes into the living room and picks up the remote control from the coffee table. She presses stop on the DVD player, and turns the television onto another channel. I do not know what has come on the television, but it looks like a chat show. I do not like television chat shows because lots of people shout on them, and I don't like it when people shout.

I say, "I want to watch the movie."

"Tough. And it's a film, not a 'movie'. What country do you think we are in?"

I whisper, "England," very quietly.

She sits down on the armchair and rests her feet on the coffee table.

I do not like it when she is doing that, because feet are not meant to go on the coffee table because they will put germs onto it. I say, "Put your feet down, please."

Jennifer Cooper laughs, and says, "You can whistle; it's not your house."

I don't understand. I can't whistle, and I don't know what whistling has got to do with her feet being on the table. I say, "No, I can't."

She does a really big breath out, and says, "Do you plan on continually annoying me for the next few hours?"

I say, "No," because I do not plan on annoying her.

She looks at me. "Good, because if you do, you can sit outside until your dad gets back."

I do not want to sit outside because it is raining today and I don't want to get wet, so I say, "No, thank you." I do not like watching this programme, and I want to watch the end of my movie, so I say, "Can you put the movie back on, please?"

Jennifer Cooper says, "No, thank you," in the same way that I said it.

I do not like today. I am starting to feel stressed, because I wanted to have a nice day with my dad and now my dad has gone away, and I want to watch Inspector Gadget but I can't, and the television is getting very noisy because people on it are shouting, and I have to be with Jennifer Cooper, who I do not like. I am having a sad and stressful day, and my head is starting to hurt me. I feel very hot so I take off my hoodie jumper.

Jennifer Cooper looks at me, but she does not say anything.

I still feel very hot, and my head is hurting, so I say, "Jennifer Cooper, can I have a drink, please?"

"You know where the kitchen is."

I don't know why she said that, because it did not answer my question. I do not reply.

She says, "Well, go on then. And make me a coffee while you are in there."

I think that Jennifer Cooper wants me to go into the kitchen and make a drink for myself, and I think she wants me to make her a coffee when I am in there too.

"I don't know how to make a coffee," I say, because I don't.

She makes a very loud groany noise, and picks up the notepad and pen that are on the table. She spends a long time writing something down. Then she tears off the page and gives it to me, saying, "Instructions; follow them."

I take the instructions into the kitchen with me. I decide to get myself a drink first, and so I look in the fridge. I find some apple juice that I want to drink, so I take it out. I do not know where the glasses are in my dad's house, because I look in the cupboard where they were when I was a little boy and they are not in that cupboard any more. I think that my dad must not have any glasses in his house any more. I can see lots of mugs hanging from a wooden thing, and so I take one off and put my apple juice in it. I do not really like drinking my apple juice out of a mug, because I like drinking my apple juice out of a glass.

I look at Jennifer Cooper's instructions for making a coffee. They say: -

1. 'Put water in the kettle.'

I know which the kettle is, because it is a metal, circle shaped thing that is in the corner of the kitchen, so I take it to the sink and I pour some water in through the spout. I do not know how much water to pour into the kettle because the instructions do not tell me, so I fill it until no more water will fit into it. I carry it back to where the kettle goes, and some of the water spills out of the spout and onto the floor.

2. 'Turn the kettle on.'

There is a button on the kettle, so I press it and it goes red. Nothing else happens. I wait for a long time, and then decide to look at the next instruction.

3. 'While the kettle is boiling, put one teaspoon of coffee into a mug.'

I think the kettle is boiling now because it has started to make a funny noise. I get another mug and I open up the drawer that I know has got spoons in.

Now I am confused, because there are some big spoons and some little spoons in here. I do not know what a teaspoon is. I remember that when I eat my pudding after my tea I use a big spoon, so a big spoon must be a 'teaspoon'. I see a pot that says 'coffee' on it, so I open it up, get a spoonful of the coffee out, and put it into the mug.

The kettle is making a hissing and a bubbling sound now. I think, maybe it has boiled.

4. 'Pour water from the kettle into the mug.'

I reach out to take the kettle. I put my hands around it and pick it up. It feels funny. About a second later I let it go, because it is making my hands sting. A lot. The kettle drops to the floor.

I scream very loudly. It is a shock because it is so painful on my hands. I scream again. I am feeling more feelings than I have ever felt before, because I don't feel pain very often, and it feels good and horrible at the same time. I wave my hands about in the air. Now it is painful on my feet too, because the hot water from the kettle is running onto the floor and I have not got my shoes on.

I jump up in the air, but when I land the hot water is still there, and it splashes even further up my leg. I can't help screaming again because it hurts a lot, but I never knew that my hands and my feet could feel this many feelings. My body is making me jump up and down to get out of the hot water, and it is making me wave my hands to help them to cool down, even though my brain is saying that it feels good. My hands and feet are not cooling down.

Suddenly, the kitchen door opens, and Jennifer Cooper is there. She shouts, "You idiot! What have you done? You stupid boy."

I cannot answer her because it is very hard to breathe. I feel very funny, and I am in lots and lots of pain. The water around my feet feels like it has cooled down a little bit now, but my feet are still burning, and my hands are still burning, and the bottom of my legs are still burning too.

Jennifer Cooper picks up the kettle by its handle and says, "Look at what you have done to the floor; there's water everywhere. Have you burned yourself, too? Stupid boy."

I take as deep a breath as I can, but it is getting very hard to breathe. I need to lie down, so I sink down to the floor.

Jennifer shouts, "Don't lie in it, you absolute lunatic. You've got all your clothes wet now. You complete idiot."

I am finding it hard to hear her now. Her voice sounds very quiet and far away. I feel like I am spinning around the room, but I am not, I am lying on the floor. I feel a little bit cold where I am lying in the water, which doesn't make sense because the water was really hot.

I hear a noise at the front door, and a voice says, "Only me. I'm not really here, I just forgot my wallet." I know that it is my dad's voice.

My hands and my feet hurt so much, but I can't cry. I don't have the strength... even... to...

***

My eyes are closed, but I am starting to hear something. It sounds like a man and a lady are talking. I think I must be having a dream, but my bed doesn't feel very comfortable. My bed feels hard and cold, and wet too. My hands and my feet are stinging a little bit. Now the talking is getting louder, and my hands and feet are hurting more and more. I think that the talking I can hear might be shouting. I can hear my dad's voice. I am not sure where I am, but I must be with my dad. I think that the lady's voice might be Jennifer Cooper's, because it sounds like her.

I can hear my dad say, "What have you done to my son?"

The lady, who I think is Jennifer Cooper, says, "What have *I* done? Excuse me, but he got into this mess all by himself."

"You were supposed to be watching him."

I feel somebody tapping my arm and stroking my face.

"Matty. Matthew, wake up, Son."

"I was only in the other room, John. It wasn't like I left him alone."

"I really don't want to hear it. Have you called an ambulance?"

"He doesn't need an ambulance, it's just a bit of water. He'll be fine in a minute."

"You get that phone, and you call an ambulance, now." Dad sounds very cross.

"Don't tell me what to do."

I can hear every word very clearly now, and I think I know where I am. I remember that I was in the kitchen at Dad's house when I hurt myself and fell asleep. But I don't understand why my dad is here, because he is supposed to be at his work.

I hear him call Jennifer Cooper a very rude name as he tells her that, if she doesn't call an ambulance right this minute, then he won't be responsible for what he does. I don't know what that means. I can't hear Jennifer Cooper any more, but I can hear my dad saying, "Matthew, can you wake up for me? Wake up."

I open my eyes a little bit, because Dad told me to wake up. I am very cold, and I feel that I am starting to shiver. My hands are hurting a lot, and so are my feet.

Dad says, "You're awake. It's okay, Son. I'm here." I can see him taking off his coat, and he lays it over my body. I feel bad, because his coat and his trousers must be getting wet now because he is kneeling on the wet floor, and his coat is lying over me and touching the wet floor.

I say, "Sorry, Dad," because I can tell that my dad is very angry because he was shouting.

Dad says, "You've got nothing to be sorry about. Just lie still for a minute. It's okay. An ambulance is coming. Did you burn yourself?"

I say, "Yes. I burnt my hands and my feet."

"Okay, just stay there. Don't worry, I'm coming back." My dad stands up, and I can hear him running the tap very fast. In a minute he comes back with a basin full of water. I hope it is cold water, because I do not think I want to burn myself again right now. Dad helps me to sit up and rest my back against the cupboard. Then he puts my feet into the water.

I make a little screaming noise because my feet sting a lot when they go into the water, because it is very cold water.

"It's okay," Dad says. "This will help the stinging, I promise." Then he stands up and opens the cupboard under the sink. He gets another basin, fills it with water, places it on the floor next to me, and helps me to put my hands into it. That stings as well, but Dad tells me that it will help me, so I believe him. He wraps his coat around my shoulders because I am still shivering. Then he shouts, "Get a blanket, Jennifer."

I am sitting with my dad, and with my hands and feet in cold water, for lots of minutes. Finally, Jennifer Cooper comes into the kitchen, and she is holding a blanket. She throws it onto me from the door and shouts, "There." Some of the blanket lands in the cold water, which is not a good thing. Then she says, "The ambulance is on its way. I'm going."

"What do you mean, you're going?" says Dad

"What do you think I mean? Are you as dim as your son?"

Then Dad shouts, "Oh, just get out, you silly little girl."

"That's what I *am* doing. This - " she points to me, and then to my dad, " - is clearly a genetic thing. Like father, like son." Then she grabs her set of keys from the kitchen table, takes one of the keys off, and throws it at my dad. She says, "I'm not coming back, so you can have that."

I don't know what key she has given to my dad, but he does not look like he is happy. He says, "Good. I'm very glad." I am surprised that he is glad, because he does not look or sound like he is glad.

Jennifer Cooper walks away, and then I hear the front door opening and closing, so I think that she must have left the house.

Dad looks at me, and he asks, "How are your hands?"

"Hot on the front, but cold on the back".

He smiles. "That sounds about right. How about your feet?"

"Hot all over."

"Just keep them in the water for a bit longer, until the ambulance comes. We will just have to take a quick trip to hospital. Don't worry, I won't leave you alone."

Hannah Pickering
October 2004

"Hannah."

Oh dear. I pull the covers more tightly over my head, feeling the cool air of my bedroom tickle my ankles, which are now protruding from the bottom of the duvet.

'Bang - Bang'

Oh double dear. I don't answer, but hear my bedroom door creaking open anyway. Do parents not understand the word 'privacy'? I tighten my grip of the duvet over my head, slightly struggling for oxygen. The stench is almost unbearable, and my eyes are stinging from tears.

"Oh, hello, Hannah's feet," says Mum, in the highly irritating tone she puts on when she's annoyed, "You haven't seen her head anywhere, have you? No? I guess I'll have to speak to you, then." How is it that mums can be embarrassing, even when there is no one else in the room? "Is there any chance you can explain to me why my bathroom stinks of bleach? Only, as far as I can see, it doesn't appear to have been cleaned."

I wait. I wonder if she is actually expecting my feet to answer. She's stupid enough.

"No? Okay, let me ask you this - why is it that I found an empty bottle of kitchen bleach in the black bin outside, along with my best towel - covered in blotches of white, and large chunks of platinum hair?"

I think she knows. I can't stop the tears from pouring now, and my mouth makes a snorty sort of noise.

"Hannah," she says, in a less harsh tone. "Let me see your hair."

"No," I mumble through the covers.

"Let me see. Maybe I can help."

I loosen my grip of the duvet slightly. She doesn't sound like she is about to murder me - although I can't see her, who knows what weapon she might be yielding out there.

"Han, come on."

I slowly peel the covers down to shoulder level, and raise my eyes to meet Mum's.

Hers are wide, and her mouth is hanging open a little.

I wait for the onslaught.

"Erm," is all that she says, and then I watch as the sides of her mouth twitch upwards. She covers it with her hand. She is shaking her head, but her eyes don't look all that angry. Suddenly, she lets out a titter, and bows her head.

I groan, and pull the covers up again.

"Han, I'm sorry; it's not that bad. What am I saying? It's hideous. What on earth compelled you?"

I feel my bed bouncing under me as her weight presses down next to my feet.

"You are such a silly girl. Your beautiful hair."

"Help," I say in a small voice.

Mum laughs. "I'm very tempted to make you go back to school like that next week. It would teach you a lesson." She is enjoying this far too much. There is silence for what feels like forever. "Fortunately, I'm not that sort of mother. I did a similar thing when I was about your age; your Nana Brady went spare at me. She *did* make me go to school like that. Those were the worst three months of my life." She slaps my bottom through the duvet, but not hard. "Right then, you, downstairs in ten minutes. We'll have a look at what we can do."

* * *

"Can't we just go to a hairdresser?" My bum hurts from sitting on this wooden dining chair for the last hour. I have had half the kitchen poured over my head, including raw eggs (for 'conditioning'), mushed up cucumber (to cover up the bleach smell - supposedly), and yoghurt (which will apparently help my hair to grow back quicker) - the old women's magazines that Mum buys have got a lot to answer for.

"No, we certainly can *not*. I'm not forking out the amount it would cost to get this mop sorted. You got yourself into this, you can deal with the consequences."

"But you're chopping too much off, I like my hair long."

"Well so did I, but as it is snapping off in my fingers there's not much I can do about that. And for the record, I also liked your hair red."

"Fine. Well, at least make it look funky."

"You've done a good enough job of that yourself, Han. Can I ask why the top two inches are still orange? Is that the 'in' look these days?"

"I didn't want to bleach my scalp," I answer. "I'm not an idiot."

Mum makes a snorty laugh, but turns it into a cough.

The front door opens at that moment. Oh good, Mr *Interesting* is here.

"Hi, Susan," calls Ian from the hallway.

"It's Sue," she says quietly, and then follows this in a louder voice with, "oh, hi, Darling. We're in the kitchen. Don't mind the smell."

Ian's footsteps get closer, and then he stops in the open doorway. "Oh, Hannah," is all that he says.

"Oh, Ian," I reply.

"Oy." Mum taps my shoulder gently.

"What are you doing to her lovely hair?" He is staring at Mum.

"Don't look at me; she did this monstrosity all by herself. I'm just trying to rescue the situation."

"Oh, Hannah. You're ten years old. You are supposed to be running around playing with dolls, not poisoning your system with chemicals. When I was your age I was..."

"Running around playing with dolls?" I ask.

"Don't be insolent."

I smile. He was probably doing crossword puzzles and watching gardening programmes when he was ten years old.

He looks at me again in what I can only describe as disbelief, shakes his head a couple of times, and then walks out of the room. We hear his footsteps drift lazily up the stairs.

"You going back to Dad yet?" I ask Mum as she snips another lock of my hair away.

"Shush, silly girl; Ian will hear you. Why would you say such a thing? Has your dad said something to you?"

"He's always asking about you. Along with all the *interesting* things that he does."

"Oh, I wish you would stop going on like that. Ian's interesting."

"Right."

"He's an extremely clever man, and *very* interesting. Deep down."

"Okay." Mum makes me laugh when she is huffing about like this. "So, are you going back to him, then?"

"Hannah, just - just don't."

I smile, but I don't say anymore. We sit in silence while she snips away, until we hear the front door opening again.

"Hi, Matty," Mum shouts. "Have you had a nice time with Raine?"

Flaming Raine.

"I can smell bleach," comes the reply. "I don't like it. It smells a lot."

Oops.

Mum sighs loudly, and puts the scissors down on the kitchen table. "Now, look what you've done," she says under her breath as she walks out into the hall.

Matthew Pickering
May 2005

"Just bunk it," Raine says to me as I walk up to the sports field in my P.E. kit.

I do not want to do sports day today. "What do you mean?"

"Bunk off. Spend the day with me."

"Do you mean leave school for the day, Raine?" I am very shocked and surprised. "I cannot do that, it is against the legal law of England. And *you* cannot do that, either."

"Of course I can. It's my last ever day of school next week; I can do what I want."

"That's not true," I tell her, because she is not allowed to do what she wants until she actually finishes school.

"Come on," she says, pulling at my right arm as we walk, "don't be a square. I know you don't want to do this sports day thing."

"I am not square," I say, wondering why she thinks I am square. "I don't want to do sports day, but I have to because I am running in a race."

"Don't do that, Squirt. You know everybody will laugh at you."

"I am a good runner," I tell her, because that is the truth. Me and Hannah are both good runners, because we got it from my Dad, who is a good runner too.

"That won't matter; they'll still laugh at you. You know they will."

She is right. I do know that everybody will laugh at me, because everybody always laughs at me. But I will not leave school when I am not allowed to, because I am not a naughty boy. "I am not leaving school," I tell her.

She lets go of my arm. "Suit yourself," she says. "At least let me come and sit with you instead of my stupid form."

"Okay," I say, and we carry on walking up to the sports field together.

* * *

My race is about to start and I am a bit nervous, but I am also a bit excited because I am a very good runner, and I think that I might win this race. My P.E. teacher must think that I am a good runner too, because he decided that I should run today. Mr Andrews says that I am representing my form in this race, and that I am racing against one person from every other form in my year, because it is the Year Nine four-hundred-metre race.

Raine is standing on her feet, and she is shouting, "Matthew, Matthew, Matthew," but I don't know why she is cheering for me because I am not in her form.

Nobody from my form is cheering for me. Everybody keeps telling me that somebody else should be running this race instead, because they think that I will lose it for them. That makes me feel sad, but I don't think that I will lose because I am a very fast runner.

I am getting ready to go. Three - two - one - the whistle blows, and I start to run.

We have got to run two times around the sports field, and I am running very, very fast. I cannot see anyone else that I am racing against, because they are all behind me. I wonder if they are a long way behind me. My legs are pushing forwards with lots of speed, and I can't even feel myself pushing them anymore.

I am now half way around the first lap of the track, and I can hear some cheering from the grass bank. I look over, and all of the people in my form are standing up and cheering. I wonder if they are cheering for me - I think that they must be. That makes me feel very happy. I turn my head, and can see that every other racer is a long way behind me now. I trip a little because I am looking behind me, so I turn my face to the front again and carry on running. I am three quarters of the way around the first lap, and I am winning.

As I get near to the part where I started the race, which means I have done one lap, I can hear the cheering even louder because I am a lot closer to everybody. I can even see that Billy Robin and Anthony Richards are standing up, although they are not cheering.

But it is getting very hard to run now. I am really, really tired. My legs are slowing down and I feel like I am getting very out of breath. My chest hurts, and it could be a heart attack. I slow down a bit more.

"Come on, Matt; they're catching you up," I hear somebody shout.

I turn around, and I can see that that person was right; every other racer is catching me up now. I wonder why they are not slowing down like I am. I turn my head forwards again and I try to keep running, but it is very hard. I start to lean forwards, and my breath is very panty. I am a quarter of the way around the second lap. My speed is not very fast at all, and I cannot make it faster, even though I am trying very hard.

Somebody passes me. That makes me sad because now I will be second and I thought that I was going to win. I hear some groany shouts from the grass bank, but I also hear some cheers, and I can see that another form of people are now standing up, while my form are sitting down. My legs are going no faster than walking now.

Another person passes me. I feel cross and sad, but I try to carry on. It is hard. Somebody else passes me, and then another person. Now I am in fifth place. My chest hurts a lot, and so does my throat. I cannot breathe.

One more person passes me. I am in sixth place, and there are only six racers, which means that I will be last.

I am half way around the track now, and I am trying to carry on walking but it is too difficult. I slow to a stop and put my hands onto my hips, which helps me to get some more air into my lungs. I hear some booing, and I wonder if it is for me. I hope that it isn't because that would be very sad. I need to sit down.

As I collapse to the floor I can hear some more cheering, and when I look across the field I can see that one person has run over the line and won the race. I feel sad. I close my eyes and lie back on the floor so I can stop feeling so tired.

I can hear lots of booing now, and when I open my eyes I can see some water bottles being thrown onto the track. I can hear some teachers shouting.

Then I hear Mr Andrews' voice, and he is shouting very loudly, "Raine Bishop, sit down now. Matthew, don't be an idiot, stand up and finish the race. Raine, I said *sit down*."

I can see something else out of the side of my eye, and I turn to look. Raine is running across the track towards me. I wonder why she is doing that, because she is not in a race. When she gets to me, she bends down and smiles.

I try to ask her what she is doing, but no words can come out of my mouth. Perhaps it is because I am having a heart attack.

"Are you okay?"

I shake my head, because I cannot speak.

"What happened?"

I breathe in as much air as I can, and manage to say, "Heart...attack."

She laughs. "Don't be an idiot, you're not having a heart attack; you're just knackered. Come on, people are laughing at you. Stand up."

"Can't," I manage to tell her, as she pulls me up onto my feet. I rest all of my weight on her.

"Of course you can," she says. "Right, let's finish this race. Give them something to laugh at, the losers." And then me and Raine start to walk very slowly around the rest of the track, and she holds me up all of the way.

Matthew Pickering
April 2007

Today it is my little sister's birthday, and she is thirteen years of age, which means that she is a teenager. I have been a teenager for three years and four and a half months already, and I don't think that it is very different from being a child. I am a bit taller than I was when I was a child, and I have got some more muscles, but that is all that is different. My mum says that I am not like most teenage boys, because most teenage boys are dirty, and smelly and untidy, but I am not any of those things because I like to keep myself and my things very clean and tidy. I do not like things that are dirty or messy.

It is a Saturday night tonight, and Hannah is having a birthday party at Harleyfield Village Hall, which is three roads away from our house. I did not have a party when it was my thirteenth birthday, and I am glad about that, because I do not like parties. I did not want to come to this party, but Mum said that she would like me to come because it is my sister's special night, and she said that Raine could come too, so I am at the party and my best friend, Raine, is coming soon.

I look very nice tonight, because I got dressed up specially. I am wearing my smart jeans and a nice red and blue checked shirt. I have put some gel on my hair and made it go to the side a bit so that it is not in my eyes, because my hair is a bit long (but not long like a girl's hair, just like nice boy haircut). Mum told me to gel my hair to the sides so that I don't cover up my beautiful blue eyes. When I looked in the mirror I decided that I looked very nice, and my mum said that I looked very nice too.

Harleyfield Village Hall is quite a big village hall. There is a very big room, which is where most of the people at the party are, and it is very loud in that room because there is a disco (even though no-one is dancing), and there are lots of balloons. There are some boys from mine and Hannah's school who are running around and jumping on the balloons to make them pop. I hate balloons when they pop because they make a very loud noise that hurts my ears and makes my head scream. But I am a sensible boy, and I know that I should not stand screaming and covering my ears, but I should leave the room so that I don't hear the sound again.

So that is what I did, and I am standing in another room that this village hall has, called the kitchen. Even though I can still hear the music from the disco, and the people shouting, and the balloons that sometimes pop, it is a lot more quiet in the kitchen because I have got the door closed, and so it is not too noisy for me.

I am by myself in the kitchen right now because Mum and Ian Hobson are standing in the party to make sure that everybody is okay, and that all of the other children and teenagers are having fun in the party room. My dad is not here yet, but I think that he is coming later. I think that he will be coming by himself, because he does not have a girlfriend. He had a girlfriend called Jennifer Cooper a long time ago, but then he made her not be his girlfriend anymore when she helped me to burn myself. Mum says that he has got a different girlfriend every week, but I don't think that he has a girlfriend this week.

The door into the kitchen opens all of a sudden, and the noise gets a bit louder for a second. I take in a deep breath and try not to cover my ears or scream. Two girls walk in, and they close the door behind them, which I am glad about because it makes the noise go quieter again. I do not know who these girls are, because they do not go to my school, but I think that they must be friends with my sister because they are at her party. Maybe Hannah knows them from her netball club. I think they have come into the kitchen to get a drink, because there are a lot of drinks in here for people to have, and a lot of cups. There are not any drinks with alcohol in them, though, because most of us are under the age of eighteen, and you are not allowed to drink alcohol if you are under the age of eighteen in England. If I lived in the United States of America I would not be allowed to drink alcohol until I am twenty-one years old.

The girls look at me when they walk into the room, and one of them makes a little giggle, but I don't know why. The girl at the front, the one who is not giggling at me, is quite a tall girl, and she has got long, straight, brown hair. She has got a very short skirt on, and she is wearing high-heeled shoes on her feet. Her shoes are red, and her skirt is black. She is wearing a red t-shirt, too. She has got a lot of red make up on her lips, and some on the tops of her eyes. I think it looks a bit silly.

The giggling girl is behind the tall girl with brown hair. She is shorter, and she has got very long, straight, yellow hair, a bit like Raine has got. She is wearing black leggings, and something that is too long to be a t-shirt, but too short to be a dress, so I do not know what it is. Both girls look like they are about fourteen years of age, but I do not know that for definite because I do not know their dates of birth.

The tall girl looks at me and she smiles. "Here's where you have been hiding," she says to me.

I wonder how she knows that I was hiding.

The smaller girl behind her giggles again, but I don't know why.

"I have been looking for you for ages," the front girl carries on.

I am confused about why she has been looking for me, because I do not know her. "I don't know you," I say to her.

She makes her left eye close quickly and then open again, like she is blinking with only one eye. I think she looks funny. "Do you want to?" she asks me.

I do not know the answer to this question, so I just lift my shoulders up and down. I have seen people do this before when they do not know the answer to a question.

The girl points her head to the floor, but looks up at me with her eyes and smiles again. I think she is very strange. "What's your name?" she asks me.

I do know the answer to that question. "Matthew James Pickering," I say.

She pulls a bit of a funny face and looks at the small girl behind her. "Don't forget the James," she says, making a bit of a laugh. "So, you're related to Hannah, then?"

"Yes," I say.

She looks at me again, like she is waiting for me to say something else, but I don't know what else she wants me to say to her.

The girl behind her giggles.

"Mine's Holly," she says. "In case you were going to ask."

I was not going to ask. I say, "Okay."

The girl that is called Holly walks closer to the chair that I am sitting on, and she bends over a little bit. "So," she says, and she pushes her hair over the back of her head with her right hand (but I don't know why she does that), "are you going to get me a drink then?"

I am confused. I am not a barman, and so it is not my job to get her a drink. She is standing closer to the drinks than I am right now, so I wonder why she wants me to get her a drink. "No," I say.

I can see her eyebrows lift up a little bit, and she stands up straighter.

The little girl starts to laugh again.

Holly looks at her and pulls a frowny face.

She stops laughing.

"So, that's how it is?" she says. "I'll get my own drink then, shall I?" She looks at the other girl. "Pour me a coke, Em."

The other girl, who I think is called Em, walks up to the counter where the drinks are, pours some coke into a plastic cup, and hands it to Holly.

"Cheers, Babes," Holly says, and then she pulls a funny face at Em. It is a face that I don't understand. She makes her eyebrows go high, and her eyes go wide, and then she looks at the door and nods her head.

Em says, "Oh... okay, just let me pour myself -"

Holly shakes her head and looks at the door again.

"Right, never mind. I'll see you in a bit."

"Bye, Babes," Holly says, as Em opens up the door and walks back into the party room.

I focus very hard on not listening to the music that comes through the door.

When Em has gone, Holly looks at me. "Just you and me now, Matthew James. That's much better." And then she does something that surprises me a lot; she puts her drink down on the table behind me, and she sits down on my knee. She puts one of her arms around the back of my shoulders, and she sits sideways so that she is looking at me.

I do not like how close her face is to my face, so I move my head back a bit. I wonder why she sitting on my knee, because there are three other chairs in this kitchen.

"You don't mind if I sit here, do you?"

"No," I say, because I don't mind it.

"So, how are you related to Hannah?"

I can feel her fingers stroking the back of my neck and I do not like it; it makes my neck feel sore. "Don't do that." I tell her, and she stops, but she looks like she is surprised. "Hannah is my sister."

"Older or younger?"

"Hannah is younger than me, because she is only thirteen."

"I know she's thirteen; it's her thirteenth birthday party. How old are you?"

"I'm sixteen years of age," I tell her.

"Snap - so am I," she says.

I am surprised." I thought you were fourteen," I tell her.

"Why did you think that?"

"You look like you are fourteen."

Holly looks a bit cross with me, but I don't know why she is a bit cross.

"Sorry," I say.

"I don't look fourteen. My brother's mates say I could pass for eighteen if I wanted to - if I put enough make up on. Don't you think I could pass for eighteen?" She starts to move her fingers through my hair.

I do not like the feel of it, and I don't want her to mess my hair up. "Stop it," I tell her, and she stops it.

"You know, 'treat 'em mean, keep 'em keen' doesn't work for me," she says, but I don't know what she means when she says this. "I like to call a spade a spade. If you want me, you can have me - simple as that. Are you seriously going to turn me down?"

I do not know how to answer her question because I do not understand it.

"Last chance. Going, three... two..." She pauses.

I look at her face.

Then Holly sits up straight. "One," she says. "Look, one of three things is happening here. Either you don't like *girls*?" She looks at me and I look back. "Or you're a bit of a bad boy?" She smiles and sticks her thumbs up. "Or you're a bit special?" She pulls a frowny face and turns her thumbs down. "Tell me you're a bad boy."

I do not want to tell her I am a bad boy because I am a good man, so I do not answer her.

She smiles. "I knew it. Well, you can be as bad as you want with me." And then something else happens that I am not expecting; Holly is kissing me on my lips. Nobody has ever kissed me on my lips before. This must mean that Holly loves me. This is very exciting, because a girl has never loved me before. I do not know if I love Holly, but I am having a kiss with her, so maybe I do love her. I have never loved a girl before.

My tummy is feeling very funny, a bit like when I am very hungry. I feel a bit sick, but I don't think that I am going to be sick.

Holly closes her eyes, and so do I.

I don't know how long she is kissing me for, but it feels like lots of minutes. My lips are getting tired, and my legs feel a bit sore because she is squashing them a little bit. Then I hear that the door is opening because I can hear the music again, but I do not know who has come into the kitchen because my eyes are closed. I hear the door close again.

"Matt?" I know whose voice that is.

Holly stops kissing me, and I open my eyes.

Raine is standing near to the door, and she is looking at me. Her hands are on her hips, and she has got a cross face on. I do not know why she is cross.

"Who are you?" Holly says to Raine.

"His girlfriend. Who are you?"

Holly stands up from my knee straight away.

I do not know why Raine said that she is my girlfriend, because that is not true.

"You didn't tell me you had a girlfriend," Holly says to me, and she has a cross face on too.

"I don't," I say. I am confused.

Raine and Holly are looking at each other.

Holly starts to laugh. "Hear that, Love?" she says. "He doesn't think you're his girlfriend, so as far as I'm concerned, he's up for grabs." She sits back on my legs and puts her arm around me again.

Now Raine looks even crosser. She walks over to us very quickly, reaches out to Holly, and pulls her up onto her feet.

Holly screams. "Get off me, you hippy freak," she says loudly.

"You get off him then, you cheap cow."

Raine and Holly are standing very close to each other and they are shouting.

I do not like it. I cover my ears up with my hands, but I can still hear them.

"What did you call me?" Holly says.

"I called you a cheap cow, because that's what you are."

I see the door opening another time, and my dad walks into the room. I think that he must have arrived at the party now. He walks over to the two girls. "Hey," he shouts, "what's going on? Cool down, girls."

Raine's face is very red. She steps back from Holly.

Holly looks at me, and then she pulls a face. "Why are you covering your ears?" she asks loudly. "You weirdo. I was right when I asked if you were special, wasn't I? You're a nutjob."

And then I see something else that makes me surprised. Raine makes her hand slap Holly very hard in her face.

Holly screams.

"Don't you *dare* call him that," Raine shouts at her.

"Raine!" Dad says in a surprised voice.

Holly covers her face up with her hand. She looks at Raine, and then she pushes past her and walks out of the door. She doesn't even look at me one more time.

When the door closes I take my hands off my ears.

Raine is looking at me, and my dad is looking at her.

"What was that all about?" Dad says. He turns to face me. "I can't believe you are still letting other people fight your battles, Matthew."

"I wasn't having a battle," I tell him. "I was having a kiss."

He closes his mouth and stares at me.

"Having a kiss?" He looks around at Raine, and then back at me. "With who, that girl?"

"Yeah, that skanky tramp," is what Raine says.

Dad looks back at her. "And why does it bother you?"

She looks at the floor. "It doesn't." Then her face looks up again, and she looks like she is angry. "But that cow was all over him."

"How do you mean, all over him? Were they fully clothed?"

Raine nods her head.

"Well, what's the problem? I'm pleased he's acting like a normal teenager for once." He puts his hand on my shoulder and smiles at me, and then he makes a frowny face at Raine. I still don't understand why it upset *you* so much?"

"It didn't," she says. "I don't care what he does, I don't care about him, I just didn't think it was appropriate for a thirteen year old's birthday party."

"You said you were my girlfriend, but you are not," I say to Raine.

One of Dad's eyebrows lifts up, and he looks at her.

"I didn't say that," she says, but that is a lie because I heard her say it. "I said I was your friend."

"You did say it. I remember," I tell her.

Dad rubs his eyes with his hands, and then stares at Raine. "You said you were his girlfriend? So is this a jealousy thing? Do you *want* to be Matt's girlfriend, is that it?" Dad is not smiling.

"No. You know I don't." Raine's eyes have gone very big and she is looking at my dad.

"I don't know what you want, and I'm not sure you do, either. You're eighteen, Raine; don't you think it's about time you grew up? I'm getting really sick of this." Dad starts to walk to the door, and I prepare myself for the music to go loud again.

"Oh whatever, John. You're not the boss of me. Just because you're ancient, you expect everyone else to act as old as you."

He turns around and stares at her. "I'm going to see my daughter on her birthday, because I don't even want to be near you right now. Just stay here with Matt, and why don't you do some kissing of your own?"

"Why are you being like this? It's *you* that said you didn't want anything serious. It *you* that told *me* to back off."

"Yeah, well I see you took me literally. Just do what you like, Raine. I honestly couldn't care less." And then my dad walks out of the kitchen, and the room gets very loud again for a few seconds.

Raine looks like she is angry. I don't understand why she was arguing with my dad, but I can see that the argument made her feel cross. I wonder why she said that she was my girlfriend. Perhaps that is what she would like to be? I think that it would be very nice if Raine was my girlfriend because she is very, very pretty, and she is my best friend, along with Rose. I think that I love Raine.

"Do you want to be my girlfriend, Raine?" I ask her, because I think that she wants to be my girlfriend.

She puts her hands up, and puts her head down to meet them. She covers up her face with her hands, but I don't know why she does that. Then she is quiet for a long time.

I do not understand.

She finally answers me, and she says, "That's not..." She lifts her face out of her hands and looks at me. "That's not what I wanted. I didn't want you to... Matt."

I don't really know what Raine is trying to say to me. "What are you trying to say to me, Raine?" I ask her.

"I..." Then she stands up and walks to the door. "Why did you have to do this? Everything was great before. I won't change, you know? I can't."

I do not want Raine to change.

"I don't feel like that about you, Matt; or anyone else. I don't care about anyone, and I don't need anyone."

I don't understand what Raine is saying, and I don't know if she wants to be my girlfriend. "Do you want to be my girlfriend, then?" I ask her.

"No, I'm sorry. No." She opens the door. "Sorry," she says again, and she walks out.

The door closes and I am alone again. I feel confused, and I feel a little bit sad.

Hannah Pickering
April 2007

"Happy birthday, Princess." My dad walks over to me, and gives me a kiss on the cheek and a card. No present. He smells very strongly of aftershave, but doesn't look like he is embracing the party spirit. In fact, he looks pretty miserable. "How does it feel to be a teenager, then?"

"Well, she's been a fair few years in practice. Hi John." Mum is now standing next to me.

"Susie, hi. You look great."

I take the card, turning away from the embarrassing kiss he plants on my cheek.

Mum smiles. "Thanks," she says, "so do you. I always loved that jacket on you."

"Actually, it's new."

"Oh. Well, I like it. Where have you been, anyway? I was wondering if you were coming."

"I was just talking to Matt in the kitchen. I caught him... " Dad is looking over at the kitchen door now, and Raine is walking out of it. So she had been with Matt, too. Just like she always is.

"You caught him doing what? John?"

Dad coughs, and turns back around to face me and Mum again. "Oh, nothing. Just, being Matt. Will you excuse me a moment? Bye, Princess."

Mum is looking confused, as Dad kisses me on the cheek again, and then walks away.

I wish they would just sort themselves out, and then we could all move back in with Dad. Don't get me wrong, it's not that I don't like Ian, but living with him is as exciting as - as being dead. His voice is boring, and his hobbies are boring. Even his clothes are boring. And I *know* Mum agrees with me, even if she won't ever tell me that. Matty thinks he's great, however. Largely because he watches The Simpsons with him, and talks about America with him, and takes him on long, boring walks along rivers and around lakes and things. All the dull things Matty's into.

I am watching Ian across the room right at this moment as he's saying something to the DJ. Seconds later, the music turns to about half its original volume.

"Are you enjoying your night, Sweet Girl?" Mum asks me. "You look so pretty, although I do wish you'd wear a dress one day."

"I don't do dresses," I tell her. Personally, I think I look nice in my shorts and cropped top. My hair looks awesome, too. Mum refuses to let me dye it again until I'm sixteen, but actually, I'm starting to think the red is pretty funky. I have had it cut short and spiky since my hair disaster when I was ten, because I found out that this style actually suits me. I get it done at the hairdressers now though, rather than by my clumsy mother. "I'm - er - just going to wait for my friend outside."

"Okay, but don't be long. And don't get cold." She shouts the last instruction at me as I walk away.

Mum and Dad are never going to get it together again without my influence, and I know from experience that Mum won't let me talk to *her* on the subject. Dad, on the other hand - I've never tried. I've just seen him walking through the doors to the car park, so I quicken my pace across the room to catch up with him.

As I pull open the door into the entrance hall I hear him shouting something just outside the door.

"Raine, wait!"

I stop still and listen. I'm not sure why Dad would want to speak to Raine.

"Oy, wait. Are you crying?"

I hear someone sniff. "No. For your information, I've got a cold. I've never cried in my life."

"Come here."

I walk closer to the door, and can see the silhouette of my dad embracing somebody - embracing Raine. I duck back a little, but make sure I can still just about see.

"Okay, so let's talk about this. What really happened back there?" he asks.

Raine pulls away from him. "I - I think I've just really hurt Matt."

"How do you mean? Did you hit him, too?" Dad sounds worried.

"No, don't be an idiot. I mean emotionally. He asked me to be his girlfriend."

"Oh."

"Yeah."

"You said no, I take it?"

"Of course I did. What do you think I'd say?"

"I don't know, Raine. I don't know what to think with you. I do think you feel more for Matthew than you're letting on."

"I don't."

"I think you do."

"Think what you like. This is getting too hard; I don't want him, but I don't want to hurt him, either. What we are doing is hurting him."

"Only if he finds out."

"Well, I can't keep lying to him forever."

"Who said anything about forever? It's just a bit of fun, right?"

I see Raine's head nodding.

"It doesn't need to get any more complicated than that. It's not like you are in love with me, is it?"

"I don't love anyone."

"That's fine then, as long as we both agree."

"Are we going to stop this, then?"

There is a pause.

"Is that what you want?"

Another pause.

"What do you think?" And then Raine reaches forwards and kisses my dad, square on the lips. Then she pulls away, takes his hand, and leads him out of the car park.

I am glued to my spot. I feel like my eyes have been burned, my mind poisoned. I feel nothing but contempt for that girl, and I don't even know *what* to feel for him. I don't quite believe what I have seen. I almost feel like crying, I have just witnessed all my hopes for my family's future shattering in front of me.

It is only now that I realise I am gripping the doorframe with such force it could potentially snap off in my hand.

"Han?"

I turn around quickly and see Mum standing at the entrance to the hall, watching me.

"Mum." I let go of the frame and stand taller. "How long have you been there?"

"Why? What have you been up to?" She grins. "Don't look at me like that, I'm only joking. I've just come, I promise. I just wanted to check you're okay. Shall bring your coat out for you? It's cold."

"No... I'm fine." I shudder a little, but not with cold. "I'm coming in now."

"What about your friend?"

"What? Oh, I don't think they are coming after all. Let's go in."

"Come on, then."

I follow her inside, feeling numb all over.

Matthew Pickering
May 2007

Raine is at my house helping me to revise for my GCSE examinations, because I have got to do some of those this year. They are very important examinations, and they will help me to get a good job. I want my job to be an actor when I am older because I want to be a movie star in Hollywood, in the United States of America.

Raine is very clever at passing examinations, and she got five A star grades and six A grades when she did her GCSEs two years ago. She went to college then, and in October she is going to a place called The University of Sheffield, because she wants to learn how to be an ecologist. I don't really know what an ecologist is, but Raine says it will mean that she can help the environment. Raine is very, very good at science, and especially at biology. I am very good at science too, and Mr Appleton, who is my science teacher at school, said that I could easily win an A star grade in my GCSE examination if only I was clever enough to write my answers in plain English. I do not know why he said that, because I always write my answers in English. I do not know any other languages to write in.

I am only taking five GCSE examinations, because I do not have to take as many as the other people in my school. Billy Robin says that this is because I am brain dead, but that is silly, and a lie, because I am not brain dead. If I was brain dead, I would be dead. I think that Billy Robin is very stupid.

The five GCSEs that I will be taking are called English, science, maths, ICT, and drama. I have got to take the ones called English, science, and maths by the law of my school, and my ICT teacher said that I should take the ICT examination too, because she thinks that I will get a good grade in it because I am good at computers. I wanted to take drama as a GCSE because it might help me to get a job as an actor when I am grown up, so I did.

My teachers think that I will get an F grade in English, but I do not want to because F means 'fail'. They think that I will win a D grade in science and in drama, a C grade in maths, and an A grade in ICT, because I am very good at computers.

Raine has come to help me with my revising, but I don't want to revise, and I don't think that Raine wants to revise either, because she keeps looking at her mobile telephone and she looks sad. I wonder why Raine looks sad.

"Are you sad today, Raine?" I ask her, as I see a tear falling out of one of her eyes.

She makes her fingers wipe the tear away from her face, but I already saw it. "No," she tells me, but I know that this is a lie because I know what tears mean. She flicks her long yellow hair over her shoulders so it is not in front of her face anymore. "Come on," she says. "Plant cells - what do you get inside them?"

I do not need to look at my books to know what is inside a plant cell, because I can remember it in my head. I say, "There is a cell wall on the outside, and inside the cell wall there is something called a membrane. Inside that there is some cytoplasm, and lots of things live inside that, like a nucleus, and mitochondria, and lysosomes, and a golgi complex. And inside the nucleus is something called a nucleolus."

She makes a very little smile and says, "Tick," which means that I am right. She is reading one of my schoolbooks that has got the answers in, because she is not clever enough to know if my answers are right in her head. "Next," she says, "can you explain the process of photosynthesis? Write it down." She hands me a pen and a piece of paper.

I look at her. I know all about photosynthesis. I know how the chlorophyll makes glucose from the sun, carbon dioxide, and water, but it is very hard to explain it in writing. I pick up the pen and put it on the paper. Raine's telephone makes a beeping noise. She picks it up, looks at it again, and then throws it onto my bed from where we are sitting.

Rose, who is sitting on my bed, lifts up her head, and reaches out her paw to touch the phone. Rose does not do lots of things any more, because she just likes to lie on my bed. She does not really play with me a lot anymore, but she still likes me to cuddle her and stroke her, and I still love her very much. Mum says that she is just tired because she is getting old, but she is not that old, because she is only eleven years of age.

I look at the paper, and write, 'Photosynthesis is - '
I scribble it out.
I write 'A plant photosynthesises - '
I think, and then I scribble it out.
'Light and chlorophyll - '
I scribble this out too. I am getting very cross.
I eventually write, 'Light. Water. Carbon Dioxide. Chlorophyll. Photosynthesis. Glucose.'

"Done," I say, and I hand the piece of paper to Raine.

She reads it. "Rubbish," she tells me, "you've just failed, Matthew."

I feel cross, and I throw the pen at the window in front of me. It makes a funny pinging noise, and bounces back. I stand up, walk quickly over to my bed, and fall onto it, making a loud grunty noise.

Rose moves a little bit closer to where I landed, and rests her head on my back.

"I don't want to revise," I say, with my face looking into my duvet. Then I roll onto my side and look at Raine.

She says, "Neither do I," and sits next to me on my bed. She still has a sad face on.

"Why are you sad?" I ask her. She lifts her feet onto the bed too, and I am very glad that she has not got her shoes on. She rests her back against my headrest and stretches her legs out in front of her.

I sit up too, and Rose follows me up to the top of my bed.

"You don't want to know," she says. I think that is a silly thing to say because I wouldn't have asked her if I didn't want to know.

"Yes I do."

"Well, I'm not sad, so there's nothing to tell you. Oh just get lost," she shouts, as her telephone makes another beeping noise. "Not you," she continues, looking at me. "Alright, do you want the truth?"

"Yes," I say, because I would like her to tell me the truth.

"Do you know what an abortion is?"

"Yes, it's an operation that girls have when they have poorly tummies. Like you did last year, remember?"

She looks up at my ceiling.

I look up too, to see what she is looking at, but there is nothing there.

"I remember. I have to decide if I want another one or not. If I don't... well university's out the window - "

I look out of the window.

" - As is the rest of my life."

I look back at Raine, and her eyes are very red coloured.

"But if I do have another...operation... The thing is, I don't really want to do that."

"You shouldn't do anything you don't want to do, Raine," I tell her.

She smiles a tiny bit, but there are little tears coming out of her eyes. "Someone else wouldn't necessarily agree with you."

"Who wouldn't agree with me?"

"Someone you don't know about," she says.

I don't know what she means.

She picks up her telephone, and then shows it to me. "He sent me this today," she says.

There is a text message on the screen that I read. It says -

From:JP
Talk to me. How are you feeling? I want to see you. Xxx

I wonder why she is showing me this message, so I say, "Why are you showing me this message, Raine?"

"Not sure," she says, "I suppose I need someone to talk to."

"But JP wants you to talk to them," I tell her. "You should talk to them, because they are telling you to."

"You don't get cleverer, do you?" she says. "If you read that message properly you'd know what I'm trying to tell you. What I have been trying to tell you for months."

I don't understand. I did read the message properly. "I did read the message properly," I tell her.

"Sure," is all that she says. She reaches her hand towards me, and she puts it on my right arm. It feels nice. She smiles at me a bit more this time, and I think that she has got a very pretty smile. "I wish I could tell you the truth," she says.

"You can tell me the truth."

"No, I can't."

I wonder why she can't tell me the truth, but I say, "Okay."

Raine smells very nice today. She smells like flowers, and I think that she must be wearing a perfume that smells like flowers, because I don't think that any human can smell like that without wearing a perfume. She looks very pretty, too. She has got a little blue headband on, but it has fallen down and it now goes across her forehead and ties round the back of her head, which I think is a bit silly. Her hair is very long and pretty. She has got some brown eyes, and they have got big black lines around them. I think that Raine painted the black lines on with make-up because they are not always there. She has got red lipstick on her lips too, which makes them look very nice.

"How does make-up work?" I ask Raine.

She laughs at me a little bit. "You do ask some funny things," she says to me. "What a random question when we're talking about... You make me laugh."

I am glad that I make her laugh. "But how does it work?" I ask again. "Why do you look more pretty when you have got make-up on?"

Raine is still laughing a bit. "I don't know, maybe it's because I am just so ugly without it?"

"Maybe," I say, although I don't think that that is the reason because I don't think that Raine is ugly.

She picks up a pillow from my bed and throws it at my face. I don't know why. It doesn't hurt me, because it is only a pillow. "I do love you, you little squirt," she says.

Something inside my chest feels a bit funny. It feels like my heart is beating a bit faster, but I do not know if that is possible. I also have a funny feeling in my tummy, but it is not a nasty feeling.

"I didn't know that you love me," I say, because I did not know this and I am surprised.

"Of course I do. You're my best mate, aren't you?"

I am a little bit confused, because Raine does not care about anybody, but I think that if you love somebody you have got to care about them. I think that it is impossible to love somebody and not care about them. "But you don't care about anybody, Raine," I tell her.

She smiles a bit, and she looks towards my window. "I guess you're the exception," she says. "Don't go leaving me, though, like my mum did."

I hope that I will not leave Raine like her mum did, because Raine's mum died.

"Promise?"

"No," I say. "I can't promise that, because I do not know the future. But I hope that I don't leave you like your mum did, Raine." I put the pillow that Raine threw at me behind my head, and rest back against the wall.

Raine then says, "What if I did something horrible to you?"

"You wouldn't do something horrible to me, because you love me."

She doesn't say anything, but she looks like she is starting to cry again.

"Why are you crying?" I ask her.

She looks at me now, and her eyes are very red coloured. "I need to ask you something, Matt. Is that okay?"

I nod my head, which means yes.

"What do you... er..." She looks down at her fingers, which are twisting the bottom part of her top round and round, and then twisting it back the other way. "What do you see me as?"

I don't understand what she means. I see her as a girl, but I don't think that is what she means.

"A girl," I say, but I don't know if that is the right answer.

"Wrong answer," she says.

I scrunch up my face, because I am annoyed that I got it wrong.

"I mean, do you see me as a friend, or... more?"

"You are my best friend," I tell her.

She lifts her head up for a second, and then she looks down at her fingers again.

"And, that's all? You don't see me as, I don't know..." Raine's cheeks have turned red, and my sister says that when people's cheeks turn red it means that they are embarrassed. I wonder why Raine is embarrassed. "It's just - sometimes, you seem to see me as more than I see you. Do you want to be my boyfriend? Is that it?"

I am very surprised. I love Raine very much, but last month she said that she did not want to be my girlfriend, but now she is asking me to be her boyfriend. My chest starts to feel a little bit funny, and it is a little bit harder to breathe. Maybe I have got a lung disease. I feel very excited about being Raine's boyfriend, and I can feel that I have got a big smile on my face. "Yes, please," I say.

She looks at me. "What do you...?" She stops, and her mouth opens a little bit. "Oh, no. I didn't mean... I wasn't asking... I'm sorry, Squirt, I'm a horrible person." She stands up from my bed, and she picks up the jumper that she put on the back of my chair when she got too hot. She walks to my bedroom door, and I wonder where she is going. "I'm sorry." She walks out of my door, then she closes it, and I can hear her running downstairs.

I am excited. I have never had a girlfriend before, and I am very glad that Raine is my girlfriend now. I lay my body down next to Rose and cuddle her tightly. I am smiling a big smile, because I am very excited.

* * *

"How do trainers work?" I ask Hannah, as we walk from the bus stop to school the next morning. I am looking at my trainers.

"I don't know what you mean," she says. I think she is a bit silly.

"How do they work?" I repeat.

Hannah looks at my trainers as we walk along, and then she looks at me. "They're just shoes, Matt."

"But how do they work?" I step into a puddle that has been made by the soft rain that is coming down this morning. "How do they stop the water getting to my feet?"

"They're waterproof. What else do you want me to say?"

"How are they waterproof?"

Hannah makes her bag lift higher up onto her shoulder, and the water from her umbrella shakes off a little bit. Some of it lands on me. She makes a loud breathing noise. "I don't know, Matthew," she says.

I wonder why she doesn't know. I look back at my trainers. "How do people make trainers? Are they made with glue, or sewing?"

"Matt, I don't know." I think that my sister does not know very much.

We walk quietly for lots of seconds. Hannah is walking in front of me now because the pavement is very thin here. I am watching her black umbrella bobbing up and down.

"Hannah," I say.

"Yes?"

"How do umbrellas work?"

She makes a funny noise. "Matt, I don't know. Can we talk about something else? How is your revision going?"

I wonder why she is asking me about my revision when I was asking her about umbrellas, but I answer her and say, "It is okay."

"Do you need any help with it? I can help a bit, if you like?"

"No," I say, "Raine is helping me with my revision."

Hannah makes another funny noise, but I do not know why. "Oh," she says, "still got time for you, has she?"

I don't know what she means, so I don't answer her. We walk quietly for two minutes. We are nearly at my school now, and are walking down the hill that the school gates are on.

Suddenly Hannah says, "I don't like rain."

"I don't like rain, either."

"No, Raine. Your friend, Raine. I don't like her."

I am confused. Hannah and Raine like each other a lot, so I don't know why Hannah is telling me that she doesn't like Raine. "Yes you do," I tell her, because I know that she does.

"I'm telling you, I don't. She's not a good friend to you."

"Yes she is a good friend to me because she is my girlfriend."

Hannah stops walking suddenly, and she turns around. Some of the water from her umbrella spins onto me again as she turns. "What?"

"Raine is a good friend to me because she is my girlfriend," I repeat for her, a bit louder this time.

She puts a cross face on. "Yes, I heard you," she says, but I don't know why she said 'what?' if she had already heard me. "Raine is your girlfriend?"

I nod my head, which means yes.

"Well that's... it's ridiculous. When did that happen? Does she *know* she's your girlfriend?"

I think that Hannah asked me a very silly question. "Of course Raine knows that she is my girlfriend, because she loves me, and she asked me to be her boyfriend."

She makes her umbrella point to the floor as her hands move to by her sides. I think that this is silly because now her hair is getting wet. My hair is not getting wet because I am wearing a hood on my coat.

"When?" she asks.

"Yesterday, when she was in my bedroom with me."

Hannah's eyebrows go high. "Did she ask you anything else when she was in your *bedroom* with you?"

"Yes," I say, "she asked me to explain the process of photosynthesis."

Hannah's eyes look up to the sky. "So you just revised - the whole time?"

"No, we revised for a little bit, and then we got on my bed."

She puts a very cross face on, but I don't know why.

"Sorry," I say, because she looks cross that I just revised for a little bit. "We got on my bed because Raine was crying."

"She was crying? Why?"

"Because she might have to have an abortion operation."

Now her umbrella drops onto the floor and her bag falls from her shoulder. She catches it on the bottom part of her arm. "A what? An abortion?" Her face looks cross again. "Matthew, do you know what an abortion is?"

"Yes," I say.

"Is it yours?"

I don't understand what she means, because I do not know what she is talking about. I do not answer her. I feel confused, and I think that I have got a confused face on.

"Matthew, is it yours?"

"Is what mine?"

"The baby."

"What baby?"

"The... what do you think an abortion is?"

"It's an operation to make Raine's poorly tummy better."

Hannah has a funny look on her face now, and I don't know what it means. "Have you - have you and Raine done anything?"

"Yes," I tell her, because me and Raine have done lots of things.

"Matt, this is important, you have to answer me sensibly. Have you done anything rude with her? Without...without your clothes on?"

My mouth is very wide open. That is disgusting. I would never take my clothes off in front of other people because that is very naughty. And I would never do something that is rude because I am a good man. "No," I tell her, "I am a good man, Hannah."

She reaches out her hand and touches the arm of my coat. "I know you are, Matty. Don't worry. Look, has Raine spoken to you about our Dad, at all?"

"No." I wonder why Hannah is asking me that question.

Her face looks cross at my answer.

"Sorry, Hannah," I say, to stop her feeling cross with me.

She takes a big breath, and says, "Don't *you* be sorry." She lifts her bag back onto her shoulders. "It's that cow that should be sorry. I'm going to... I hate her, I really hate her. And I hate *him* for doing this to you."

"Who is him? Why do you hate her and him?" I ask.

"Ask your girlfriend," Hannah says, as she picks her umbrella up from the floor (but I don't know what is the point of this because she has already got wet hair). "Before I get to her."

Matthew Pickering
August 2007

We are standing in the big hall of my old school; Me, Mum, Ian Hobson, Hannah, my dad and Raine. Raine and my dad are standing a long way away from each other, but I don't know why. Raine keeps looking at him, but my dad is never looking at her. My mum keeps looking at my dad too, but he just keeps looking at the floor. Hannah is looking at my dad *and* at Raine, and she has got a cross face on, but I don't know why. Ian Hobson is not looking at anybody.

"Claire O'Neal," says my old teacher, Mr Andrews, and Claire walks up to the table to get her GCSE results. I am starting to feel very nervous, because I always come after Claire O'Neal on the register, and so I will be going to get my results next.

Mum grabs my hand, squeezes it, and makes a squeaky noise. "Eeee, Matty, it's you soon. You don't need to worry, Angel, I know you will have done well. And even if you haven't, that's okay too, lots of people fail their GCSEs and go on to get good jobs - "

"He's not going to fail, Mum," says Hannah, rubbing her short hair up into spikes at the front. I think it is very silly that my sister has got short hair, because she is a girl and not a boy, but she says that she likes her hair when it is short and spiky.

"No, of course he isn't, and that's why I've got him lined up for A-levels in September, but I'm just saying-"

"I don't want to do A-level examinations."

" - And your dad can get you a job at his factory if all else fails, so you really needn't worry."

"I don't want to do A-level examinations."

"Oh, don't be silly, Matthew. If you can do GCSEs, you can do A-levels. Of course, it will all depend on your grades today."

"What happened to enrolling him on that drama course?" Hannah asks. "Something that he actually *wants* to do."

"Oh, Hannah, just shush, would you?" says Mum.

"Matthew Pickering."

That is my name, so I start to walk to the desk that Mr Andrews is standing behind.

"Good luck, Son," says Dad, and I hear lots of other people say good luck to me too.

"There you go," says Mr Andrews when I reach the table, handing me a sealed envelope that says Matthew James Pickering on the front. "Just don't blame me if you're not happy with them," he continues, as I take the envelope and begin to walk away, "some people are very difficult to teach."

I think that he is right; some people are probably very difficult to teach.

"Well?" says Mum when I get back to her, and she holds her hand out for me to give her the envelope.

"It's for me," I say, pointing to my name on the front, and I begin to open it.

She puts her hand back down again.

I am very careful not to rip the envelope as I pull the piece of paper out of it and read what it says. I am very happy with lots of my results.

"How did you do?" Hannah reaches to take the paper out of my hand, but I hold onto it tightly.

"It's mine," I tell her. "I did very well, and I won lots of good grades."

"You did? Oh Matty, I'm so pr-"

"Mum, shush. What did you get?"

I read the paper again to make sure that I am right, and I am. "My maths teacher thought that I would win a C, but I have won a B grade."

"That's my boy," says Dad, and Mum and Hannah cheer. Raine and Ian Hobson are smiling. "What else?"

"I won an A grade in ICT, because I am good at computers." I say.

"Well done, Angel."

"Well, we could have guessed that one," says Ian Hobson. "Brilliant."

"What about drama?" says Hannah.

"And English?" says Mum.

"And science?" Raine asks.

"Let the poor kid speak. Go on, Son."

I look at Hannah. "I won a C in drama."

"A C? Fantastic. Now you can do that drama course you wanted to do."

"Hannah, please. He's not studying acting; what a waste of his education that would be. What did you get in English, Sweetie?"

I feel sad, because I want to study acting so that I can be an actor in Hollywood for my job. I also feel sad about my English grade. "I lost," I tell Mum.

"Sorry?"

"It's okay."

"Do you mean you failed? Oh, Darling, what a pity; English was so important for getting you onto your A-levels."

"I don't want to do A-levels."

"But never mind, you have done very well on everything else. What about science? Has everything that Raine taught you gone in?"

Hannah makes a cross face at Raine, but Raine is just looking at me.

"I did very well in science," I tell them. "They said I would win a D, but really I won a B grade."

I can hear lots of cheering, but I cannot see who is cheering because Raine has given me a big, hard hug. Then she kisses my cheek five times, and now she is kissing me on my lips. It is a long kiss, and I like it a lot. Raine has never hugged me or kissed me before, even though she is my girlfriend. It feels very nice and exciting.

I can hear my mum saying, "Aaah."

Raine stops kissing and hugging me, and then she stands back. Her face is red and she is not really smiling. "I'm really proud of you," she says, quietly, and then she turns around to face my dad.

He just shakes his head, but I don't know why.

Hannah has got a red face too, and she looks cross, but I don't know why about that, either.

Then Raine looks back at me, says, "Sorry," and starts to run towards the door.

"It's okay," I say, but I do not understand what is happening.

Hannah Pickering
August 2007

"Raine! Stop, you coward." I follow her across the car park. Perhaps she underestimates the speed at which Pickerings can run, but I have caught up with her within seconds.

I reach out to grab her arm, and she spins around, slipping on the puddled floor. She screams as she falls.

"Oh, shut up," I tell her, "you're not hurt."

She looks like she is about to cry. Let her.

"Get up. I want to speak to you."

She puts her head into her hands and starts moaning about something. I have never seen her vulnerable like this. I am almost concerned.

"Raine?" I say. "Are you - alright?"

She looks up. "I don't know," she hisses at me. "I don't know if I'm alright."

I reach my hand down to help her up, but she ignores it and slowly pushes herself to her feet.

"What was all that about?" I demand. "Were you using Matt to make my dad jealous?"

"What?" She looks shocked. Rumbled.

"You heard. Fancy a trip to Jeremy Kyle? You'd be brilliant on there. 'I convinced my best friend that I am his girlfriend, while having a secret affair with his forty-odd year old father'. Yes, I know all about that. I know all about everything. If you're determined to screw with my dad then fine, he's old enough to handle you, but do *not* mess with my brother."

She is suddenly white. "Don't - don't tell Matthew," she pleads with me.

"Of course I'm not going to tell him; do you think I want to see his heart shatter?"

"I never said I was his girlfriend - he just assumed."

"Oh, assumed, did he? And did he assume that you just snogged his face off in the school assembly hall?"

She is examining her shoes. "I didn't mean to do that, I was just so proud of him, and I, I got carried away."

Ha. "Carried away? I was proud of him too, Raine, but I didn't need to shove my tongue down his throat to show him that."

"Don't be vile," she says, looking a little wobbly on her feet.

"I just can't believe your audacity - to carry on with his dad while he is blatantly in love with... Raine? Are you... why are you holding your stomach?"

She is suddenly doubling up, her hands clenched tightly to her middle.

"What's going on?"

She is starting to cry.

"Do you need an ambulance or something?"

She straightens up a little, panting. "No, I'm fine. Please don't call an ambulance."

She is clearly in pain, and that pain appears to be focused in her lower abdomen. A light bulb clicks on in my head.

"You're pregnant. You are. That's why the fall... I can't believe it."

She is fully upright now, but is steadying herself on a silver Fiesta, still looking ghostlike. "Don't say anything."

"You never did get that abortion, did you?"

"How did you...Hannah, please don't... "

I feel sick. "I'm calling you an ambulance." I pull my mobile out of my pocket and begin to dial the nines.

"Don't; I'm okay. I don't want anyone to find out."

I sigh, cancel the numbers for the time being, and guide Raine to the nearest bench. "Don't you think it's going to be pretty obvious when you start to balloon out like a pig about to litter?"

"I know." Her breathing is arrhythmic. "That's why I'm leaving. I'm giving up my place at university, and I'm going to go away. I don't know where yet, but I can't put Matt through this."

My hatred for this girl is growing by the second. "But you can put him through you completely deserting him? His girlfriend disappearing for no apparent reason."

"I'm not his girlfriend."

"In his eyes you are. I knew you were a lot of things, Raine, but selfish and cowardly? They're news to me."

"Please don't tell him what I've done. Don't tell anyone; including John. No-one can know."

I shake my head in disbelief as I begin to dial the numbers again.

"No, not an ambulance."

"Look," I say, frustrated, "I'm assuming that is my little brother or sister in there? Or could it be anyone's little spawn? ..."

She turns her eyes to the floor.

"... And if it is my brother or sister, I want to make sure they are okay, okay?"

"It's not," she says after a long pause, as I am lifting the phone to my ear. "It's not your brother or sister," she clarifies. "You were right, it could be anyone's, but it's definitely not your dad's."

I press the cancel button on the phone and return it to my pocket. "Forget you, then." I walk back inside to find my brother.

Matthew Pickering
September 2007

I think that Margaret is telling me a lie. I push open the front door and walk quite fast into the house. She nearly falls over because she was standing behind the door; but she manages to grab the handrail at the bottom of the stairs, so she does not fall.

"Raine," I shout, taking my shoes off as I enter the hallway.

"Matthew, I have been telling you for weeks, she is not here."

"I think you are lying to me." I run up the stairs to Raine's bedroom so that I can find her.

Her grandma is following me up the stairs, but she is a very slow walker so I get there a lot quicker than she does.

I knock on the door and wait for Raine to say, 'come in,' because that is the polite thing to do, and I am a polite man. Raine does not answer me, so I knock again and wait.

"She isn't in there," Margaret tells me as she reaches the top of the stairs. She slowly walks over to me and opens Raine's bedroom door.

I look inside the room. "Where are all of Raine's clothes?" I ask, because I can see that her wardrobe is open, and that it is empty.

Raine's grandma looks sad. "Probably where all of my retirement savings are." She walks slowly into the bedroom and sits down on the bed. I watch her pick up Raine's pillow and put it to her face. I do not understand why she does that. Then she puts it down again, and I can see that she is starting to cry.

"Why are you crying, Margaret?" I ask

"First my daughter, my beautiful daughter, and now... I thought she respected me... I thought she appreciated everything that I have done; everything that I have given up for her. She is such a clever girl, and she worked so hard to get her wonderful grades. Turns out it was all for nothing. She has two weeks to return before she loses her place at university - the stupid, stupid girl. And to steal - not only to steal, but to steal from family - to steal from me. Where did that innocent little girl go?"

"I don't know," I answer, because I do not know where Raine has gone. I have not seen her in nearly three weeks, and I miss her very, very much. I miss playing in my garden with her and Rose, and I miss her telling me all about animals and how they work. I miss how pretty she is, and how much I love her. I miss her protecting me when we take Rose for a walk around the park and people shout nasty things at me. I feel very sad when I think about Raine, and I wonder why she doesn't want to see me anymore. I wonder if I am dumped. It makes me very, very sad to think that Raine might have dumped me from being her boyfriend.

"No, me neither. She was such a good little girl before everything happened with her mum, but that messed with her head so much. You can understand it, but to do this to her own grandmother... it's just cruel. I feel like I don't know her any more."

"Where is Raine?" I ask, because I want to know where she is.

"I only wish I knew, Matthew. I thought she would have told *you* where she was going, or at least said goodbye, but it turns out I didn't know her that well after all. I called the police when she first went..."

"Did you want to get Raine arrested because of her stealing?"

"But they said she had clearly gone of her own accord, and as she's eighteen she is technically an adult. I didn't want them to know about the money, I didn't want her to get into trouble." Some tears are rolling down Margaret's face, and she wipes them away with a handkerchief. Then she blows her nose on it. "I just hope she is okay. I can't help picturing her lying in a ditch somewhere, or locked in some mad man's cellar. Oh, Matthew, do you think she's safe?"

"I don't know," I say, because I do not know if Raine is safe. My heart hurts when I think about her lying in a ditch, or locked in the cellar of a mad man. Maybe I am having a heart attack again. I try to say some more things but my throat has got blocked up and I am finding it impossible to talk. I don't know what is blocking my throat, but I wonder if I might be dying.

* * *

I am very out of breath, because I have run some of the way home from Raine's house, which is almost three miles away. That is a long way. I don't mind being out of breath though, because the running has helped the pain in my chest and the blockage in my throat to get a bit better. There is some banging in my head though, and a little bit of screaming. My girlfriend, who I love very much, has dumped me and run away from me, and I don't know where she is. I feel like I would like to cry, but I am too out of breath to do that.

When I get inside my front door I slam it closed, take off my shoes, and run up to my bedroom to find Rose, because she usually sleeps on the bottom of my bed.

"Matty, are you okay?" Mum is saying as I run up the stairs.

Hannah comes out of her bedroom when I get to the top, and she is looking at me. "Matt?" is all that she says.

I run into my room and fall onto my bed so I am lying next to Rose. She looks at me, and I think she is smiling to make me feel better. I put my left arm over her body and she feels very warm. She lifts her paw and puts it over me, like she is giving me a cuddle. Then she licks me on my face. I know that Rose has not got any germs, because she has not got a cold, so I don't mind if she licks me.

"Matthew, can I come in?" It is my mum.

I bury my face into Rose's warm chest as tears start to run out of my eyes. Then I hear the door opening, but I don't know why, because I did not say that my mum could come in.

"Did you find her, my darling?" I can hear her asking me. "What did she say?"

I am crying and I cannot breathe, so I cannot answer her.

"Has she gone for good, then?" That was my sister's voice.

"Hannah."

"Don't worry, Matt; you're so much better off without her."

"Hannah, you're not helping. Be quiet or go back to your room."

Rose makes a little noise, and I think she is trying to make me feel better. I feel my bed moving as somebody sits down on it, and they start to stroke my back.

"I understand how you must be feeling, Angel," Mum says, "but you will be able to make plenty of new friends at college next week. I know Raine was a good friend to you, but there will be lots more, I promise."

I do not want to go to college, I do not want to do any more examinations, and I do not want to go somewhere where Raine and Hannah cannot protect me from bullies.

"He doesn't want to do stupid A-levels, Mum."

"Hannah, please. Would you just go?"

"Fine, make him unhappy. As long as you can say with pride that your son didn't drop out at sixteen. As long as you don't have to admit that things are a bit difficult for him, and that he needs to be treated a bit differently."

"How dare you say that to me? I know very well that he needs to be treated differently, but he can achieve so much more than this."

"Of course he can, but let him do it in things he *wants* to achieve in. Like drama, or animal care - something like that."

"He can do A-levels like I did. Like lots of boys his age do."

"You do realise you're talking just like Dad, don't you?"

"Yeah, well perhaps your dad had a point. Maybe Matt does need to start living life a bit more normally now. He proved he can do it with those marvellous grades he got in his GCSEs."

"Yes, because he did a reduced number of them and he had support in the exams. You put him into college to re-sit English *and* do two full A-levels, and you are setting him up to fail. Is that what you want?"

"Leave the room, please, Hannah."

"I'm just saying it as it is. You know, I reckon you and Dad were made for each other after all."

Then I hear my bedroom door slamming closed.

I am stopping my crying now, because my cuddle with Rose is making me feel a bit happier.

"Are you okay, Angel?" My mum is stroking my back again.

"No," I answer her, because that is the truth. "I am sad."

"Do you want to talk about it?"

"No.

She is quiet for lots of seconds. "Okay," she says, "but I want to help you."

"I don't want to do A-levels," I tell her, because it is making me worried that Mum is going to make me go to college to learn some A-levels.

"You might think that now, Darling, but trust me, it will really help you in the future if you do just a bit of hard work now."

"I have done too much hard work already. I want to be an actor in Hollywood."

"Well, perhaps you could pursue your acting career after your A-levels?"

I don't think that she is listening to me. I am feeling stressed again. I start to make my train noise into Rose's chest, and she begins to kick her legs because I think it is tickling her.

"Oh, oh, Matty..." My mum's voice sounds different this time. "Okay, Sweetie, don't get upset. We can maybe discuss it another time?"

"No," I shout at her, and Rose jumps back from me a little bit. "No A-levels. No A-levels."

"But I already enrolled you."

"No A-levels."

She is silent again. "Okay," she tells me after a very long pause. "Okay, no A-levels."

I stop my train noise straight away, and Mum starts to stroke my hair with her hand like I am a dog. Like I am Rose.

"You should do something though, Baby. Your dad thinks he could get you a job at the factory if you fancy it? You can't just sit at home all day, can you?"

"Will it be a job as an actor?"

"No, Darling, it will be a job printing things, like your dad does. But it would be good, don't you think? You could get some money to buy things you like. Or maybe you could save up for a trip to America, or something? Would you like that?"

I say, "Yes," because I would like to get some money from doing a job, and I would like to save up my money for a trip to America.

"Good man," Mum says.

Matthew Pickering
November 2007

Today is my eighth day at my new job. I am excited that I have got a job, because I like to get paid money. It is a job working in the factory that my dad works at, and that is how I got the job, because my dad told his boss that I would be a good worker.

My dad is one of the managers at this factory, but he does not manage the team that I am working on because he is not allowed to, because I am his son. I do not really understand, but I know that this is the rule. Dad is not at work today because it is my team that is working today and not his team.

I am very good at my new job. The factory that I work at prints words and pictures onto things like pens, and it uses special machines to do it. I am very good at using the printing machine, and I can use it very fast. I can print one hundred pens every hour, and ninety notepads every hour. It takes a bit longer to print onto mugs because they are a bit harder to print on and you have to be very careful not to break them. I can only print sixty mugs in an hour.

There are five other people on my team, and I am a lot quicker at printing things than they are because they all sit and talk for nearly all of the day. I think that this is very naughty because they are paid to print things and not to talk, but when I tell them that they get cross with me.

That is the thing that I don't like about my job. I do not like the people on my team, because they are not very nice people. They always talk about me, and they call me a robot, because I work very fast and they say that I talk like a robot. I do not talk like a robot, because I am a human. They laugh at me a lot too, and they have told me to quit because they say that they don't like me working here. That makes me sad. I do not want to quit because I am very good at my job.

Today I am printing onto mugs, and I am being very careful so that I do not break them. I am sitting at the machine next to a lady called Kayleigh, and she is five years older than me. There are four other people in the room on machines too. I have got my earmuffs on so that I cannot hear the noises from the machines, but there is only my machine that is working anyway, because everybody else is just drinking hot drinks and talking. I do not think that this is right, but I try to ignore them because that is what my mum has told me to do.

I am printing lots and lots of mugs, and I am stacking them carefully into a big box next to my chair when I have done them. I have printed three hundred and seventeen mugs so far today, and I have filled lots of boxes, which are all next to me. Kayleigh has printed twenty-five mugs. Everybody else's boxes are nearly empty of printed mugs because they are not doing any work. People keep throwing things at me, but I am used to people throwing things at me, so I ignore them.

It is the afternoon, and I am very desperate to go to the toilet because I have been working for a long time without a break. I decide that I have got to go to the toilet, so I go, but I go very quickly so that I don't waste any time. I walk past the office where my team's manager is, and he is looking at a computer. I can see this because there is a window in the door. He looks up, and he pulls a frowny face at me through the window, but I don't know why he does that. When I pass the office again on the way back from the toilet he stands up and opens the door.

He says, "Where did you go?" to me.

I tell him that I went to the toilet. He looks cross so I say that I am sorry.

He puts one of his hands on the doorframe and leans against it. "Do I pay you to whizz?" he asks me, but I don't understand the question. "Just because you're the new kid and your dad's a gaffer here, don't reckon you can screw me over."

I still don't understand what he means.

"Have you printed many mugs today?"

I understand this question, so I say, "Yes," to him, because I have printed a lot of mugs today.

One of his eyebrows lifts up, and he stands up straight, letting go of the doorframe. "Come on then," he says. "Prove it." He points his arm down the corridor to the room where the machines are, and I think he wants me to walk that way, so I do. He follows me.

When I open the door everybody is standing up near my machine, but when they see the door opening they all sit down in their chairs quickly. By the time my manager gets to the door, everybody is in their chair and they are looking at their machines.

I notice something strange. Around the bottom of my chair are lots of mugs - lots of smashed mugs. I think there are about ten mugs on the floor near my machine, and they are all smashed.

"What are these?" my manager says, and he looks at me with a very cross face this time. He is pointing at the mugs.

"Oh don't be cross with him," Kayleigh, my machine next-door neighbour, says, "he's just a bit butterfingered, that's all." She smiles at me.

I do not understand how those mugs got broken around my machine.

"Butterfingered, is he? Well, that's a cut to your pay slip, Pickering. Let's see what you actually managed to get into the box in one piece, shall we?" He walks over to my machine and looks in the boxes next to it. He won't be cross anymore once he sees all of my hard work. "What the...? What have I been paying you to do all day?"

I am confused.

"Four empty boxes, and one-two-three-four cups in this box. Four cups. That's all you have managed, in six hours? Four printed cups, and a dozen bust ones."

I did not print only four mugs; I printed three hundred and seventeen mugs. Why is he saying that I only printed four?

Kayleigh is smiling a big smile.

I walk over to my boxes, and I can see that there are only four cups in it.

"Well?" my manager says, "are you going to explain yourself?"

"I printed three-hundred and seventeen mugs," I say, because that is the truth.

"Oh yeah, so where are they?"

I do not know where they are. They were in my boxes when I went to the toilet.

"Kayls, how many cups have you seen Mr Exaggerate print today?"

Kayleigh looks at him. "Just those four. Sorry, Matt, but I have to tell him the truth. He did those, and then he just kept breaking them. The rest of the time he was trying to talk to us lot." She is not telling him the truth, like she said that she had to, because she is lying to him.

I am sad about this.

"Oh yeah, and I suppose you all got on with your work, and none of you talked back?"

"Look in our boxes if you don't believe us," Kayleigh says.

My manager walks over and looks into her box.

I look too.

Kayleigh does not only have twenty-five mugs in her box anymore. Now it looks like she has got about one hundred mugs in her box. That is impossible. Everybody else's boxes look a lot fuller than they did when I went to the toilet, too. I don't understand this, because they could not have printed so many mugs in the few minutes I was out of the room. It is impossible.

"Hmmm," says my manager, "still not loads, I must say, but a lot better than the new kid."

"Yeah, well he kept distracting us, didn't he?"

"So, you're saying that if he wasn't here you'd be a lot more productive?" He has crossed his arms over his body. "Just like you were before he started here?" He raises his eyebrow up again, and I can see that he is smiling a little bit.

Kayleigh smiles back at him. "A *lot* more."

They look at each other for some seconds, and then he looks at me again. His face is not smiling now. "Ever heard of unfair dismissal?" he asks me.

"No," I say, because I have never heard of that.

"Right, good. You can go home now."

"Is it five pm?" I ask him.

He puts his hand onto the back of Kayleigh's chair, and leans onto it. "Nope, but you have finished working here. Finished for good, I mean. You can't come back."

"Why can't I come back?" I ask him, because I want to come back.

"Oh, I don't know; damage to company property, distracting other employees, laziness, lack of productivity. Do I need any more reasons?"

I am sad and confused. "But, I printed three-hundred and seventeen mugs," I tell him.

"Prove it," he says, with a funny little smile on his face. "Look, Matthew, I'm a reasonable guy, and if I liked you or thought you were a valuable member of the team then I might have given you the benefit of the doubt here. But as I don't, and you are not, and you have got no evidence to back up your story, you can pack your bag and go home now."

All of the people in the room are smiling now, and one man is laughing a bit, which I think is not a very nice thing to do because I feel sad.

"Tell your dad I'm really sorry, but I gave you a chance like he asked and you just threw it back in my face. Will you tell him that?" he asks.

"Okay," I say, and I go to get my bag, with a sad face on.

* * *

When I get home I am very surprised to see that my dad's coat is hanging up on the hook in the hall and his shoes are by the door. That must mean that my dad is here, but that is very surprising because my dad does not live at this house. I am going to have to tell my dad that I have not got my job anymore, because my manager gave me a chance but I threw it back in his face. I do not want to tell him that because he will be cross with me for losing my job. I am feeling very sad.

"Hello?" Mum shouts from the living room. "Ian?" I walk into the living room.

"No, I am not Ian Hobson."

My mum and dad are sitting on the settee together, and Dad has got his arm around Mum, but he pulls it away when I walk into the room.

My mum's face looks funny. Her eyes look swollen and red, and her skin looks a bit paler than usual. She rubs her eyes with her hands and looks at me. "Oh, Matt, you're early. Baby, you look sad, are you okay?"

"No," I say, because I am not okay.

Mum stands up and walks over to me. Then she gives me a big hug, and then pulls away, leaving her hands on my shoulders, and looking at me. "Darling, it's okay. How did you find out?"

"My manager told me."

She pulls a funny face. "Your manager? But how did he... John, did you tell his manager?"

Dad shakes his head, and then stands up too. "Er, no. Matthew, what did he tell you?"

I feel sad. "That I have finished working there," I answer, "and that he's sorry, but he gave me a chance and I threw it back in his face."

"Oh, Darling." Mum hugs me again, and I feel like my eyes might cry a little bit.

"What did you do, Matt?" Dad looks cross.

"John."

"What on this earth did you do?"

My mum is still hugging me, and she is rubbing my back, but her face is turned to look at my dad.

"I don't know," I answer, because that is the truth. "I printed lots of mugs, but somehow they got smashed."

Dad covers his hands with his face, and makes a loud breathing noise. "Oh, that's great; thanks, Son. Now I'm going to look an idiot with the other gaffers. An idiot with a clumsy oaf of a son."

"John, please." Mum sounds like she is sad. "The more pressing issue..." Her eyes are very wide as she is looking at Dad.

His face suddenly goes less cross. "Right. I think you should sit down, Son."

"Why should I sit down?"

"Just... just sit down, okay?"

Mum lets go of me and I sit down on the armchair.

Mum and Dad sit on the settee opposite me, and Mum starts to cry.

"Why are you sad, Mum?"

She doesn't answer me.

"Matthew," Dad says, "your mum asked me to help to tell you something; she thought you might get a bit upset. The thing is, Mate... Oh man, this isn't easy. Okay, the thing is... you know Rose was very old..."

"Rose is only twelve years old, and that's not very old," I disagree, "because I am seventeen and I am not old yet, and that is much older than Rose is."

"But dogs don't live as long as people, Mate; and for a greyhound like Rose, twelve is very old."

I think my dad is being silly.

"And she has been quite poorly, remember, Darling?" Mum says, wiping her eyes with her hands again. "She wouldn't really play with you anymore, would she?"

I do remember that, because it made me sad. Now that Raine has run away Rose is my only friend to play with, and she won't play with me anymore, but it is okay because I still love her very much.

"Anyway, I – well, I took her to the vets today; I wanted to see if he could make her better for you. Your dad came with me; Ian was at work, and I didn't want to go alone in case... She was really, really poorly, Matt. The vet said it was cruel to keep her al..." Mum covers her face up with her hands, and Dad puts one of his hands onto her leg.

"It's okay, Susie," he says. "Matthew, it's not good news, Son. The vet had to put Rose to sleep."

I stare at my dad, and he is staring at me. I am not sure why it is not good news that Rose went to sleep. "Is she awake again, yet? Can I see her now?" I want to see Rose, because she is the only thing that will cheer me up about my horrible day at my job that is not my job any more.

Mum looks up at Dad, and he looks back at her.

"It's okay," he says, and then he turns back to face me. "No, she isn't awake. Rose died, Matt."

I feel like somebody has punched me in my tummy. I feel sick. My mouth fills up with saliva, and my whole body feels funny. Rose can't have died, but my dad says that she has. I bend over the side of the armchair and lots of sick comes out of my mouth. My mum took Rose to die. And my dad helped. I am sick again, and I begin to cough.

My eyes are closed, but I can feel some arms wrap around me. They must belong to my mum or dad, but I do not want them to touch me. They killed my dog. They killed the only best friend I had got left. I stand up very fast, and push them away from me as hard as I can. When I open my eyes I see my mum falling onto the floor, away from me. Good.

"Matthew!" my dad shouts.

"It's okay, he's upset."

Dad helps my mum to stand up, and she runs over to me and tries to put her arms around me again.

"Matthew, Sweetheart, I know this is hard for you..."

"You killed my dog." I quickly and tightly grab onto her wrists, pull her hands away from my arms, and push her as hard as I can.

She falls backwards and lands on the settee, lying on her back. She screams as she falls.

My head is screaming too.

As soon as I have pushed Mum I can feel myself being pushed back against the wall, and my dad is pressing his body against me. "Don't you ever..." he is shouting at me.

I think I have got a very cross face on. I think that my head might explode. It is banging, and banging, and banging. I think I am having a stroke.

In the background I can see Mum standing up. "John, don't! He's upset."

Dad keeps staring at me, and I keep staring at him.

My mum walks over to my dad. "John, listen to me. Let him go. I'm fine. Can't you see he's upset?"

"It was a flaming dog," my dad shouts.

I let out the loudest scream that I can, and I use all of the force in my body to push him away from me. Then I scream again, maybe even louder this time, and I use as much strength as I have to throw my fist behind me, and then into his face.

Mum screams, and Dad falls backwards. Mum catches him. "Matty, no," she shouts, and she puts her hand out towards me like she is telling me to stop.

I cannot stop. I throw my fist out again and I catch my dad's nose. I can feel a crack through my knuckles, and I think that I might have broken his nose.

He puts his hands over his face, so this time I kick him, and my kick lands on his stomach.

Mum shouts, "Stop, please," and she is starting to cry.

My dad is making some funny coughing noises.

I turn around and run through the door, leaving them in the living room. Mum is crying very loudly now, but the screaming in my head is making it harder to hear. I close the door very hard, and I run into the kitchen. I need something to take this pain away from me. I need to feel something else to take the pain in my heart away.

My dad is shouting, "Susan, leave him! He's getting a knife."

I am not getting a knife. I run to the corner of the kitchen where my mum keeps the kettle, and pull it from its base. I remember what it feels like when hot water spills all over you, and it hurts a lot, and it takes away everything else that is in your head. I tip it over my body as I hear a loud scream from my mum, who has run into the room.

But the kettle is empty. I throw it to the floor.

"Angel, Sweetheart, calm down."

"Matthew. Calm down, now."

"You killed my dog," I shout, as I hit my fist against my head as hard as I can. I don't feel anything, other than the painful feeling in my chest and the sound of screaming in my brain.

I can hear the front door opening and my sister's voice shouting, "Hello."

Then I hear footsteps running to the kitchen, and Mum shouting at Hannah to go upstairs.

I pull open the cupboard door under the sink and wrap my fingers around the edge of it. "You killed my dog," I shout, and slam the door shut as hard as I can, feeling my fingers crush behind it. It feels good. The screaming in my head goes quieter, and I pull the cupboard door open again.

Dad, who has got blood pouring out of his nose, runs towards me as I slam the door shut again and another sting of pain shoots up my arm. The screaming gets even quieter, and it feels good. I can feel him wrapping his big arms around me from behind, and pulling me away from the cupboards. He is very strong, and he lifts me up from the floor.

I cannot move my arms because Dad has pinned them to my sides, but I kick out in every direction, and I feel my feet kicking his legs. "You killed my dog," I shout, as the kitchen door opens wider and I see Hannah running in, and hear my mum screaming and crying.

Hannah runs in front of me, and I can see her looking at me.

I kick out, and I hit her legs with my feet.

"Hannah, come here," Mum is crying.

"Go upstairs," Dad shouts.

"Matthew," Hannah says in a loud, but nice voice.

My head stops screaming a little bit more. I look at her.

"Matthew," she says again, a bit quieter this time, "it's okay. You are okay, everything is okay." Her face is calm, and it makes my legs stop kicking.

I stare at her, and she smiles a little bit at me.

"They killed my dog," I say in a little voice.

Hannah looks surprised, and turns to look at Mum.

"The...the vet..." Mum says, and then she starts to cry again.

"Oh, Matt," Hannah says, "I'm so sorry. But it's okay. I promise, it's okay." She looks into my eyes for lots of seconds, and I start to feel calmer. Then she looks at Dad and says, "You can put him down now."

I don't feel Dad putting me down.

"I am telling you, you can put him down. That look's gone from his eyes."

I can hear my mum crying in the corner as Dad puts me down on the floor. He still has his arms around me, but they are not as tight now.

I say, "I'm sorry, Hannah."

"I'm not cross," Hannah says. Then she looks at my hand. It is covered in red blood. "What did you do, Matty?"

I look at my hand, and wonder why it is covered in red blood. "I can't remember," I answer.

"It's okay," she says, and moves a chair out from under the table.

Dad lets go of me, and Hannah makes me sit down.

"Everything is okay, Matty. It's okay."

I close my eyes and let my head drop forwards. Everything is not okay, because I have been fired from my job, and my girlfriend has run away because she doesn't love me anymore, and now my mum and dad have killed my only other friend. My heart hurts, and I start to cry.

Susan Hobson
February 2008

"Can I come in?"

He sighs deeply, and opens the door a little wider. "Do you think you should?" he asks.

"No," I answer, walking past him into the house, and making my way to the kitchen fridge.

"Looking for something?"

I find two bottles of lager cooling there and pull them out, passing one to John.

"Thanks, Suse. Very generous of you."

I smile wryly, and remove the bottle opener from the top drawer.

"Not that it isn't lovely to see you, but - "

"I needed to get away." I march into the living room, throw my open bag onto the floor, and fall into the corner of the settee.

John follows, and takes the seat next to me. He looks undeniably hot tonight. Who says men shouldn't wear denim shirts anymore?

I take a swig from the bottle and feel instantly refreshed, and slightly chavy. It makes a nice change from Ian's sixty-pounds a time red wine.

"How's your mum?" he asks, placing his feet up onto the coffee table. It's a good job Matthew isn't here.

"Don't ask; I don't even want to talk about it."

"Okay..." He looks confused. "What *did* you come to talk about?"

"Who says I came to talk? Oh, don't look at me like that, I didn't come to do that either." He is disgusting.

"Right. So why did you come?"

"Who knows? I needed to get away, and you were the only person I could think of that I could come to. Shows how many friends I have got around here."

"Oh cheers, I'm honoured." He is grinning. "The old man driving you crazy, is he?"

"Ian isn't old. And no, he's great, as a matter of fact. It's him that's watching the kids now - on his night off."

"Good old Ian."

"Don't."

His smile fades a little.

"Ian *is* good; he's a good man. Far better than you."

"Well, if you've just come to insult me - "

"No, I'm sorry." I place my bottle onto a coaster on the table. "It's me that's the problem; I'm a terrible person. Do you know where I told Ian I was going tonight? Mums. Yep, I'm using my sick mother as an excuse to come and spend time away from him and the kids, with my ex husband. Does that sound like I'm a terrible person? It does to me."

"How many of those things have you had?" He points to my lager.

"I'm not drunk, John; far from it. Although I sort of wish I was. Want to get drunk with me?"

"How would you explain that one when you go home later? You and your dying mother were partying all night?"

I could tell him off for pointing out that Mum's dying, but it's not exactly like it's a reminder, I think about it all day, every day. "I could stay here," I suggest.

"Could you? And what problems would that solve, Susie?"

"Don't you want me to? You always go on about how you want me back - even when you are with your other girls, I know you still want me."

"That's beyond the point, Babe. Are you sure you're not drunk?"

"I'm not drunk, alright? I only had a couple of glasses before I came."

He holds his hands up in front of him. "Alright, I'm sorry. Come on though, talk to me. What's bothering you?"

"Besides Mum?"

"As well as that, yeah. I know there's more to this, you're normally so strong."

I push my hair over the top of my head. "I'm not strong; even Ian knows that. Why else would he be suggesting we get carers in to look after Matt?"

"Carers? He's not that bad is he? I know that thing with the dog upset him, but - "

"Tore him apart, you mean? Out on one of their walks last week Ian literally had to manhandle him all the way home after they passed a lady out walking her greyhound. And every blonde haired girl he sees, he goes running up to them thinking its Raine. He's totally covered himself in cuts and bruises."

John groans loudly. "That girl's done so much damage. Maybe a bit of help for him isn't such a bad idea."

"You've changed your tune. It's not long since you were denying there was even anything wrong with him."

"You're talking more than a decade ago, Suse; a lot of water has gone under the bridge since then."

I smile slightly, and nod my head.

He looks thoughtful. "I could spend more time with him myself, you know."

"I do know."

"Alright, don't get narky; I'm suggesting something here. Maybe I could do a bit more woodwork with him or something? He loved it when we made that kennel together."

"A great lot of use that is now."

"He enjoyed making it; isn't that the point? It kept his mind occupied. Maybe it would help him again?"

"Well it certainly wouldn't harm him, spending a bit more time with his dad." I look pointedly at him, expecting him to fervently deny his past as a useless father figure.

"You're right," he says, staring at me. "You're always right."

"Okay, why are you looking at me like that? What's wrong?"

He turns away slightly and picks up his lager. "Nothing's wrong, it's just so nice to be spending time with you again. I miss you."

I give a small smile. He's right; it is nice. I can connect with John in a way I have never been able to with Ian. It's not like we get on amazingly all the time; in fact, I have probably had more arguments with him in the last year than in my entire marriage to Ian. Perhaps that shows something, though? At least there's passion between us; a fire that was never fully extinguished. I cough, and turn away myself. "I should probably go."

"What?"

"It's not fair to leave Ian with Matt. And it's not like Hannah's much easier these days either - Little Miss Stropalot."

"She's like her mother." He smirks as I throw the bottle top at him. And then he is looking at me again. "Don't go," he says

"I have to."

"Don't. You're the one who suggested staying tonight. Do it. But not for the night… stay forever."

"Now who's the one that's drunk?"

"I'm serious."

"You know I can't do that. You said as much yourself."

"What's stopping you? Your loveless marriage?"

"That's not fair."

"I know you, Susie. I know you don't feel for Ian half of what you feel for me. Tell me if I'm wrong." He reaches his hand to touch my chin, and slides closer to me on the sofa.

"You're wrong."

"Am I?" He is looking at my lips, and then back at my eyes.

My whole body is stiffening. I cannot move. "Yes."

"Am I?" His face is pulling ever closer; inches from mine. He looks up and meets my eyes.

I can't breathe. My stomach flips over.

He pushes his lips to mine.

I pull back swiftly. "Yes." I turn away and reach for my bag, which is pouring open onto the floor by my feet. "Yes, you are. I have to go." I begin piling each item orderlessly into the bag.

"Please stay."

"I can't." I stand up, throw my bag over my shoulder, and manoeuvre my way around the coffee table to the living room door. "I'm sorry, John; I shouldn't have come. Goodnight."

Matthew Pickering
March 2009

I am at the hospital now with my mum, and my Uncle Henry, and Ian Hobson and my little sister, Hannah. The last time that Hannah came to this hospital was when she came to have her fingers put back together after I broke them for her when there was a scary storm. I feel very sad about that, because I did not mean to break her fingers. She was very kind to me after I broke them, and when I told her that was sorry she said, "It's okay, Matty; I know it was an accident." She was right, because it was an accident, because I would never hurt my little sister on purpose. Hannah's fingers are okay now, and they are all back together again, which is very good news.

Today we are all at the hospital because we want to see my Nana Brady before she goes away forever. I do not know where my nana is going, but Mum says that I will never be able to see her again once she has gone. That makes me feel a bit sad.

My mum and Uncle Henry are in my nana's hospital bedroom now and they are talking to her. I am sitting with Ian Hobson and Hannah in the hospital's waiting room. Hannah is looking at a magazine, but she hasn't turned the page for a long time so I think that she must be a very slow reader.

Her eyes are very pink and there are tears coming out of them, so I think that her magazine must be a very sad magazine.

"Are you all right, Matt?" Ian Hobson asks me.

"I'm all right," I say.

"Do you feel sad?"

"A bit sad," I tell him, "because I don't really want my nana to go away."

"She will be sad to leave you, too. She worships the bones of both of you." He is looking at Hannah now, but she is keeping looking at her magazine so she must not have heard him. "You've both given her a very happy life; I know that."

Hannah sniffs, and I wonder if she has got a cold.

"Will Nana Brady miss me?" I ask Ian Hobson.

"Of course she will, but she will always be watching you."

"What do you mean?" I ask.

"Well, I mean... she will always be with you, won't she?"

"I thought Nana Brady was going away forever?" I am very confused.

Hannah looks up from her magazine, and she sniffs again. "Wouldn't it be easier to just tell him the truth?" she asks Ian Hobson. I wonder what the truth is.

"What is the truth?"

"Han, it's what your mother wants."

"He's not a kid, Ian. He can handle a bit of honesty." She looks at me. "Matty, Nana isn't going away. Not like you think."

"Hannah, stop it," Ian Hobson says.

Hannah looks at him, but doesn't say anything.

"We need to make this as easy as we can on your mum. We can't give her any more stress right now."

"Well, how about making it easier on him?" she asks.

I don't know what she means.

"That's what she is trying to do."

Hannah wipes her eye and says, "Right, just tell him what you like then. How about, 'she will always live on in our hearts,' that's a good one. Or, 'she will never leave you, you just wont be able to see her any more,' why don't you try that? Confuse him even more."

I say, "Hannah, don't be upset," because I don't want Hannah to be upset, and I can see that she is crying now.

She smiles at me, but there are still tears falling out of her eyes. "I'm okay," she says to me, but I don't think that she is okay.

That is when my mum and my Uncle Henry, who is my mum's brother, walk in. Mum is crying too, just like Hannah, and Uncle Henry has got his arm around her shoulders. I wonder why he is doing that, because he is not her husband; Ian Hobson is her husband. I think he might get cross with Uncle Henry for putting his arms around my mum's shoulders. When Mum sees Ian Hobson she walks quickly over to him, and he stands up and gives her a hug.

Uncle Henry looks at Hannah. "Mum is asking to see you, Tiddler," he says to her. 'Tiddler' is the name that he calls Hannah, but I don't know why. He nods his head towards me. "You too, Son."

Me and Hannah stand up because Nana Brady is asking to see us.

Mum turns away from Ian's hug and says, "Will you go in with them, Hen?"

Uncle Henry shakes his head. "Mum just wants to see the kids."

Hannah says, "It's okay, Mum. We'll be fine," and she holds my hand. It makes me jump a little bit, and I do not know why Hannah is holding my hand, because she is my sister, not my girlfriend.

I say, "Hannah, you cannot hold my hand because you are not my girlfriend."

She keeps on holding my hand and says to me, "I might get a bit sad when we go and see Nana, and I might need you to look after me. Will you hold my hand to look after me, please?"

I say, "Yes," because I want to look after my little sister. I keep holding her hand.

Mum smiles at us and says, "Thanks, Sweethearts. Come out if it gets too hard." Then she puts her head back against Ian Hobson's chest, and he puts his arm around the back of her neck.

* * *

Nana's hospital bedroom is not as nice as her flat. It has not got any pictures on the walls like her flat has, and it hasn't got a carpet, but there are lots of cards on the table. There are some grapes too, and I hope Nana Brady will let me have some grapes because I like them a lot.

I am shocked when I see my nana. At first, I don't think that we have gone into the right room, because the lady in the bed does not look like Nana. This lady is very thin, and my nana is not very thin, and this lady has got no hair, and my nana has got hair. But then the lady smiles at me, and I know that it is my Nana Brady.

I say, "Hi, Nana. Where is your hair?" I hear something next to me, and I turn around to look at Hannah. I realise that she is crying again, so I give her a hug and say, "It is okay, Hannah. I'm here to look after you." When I have finished hugging her, I hold onto her hand again.

Nana says, "My little angels. Come and give your old nan a kiss."

I go and give my nana a kiss, but I do not let go of Hannah's hand.

Then Hannah gives her a kiss, and I still do not let go of her hand.

Nana reaches out and rubs Hannah's face. I think that she is wiping the tears away from her eyes.

I am still wondering where Nana's hair is, so I say, "Where is your hair, Nana?"

She smiles at me. "I had to have chemotherapy, Darling, and all my hair fell out. Isn't that rubbish?"

I say, "Yes," because that is rubbish.

Nana is talking funny. She is talking very quietly and a bit croaky, like she does when she has a sore throat.

"Have you got a sore throat, Nana?"

She says, "No, Sweetheart, nothing is sore. I'm not in any pain."

I am glad that she is not in any pain.

Hannah starts crying again when Nana says this.

I turn to face her. "Don't cry, Hannah; it is a good thing that Nana is not in any pain, and not a bad thing."

Nana reaches out to me and holds my other hand. She says, "I love you both, so much."

I say, "Thank you".

Hannah tries to say, "I love you too," but it sounds a bit funny because she is crying.

I say, "Nana, why aren't you fat anymore?"

Hannah smacks the top of my arm gently, but she doesn't say anything.

My nana laughs quietly. "That's hospital food for you; it's rubbish."

Hannah makes another crying noise, and then wipes her face with a tissue. "I'm sorry, Nana," she says, and then she cries a bit more, "I'm sorry; this isn't what you need."

"There's plenty of time for tears, Sweet Girl, but right now we should be enjoying the time we have together, don't you think?"

Hannah makes a big sniff and says, "You're right, I'm going to stop." Then she makes another big sniff. "So, have any handsome doctors been looking after you?"

Nana laughs. "A couple, yes. There are some very nice young men here to keep me occupied." She closes one of her eyes at Hannah, and then she opens it again.

Hannah has nearly stopped crying now.

"Now, Matthew, I want to talk to you for a moment."

"Yes, Nana?" I say, because she would like to talk to me for a moment.

She starts to stroke the scars on my hand. "This needs to stop, Little Angel. You are hurting yourself so much, and it needs to stop. I can't bear to see you like this, and I can't bear to go away knowing it's going to continue - knowing it could get worse. Very soon, I'm going to give you a present - you won't get it today, but very soon. I want you to use that present to get yourself happy again. I also want you to find a new dog, like Rose, that you can look after and that can be your new best friend."

"I don't want a new Rose," I tell her, "I just want Rose."

"Rose is gone, Sweetheart; you know that. But it doesn't mean you can't move on with your life and be happy again. Think about it, won't you? Whatever will make you happy, you need to promise me you will strive to achieve it, okay?"

I nod my head, "Okay, Nana."

"I'll help him," Hannah says, putting one of her arms around me like a sideways cuddle.

"Good girl. But promise me that you won't forget your own happiness. You two mean everything to me, and I have to know you are going to live long and fulfilling lives. Both of you." She looks from Hannah, to me, and then back to Hannah. "I love you both so much. Promise me you will be as happy as you have made me."

"I promise," Hannah answers.

I cannot promise this because I do not know the future. I wonder if Hannah knows the future, but I do not think that this is possible. "I cannot promise to be happy," I tell her, "because I do not know the future."

She smiles at me. "Do you promise to try?"

"Okay," I tell her.

Hannah Pickering
March 2009

There is only so much a person can cry in one week, and I think I have used up my quota for the whole year in these past seven days. That's why I'm sure I must be able to handle a frank family discussion about Nana's will. I don't think my body could possibly produce any more tears. This is what I'm hoping for, anyway.

Mum and Ian have made me and Matty sit down for a 'family chat' around the kitchen table. Ian has a pile of forms in front of him, alongside a drink of juice. No one is allowed hot drinks in this house any more. In fact, the kettle has been completely disposed of. As have most of the sharp knives; hence our meals of very chunky and clumsily cut meats and vegetables.

Ian clears his throat once everyone is seated and has a drink next to them - very official. "Okay, I wanted to gather you all together so we could have a chat through your grandmother's will."

Oh my life. I wonder if I can fall asleep with my eyes open.

"She has been very generous, and has left rather a lot to the both of you and to Louise."

"Louise who's not even her real granddaughter?" I ask, incredulous.

Mum eyes me across the table, but does not say anything. The master is speaking now, no one else must talk.

"Hannah, don't question your grandmother's motives."

"My *nana*, you mean?" Oh he does irritate me.

"Your *nana* has been very, very generous, if you will allow me to continue?"

"Fine."

"So, your Nana's will - "

"What's a will?" Matty interrupts.

"Well... " Ian coughs. How are they going to get around this one without actually telling Matt that Nana has died? "When your Nana - went away - she had to give all of her things to the people that she loved, and so she has left some of her things for you and Hannah to have."

"Oh," he says. "I thought a Will was a person."

I catch Mum smiling for the first time in about a month.

"Well, no." Ian rearranges his papers and then looks at me. "Hannah, we don't want you to be upset, because this really isn't favouritism - "

Oh great, what's coming now?

" - And your Nana has left you quite a hefty sum for you to save for university; which we will come onto in a moment - "

A hefty sum?

" - But, Matthew..." Ian reaches into his pocket and pulls out a small, silver Yale key.

Matty reaches out and takes it, looking confused.

I can't say that I am any clearer than he is, to be honest. She can't have bought him a house - she wasn't made of money. Although, maybe she has; maybe both Matt and Uncle Henry's *non*-daughter,

Louise, have got a new house out of it. But at least Ian is safe from paying university fees for me in a few years time - *if* I decide to go, that is. No favouritism there at all, then.

"What is the key for?" Matt asks.

Mum smiles and says, "It's for your Nana's flat, Darling."

Oh, so she *can* still talk. Mum looks at me, but I turn away. What does she expect me to say?

"Your Nana wanted you to live in her flat, if you want to? There's no mortgage or anything, so it would be completely free. Except for bills of course, but me and Ian can help out with those until you can find another job."

I grip my hands together tightly. I am happy for Matthew. I am. This is just what he needs. But I can't help but feel a little pushed aside.

"We have sorted you out some support," says Ian.

Clearly Mum has contributed as much as she is allowed.

"A lady called Brenda and a man called Brian are going to look after you at the flat and help you with cooking and things. They will take it in turns, and they will go back to their own houses at night time. They need paying some money; but your mother and I can help with that too, until you find a job."

Matty still looks confused. "I don't understand," he says, and he is looking at me.

I bite my tongue, and remember my promise to Nana. "You are going to live in Nana's old flat," I explain to him simply. "Is that okay?"

"But Nana doesn't live there any more."

I smile at him. "No, she doesn't; it's your flat now. You are going to live in flat number twenty-two. Is that okay?"

"Yes, that's okay."

"Some people called Brian and Brenda are going to help you when you do your cooking, and your cleaning and your shopping," I continue, watching comprehension flood his face. "Is that okay?"

"Okay." He looks excited.

Through my annoyance, I can't help but feel a little excited for him myself.

Matthew Pickering
June 2009

I have lived in my very own flat for one whole month now and I like it a lot, because it is very exciting living in your own flat. Sometimes I get lonely because I miss living with my mum, and my sister and Ian Hobson, and I miss my best friends called Rose and Raine, but I have got a new friend who is called Brian, and he comes to see me at my flat on lots of days.

Brian is one of my support workers, and he comes to help me do things like cooking and cleaning, and he takes me to places on trips. He is fifty-two years old and he likes The Simpsons, just like I do, which is good because we watch it together. I really like watching The Simpsons because it is my favourite television programme and I find it very funny. Especially when Homer says, 'D'oh!' That bit is very, very funny. My favourite character on The Simpsons is Ned Flanders because he has got a funny moustache, but Brian's favourite character is Bart Simpson.

Brenda is my other support worker, and she is a person that I do not like very much because she is not very nice to me. She does not let me watch many episodes of The Simpsons when she is looking after me because she says that it is a silly cartoon, and that cartoons are for children. I don't think that she is right though, because me and Brian like watching it and we are not children.

Brian and Brenda both like to wear very similar clothes, which is silly because Brian is a man and Brenda is a lady. They both like to wear white trainers, blue jeans, and big polo shirts that say, 'Harleyfield Home Care,' on them. Sometimes they wear a dark blue polo shirt, and sometimes they wear a dark green polo shirt.

Today Brian is taking me to a boring meeting at a place in town. He says that I have got to go to this meeting for half an hour and then he is going to take me to the park as a treat, because I like to sit by the river in the park and listen to it trickling. He has made me wear some posh grey trousers, a white shirt and a blue and grey spotty tie. I don't really like wearing ties because they are very difficult to tie up, but Brian tied my tie up for me this morning. I have got to wear my posh black shoes too, but I wish I didn't have to wear them because they are uncomfortable and they make my feet hurt.

I have got my black coat on, and we are getting on the bus to the meeting now. Brian helps me to count out some coins to give to the bus driver, and he tells me to say, 'one to town, please.'

I am standing at the front of the queue when we get on the bus, and I say, "One to town, please," and I give the man my money. He looks at it, and then presses a button that makes a ticket come out of the machine. He puts the money into his big tin box as I take my ticket.

Then Brian pays his money and takes his ticket, too. He says, "Choose where you want to sit, Matt."

I like to sit upstairs, so I start to go up the bus stairs.

Brian follows me.

When I am half way up them the bus makes a big hissing noise and starts to move, but I am still on the stairs. I don't like the hissing noise so I put my hands on my ears, but then I start to wobble because I cannot hold on to the railing and cover my ears at the same time.

Brian holds me steady and says, "It's okay, the noise has stopped. Up you go. Hold on tight."

I let go of my ears and hold onto the railing, but I am still wobbling because the bus is moving up and down and from side to side. I don't like it. I really don't like it. I think I might fall. I look down the stairs, and Brian is behind me, and there is a man behind Brian who looks about fifty-two as well, and he is holding his shopping bags.

The man says, "Come on, what's the hold up?"

The bus makes a little jolt and I feel like I am going to fall over, so I sit down on the stairs.

Brian turns around to the man with the shopping bags and says something that I can't hear.

The shopping bag man says, "Forget it," and goes and sits on a seat downstairs.

"I don't like buses, I don't like buses, I don't like buses," I say. That is not very true because I do like buses, but I don't like them when they move when I am trying to walk, because they make me fall over.

Some minutes later the bus stops again. It makes another loud hissing noise that frightens me, but Brian says, "Right, it's stopped. Jump up; up we go." He helps me to stand up, but I don't jump up because I might fall down the stairs if I did that. Then I walk up the rest of the steps onto the top deck of the bus. Brian says, "You find a seat and I will be up in a minute; I just want a quick word with that man who was behind us," and then he goes downstairs again.

The top deck of the bus is nearly empty, but there are two teenage boys and a teenage girl sitting on the back seat. They are playing music very loudly, and they are shouting and saying a lot of naughty words. I like to sit on the back of the bus on the top deck; it is my favourite place to sit. There are five seats on the back of the bus and there are only three people there, so that means that there are two more places for me and Brian, which is good.

When I get closer I can see that the teenage boy that is sitting next to the window has got his hand on the top part of the leg of the girl next to him. They are talking to the other teenage boy, who is sitting on the other side of the bus. He has got his bag on the seat next to the window, which you are not supposed to do, and he is sitting next to his bag. There is one seat free in the middle. That is my favourite seat, so I want to sit there.

When I get really close to the back the teenage girl shouts, "Oy oy!"

I don't know what that means. I sit on the seat in the middle of the back row, and they all look at me.

One of the boys says, "What the..." (I do not want to think about the next word that he says because it is a bad word).

The girl says, "What you sitting next to me for? Are you a perv or summet?"

I do not know what she means, so I do not answer her. Their music is very loud and it is hurting my ears, so I say, "Please turn your music down."

The boy that is sitting next to the girl says lots of rude words to me, and the boy on the other side of me empties his bag of crisps over my head.

I don't know why they are doing this, because I said please, but I think they are cross with me so I say, "Sorry."

They look at me with funny faces on, but they don't say anything. Then they start laughing very loudly.

The boy who is sitting with the girl starts to throw his hand about so that his fingers click together.

I wonder if they are doing nasty laughing, or if they are laughing because they think I am funny and they like me. I look at the boy who has got his bag on the chair and I say, "Excuse me, but I want to sit with my friend so please put your bag on the floor so they can sit down."

He shouts, "What? You think I'm going to move my stuff so you can sit with your ho? Get lost - sit down there with her," and he points to the front of the bus.

The girl says, "He ain't got no ho, Dumbass. He's alone ain't he?"

I don't understand.

"Oh yeah, where is this 'friend'?" asks the boy next to the girl.

"Downstairs, talking to a man," I answer.

"You wanna get that sorted," he says back to me.

I really don't understand what these people are talking about.

He continues, "You wanna get yourself down there and knock that pimp out. Then you wanna knock your (rude word) out too for chattin' up another mother." I look at him, and he says, "You get me?"

I don't know what he means, but I think that he likes me. "Are you my friend?" I ask.

The boy says, "I ain't your friend, you freak."

Then the girl says, "You is barking up the wrong tree, Mate. You wanna get out of our way."

I think that I do want to get out of their way, because I don't think that they are being very nice to me.

The girl picks up her bottle of lemonade that is stuck between the top and bottom cushions of the chair in front of her and she opens it. It fizzes out, and she holds it over the top of my trousers so that all the lemonade goes on to them. It looks like I have weed in my trousers, but I haven't done that. "Ooops, sorry," she says. "I slipped."

I say, "That's okay", because that is what you are supposed to say when someone says that they are sorry. My trousers are very wet, and I am covered in bits of crisp. I am a little bit scared of these teenagers. I think that they might be bullies.

Then I hear someone shout, "Matthew! Come here."

I look up, and Brian is standing at the front of the bus. He looks very cross, but he is looking at the teenagers and not at me.

One of the boys says, "A bit old for you ain't he, Mate?" but I don't think that he is my mate.

Brian says, "Ignore him and come here, now." So I stand up and walk to him.

The bus is moving, so it makes me wobble, but I don't mind very much this time because I want to get to Brian quickly.

When I get to him he says, "Come downstairs," and he pulls me to the top of the staircase. The bus stops again, which is good because I can walk down the stairs safely now. When I get to the bottom I see the shopping bag man, and he smiles at me. We sit down on some empty chairs, half way down the bus, and it sets off again.

***

We get off the bus after a bit, and we walk through town to a big building. Brian has brushed all of the bits of crisp off my clothes and out of my hair, but my trousers are still wet from the lemonade. When we walk into the building we go up to the reception desk, and Brian says to the lady behind it, "Hi, this is

Matthew Pickering; he's come for a... meeting. At ten thirty."

The lady looks a bit confused and says, "A meeting?"

Brian spells out a long word, and all I can work out is that it starts with 'I-n-t-'.

Then the lady makes her eyes go thin for a few seconds, and then she says, "Oh, I see. Take a seat. They will call you when they are ready."

Brian says, "Thank you. I was wondering, would it be possible for me to sit in with him? Just to help with his nerves?"

"That might be difficult, Sir. It's not exactly company policy."

"Yes, but he is autistic and - "

"We are aware of that. Don't worry, our team are very understanding; he will be fine."

Brian says, "Okay, thank you," and then he takes me to sit on a chair. When we are sitting down he says, "Matthew, do you know why you are here today?"

I say, "For a boring meeting?"

He laughs, but I don't think it was funny. Then he says, "Yeah, kind of, Mate. The people that you are going to have a meeting with would like to give you a job working here. Would that be good?"

I don't know if that would be good.

"It would be working as a cleaner for two days a week, so you could get a bit of money to go out on more trips and do more fun things. Does that sound okay?"

"Okay," I repeat, because I like making things clean and getting rid of germs.

A door opens, and two ladies and a gentleman come out of it. They are all dressed in smart suits, and one lady says, "Thank you."

The other lady says, "It was lovely to meet you, we will be in touch."

The man says, "Good bye".

Then the first lady walks past me and out of the front door and the other lady and man go back into the room.

Some minutes later, the man comes out again, and he says, "Matthew Pickering?"

"That's my name."

He looks a bit funny at me. "We're ready for you."

Brian stands up, and so do I. He says, "You will do really well, Matt. Don't worry. Everything is okay."

I nod my head and look at the man, who walks over to me and holds out his hand.

Brian whispers, "Shake his hand, Matt."

I don't understand, but I hold his hand, and he starts to shake mine up and down. Then he lets go. I see him look down at the wet bit on my trousers, and he pulls a funny face. "Shall we go in?" he says, and he walks back to the room.

I look at Brian, and he smiles and nods his head. "Go on, follow him. I will be here when you come out."

* * *

These people have been asking me questions for a long time. I wish they would stop it, because I don't like it when people ask me lots of questions. It makes me feel nervous because I don't know what to say if I don't know the answer. The lady said that she is called Suzanne Bowers, and she is the head of the domestic team here, and then she told me that means the cleaners. The man said that his name is Mick, but he didn't say his last name. He is in charge of 'hiring and firing.' I know what that means because people get hired and fired on The Simpsons, and when you get hired it means that you get a job, and when you get fired it means that you lose a job. I wonder if I will be hired as a cleaner by Suzanne Bowers and Mick today.

I don't like these people very much. Mick has got a cross face, and I think I must be saying the wrong answers. I said sorry to him because he looked cross, but then he pulled a very strange face at me and I don't know what it meant.

Suzanne Bowers is being nice to me, but I think that she thinks I am deaf because she is talking really loudly and slowly, like I am deaf. But I am not deaf. Maybe I should tell her that I am not deaf.

Mick looks at his piece of paper and says, "What's your time keeping like?"

I answer, "I can't tell the time."

He looks at Suzanne Bowers and she looks at him.

She smiles a little bit. Then she turns back to me, and starts to talk in a high voice with a smile on her face. "Does that mean that you are late, sometimes? That means when you don't get to a place at the time you are supposed to. Does that ever happen to you?"

I know what late means. I say, "No, I am never late," because I am never late. I don't like to be late, because that means breaking a rule, and I don't like breaking rules.

She says, "That's very good, well done."

I like that she thinks I have done well, but I think that she is talking to me like people talk to children. Maybe she thinks I am a child, but I do not look like a child because I am a man. I wonder why she is talking to me like a child that is deaf.

Then she says, "Do you have much experience cleaning? Have you ever done any cleaning before?"

I say, "Yes. I clean my flat every Sunday afternoon. I like to make it super clean because I don't want to get any germs."

"Super," says Mick in a funny voice.

I think I am answering these questions well because Suzanne Bowers keeps telling me I am doing a very good job. I think I would like to be hired as a cleaner, because I like making things nice and clean and I would like to get a little bit of money so that I can go on more trips. I feel a bit calm now. I can understand the questions that they ask me, and I think I am doing very well.

"I would be a very good cleaner," I say as the meeting finishes. "Am I hired?"

Suzanne Bowers smiles at me. "Well, we have had lots of good candidates, but we will give you a call later on today - a phone call - on the telephone - and we will tell you then if you have got the job."

Mick says very quietly, "I wouldn't count your chickens, though."

I think that that is a very silly thing to say, because I don't have any chickens. I think that he is a strange man.

They both stand up and hold out one of their hands to me. I remember that I am supposed to shake their hands, so I do.

The lady says, "It was very nice to meet you, Matthew."

The man says, "Goodbye."

They both take me back outside to see Brian, who stands up when he sees me and says, "Hey, how was it, Matt?"

"They will call me if I am hired. I think they will hire me."

He says, "Wow, well done. How was the meeting? Did you feel stressed?"

"Only a bit," I answer.

"Did you make your train noise?"

I say, "No."

Brian opens his mouth very wide and says, "Aren't you good? I'm proud of you, Mate"

I say, "Thank you."

"Come on then," he tells me, "it's home time."

"Will we be home in time for The Simpsons?" I ask. "It starts at six pm, on Four."

"We haven't had lunch yet, Matt."

I am not sure what lunch has got to do with The Simpsons, so I ask again, "Will we be home in time for The Simpsons?"

"It's only 11am, and The Simpsons doesn't start until, what time?"

"Six pm, on Four. Will we be home in time for The Simpsons?"

"Yes, we will."

I am glad.

* * *

I am back in my flat now, and Brian has gone back to his house. My flat is very nice, because my mum and Hannah decorated it for me. It doesn't look like my nana's flat any more because it is not decorated the same, but it still makes me think about her. It makes me think about Rose too, because she used to live here as well. I loved Rose very much, and I miss her a lot.

My living room has got cream paint on the walls, and it has got a blue carpet, because I like blue because I am a man. It smells like a plant called lavender in my living room, because I have got an air freshener that smells like lavender in here because I like that smell. I have got Nana's old settee, but my mum covered it in blue material so that it looks nice, and I have got a small television, a DVD player and my PlayStation in here too.

My bedroom is the big room opposite my front door, which used to be Nana's pink bedroom. It is not pink anymore, but it is light blue, and it has got posters of The Simpsons up on the walls. It has got one poster of all the cast of The Simpsons, and it also has one big poster of Homer Simpson saying, 'D'oh!' which makes me laugh every time I look at it. My duvet has got a cover that has Bart Simpson on it. I chose it myself from the shop.

Brenda is my support worker this evening. Brian brought me home from my meeting about the cleaners job this afternoon, and at five pm Brenda came to my flat and Brian went back to his house. I do not know yet whether I have been hired as a cleaner by Suzanne Bowers and Mick, but they will give me a telephone call to tell me.

I don't like it when Brenda is my support worker, because she tells me off lots of times. I wish I could get a different support worker than Brenda, because I think that she is horrible. Brenda is forty-five years old, and she is a little bit fat. She has got long, curly, yellowy-orangey hair, and she has got very small brown eyes, which look funny on her big face. Tonight she is wearing a dark green polo shirt, and not a dark blue polo shirt. I think it is funny when Brenda wears a blue polo shirt, because blue is for men and Brenda is a lady.

Me and Brenda have just made my tea. It was pepperoni pizza, which is my favourite, but I am still hungry because Brenda ate three pieces of my pizza, and I wanted to eat it all. It was not her pizza, so I do not think that she should have eaten it. I blew air through my teeth when she took the pieces from my plate, and she said, "Stop it, Matthew", but I don't like it when she tells me to stop it, so I blew the air harder. "I said, stop it," she said again in a cross voice.

I don't like cross voices.

Then she said, "Stop it, or I will put the rest of your pizza into the bin and then you will be very hungry."

I didn't understand what my train noise had got to do with my pizza, but I did not want her to put it in the bin because I would be very hungry, so I picked up my plate and carried it with me into my bedroom. I locked my door.

That is where I am now. I am in my bedroom, and my door is locked. I have eaten my pizza but I am still a bit hungry. I can hear that Brenda is watching my television in my living room, and she is laughing very loudly. I think that she must be watching a funny programme. I wonder if she is watching The Simpsons, because that is a funny programme and it is on at six pm, on Four. I don't know what time it is now.

I open my door a little bit and listen, but it doesn't sound like Brenda is watching The Simpsons. "What time is it, Brenda?" I ask, putting my head through my bedroom door and looking at Brenda, who is sitting on my settee in my living room. The living room door is open.

"Have you stopped being naughty?" she asks back.

I don't know what she means, because I have not been naughty. "I am a good man," I say.

Brenda says, "Hmmm."

I wonder what that means. "What time is it, Brenda?"

"You already asked that," she says.

"You didn't tell me the answer. What time is it, Brenda?"

She looks at the big clock on the wall in my living room. "Quarter past six," she says.

"Is it quarter past six am, or quarter past six pm?"

Brenda says, "Don't be silly, you know its pm."

That means that I am missing The Simpsons, because it starts at six pm, on Four. I run over to Brenda, and I take the remote control out of her hand.

She shouts, "Oy!"

I turn the television onto Channel Four, and I can see Homer talking to Mr Burns. I remember this bit, and I like it, but I am sad that I missed the beginning of the programme.

I sit down on the settee next to Brenda, but she takes the remote control out of my hand and she puts her programme back on. "I was watching this," she says, but I am cross because it is my television and I want to watch The Simpsons, and I am missing a funny bit.

I try to take the remote out of Brenda's hand again, but she holds onto it really tightly. The channels start to skip because she is pressing all of the buttons on the remote control while she holds it. The noises from the television keep changing because the channel keeps changing, and I want to watch The Simpsons and Brenda won't let me, but it is *my* television. I can feel my face turning very hot, and my head starts to hurt me. I feel very angry.

Brenda says, "Calm down, Matthew. You can watch The Simpsons another night."

But I want to watch The Simpsons tonight. I watch The Simpsons every night. When I am with Brian he lets me put my Simpsons DVD on too and we watch three episodes together, but Brenda is making me very cross when she says 'you can watch The Simpsons another night'.

"Stop being so silly and naughty," Brenda shouts at me.

My head starts to scream. My mouth starts to scream too. "I am a good man," I shout, and then I scream again. I take the pillow from the settee and I throw it at the television. It wobbles a bit. I take

Brenda's cup of coffee and throw it at the wall. It smashes and makes a very loud noise, so I cover my ears and fall onto the floor. I scream a bit more.

I don't know how long I am lying on the floor screaming for, but in the end I see Brenda press the remote control and put Channel Four on. She says, "Fine."

I stop screaming and I look at the television. Homer, Marge, Bart, Lisa, and Maggie are all sitting at the dinner table together. My headache suddenly goes and I feel happy again. Then the music starts, and the names of all the people that help to make The Simpsons come up on screen. I realise that it has finished and I have missed it. My head starts to hurt and scream again, and so my mouth starts to scream again too. I kick my legs up and down so they hit the floor really hard. This makes my head hurt a little bit less, so I keep doing it.

I see Brenda stand up and walk into the kitchen. She closes the door, so I can't see her anymore. That makes me feel a little bit less angry. Soon I am too tired, so I stop kicking and I stop screaming. I close my eyes.

* * *

I think I must have fallen asleep, because when I open my eyes it is dark outside my window. It is the month of June, and in the month of June it is not dark when The Simpsons is on, and it is not dark until a long time later.

Brenda is sitting on my settee, eating a bag of my crisps and reading a magazine. She says, "Oh, have you decided to wake up now?"

"No," I say, because I didn't decide to wake up, I just did. I sit up, and wonder what I am going to do now. "What am I going to do now, Brenda?"

"Have you calmed down?"

"Yes."

She looks at me. "Are you sure?"

"Yes, I am sure."

"Fine," she says. "Well, that company you went to today called while you were tantrumming. Did you want to be a cleaner?"

I say, "Yes," because I did want to be hired as a cleaner by Suzanne Bowers and Mick.

Brenda smiles at me, but it is a funny smile. "Did you *really* (she makes that word very long) want to get that job as a cleaner?" she asks.

I say, "Yes," again, and I am getting annoyed because I have already told her that. "Am I hired?"

"What do you think?"

"I don't know."

She looks at me, and takes another handful of crisps out of my crisp packet. She eats them. "Do you think they would trust you enough to give you a job?" she asks me.

"Yes, I do."

She puts on a silly sad face and says, "Oh dear, you really do think that, don't you?"

I am fed up of answering her questions, so I don't answer her this time.

She smiles again. "Nope," she says, "you didn't get it."

I think she is saying that I have been fired from the cleaner job. I look at her, and I take a deep breath. "Did I get fired?" I ask her.

"What did you expect?" she says.

I don't understand. "Did I get fired?" I ask again.

"Don't you understand English?" she asks me, which is a very silly thing to say because she knows that I understand English, because it is my language.

I am feeling very cross with Brenda.

"You can't get fired," she continues, "because they wouldn't hire you." She makes a laughing noise.

I am confused. "Did Suzanne Bowers and Mick hire me as a cleaner?" I ask again, because I want Brenda to tell me an answer that I understand.

She laughs again, and it is a loud laugh this time; it hurts my ears.

I do not like Brenda.

"Of course they didn't," she says. "The guy phoned and said you were a freak - well, those weren't his exact words, but it's what he meant. Brian was an idiot taking you to that interview today. Like you could ever amount to anything." She laughs again.

The only part of what Brenda just said that I understand is that Suzanne Bowers and Mick did not hire me as a cleaner, and that Brenda finds that very funny. My head starts to pound and scream quietly, and then louder and louder. And then, my whole world turns red.

Matthew Pickering
November 2009

Today, Brenda is taking me to something called Amateur Dramatics, which means acting, and I am very excited about it because I want to be an actor as a job. Hannah found me this amateur dramatics class, and she told me that it will be a hobby and not a job, but that is okay because I will be learning how to be a very good, famous actor, so I can get lots of money when I am older.

I am going to an acting club called Billsford Amateur Theatrical Society, because it is in Billsford Village Hall. They call it BATS for short. BATS starts at one thirty pm, and it is one twenty-five pm when me and Brenda get off the bus in Billsford. I know that this is the time because I am looking at my new watch, which Hannah gave to me as a present for my nineteenth birthday. It is very easy to tell the time on my new watch because it is called a digital watch, and it tells you the time in numbers and not with a round clock.

I walk straight in to the village hall when we arrive there at one twenty-eight pm, and Brenda follows me. There are lots of people in the room that are standing around talking to each other.

I say, "I am here for doing acting," in a loud voice.

Everyone in the room looks at me, and Brenda goes a bit red on her face. She says, "Sorry; he's autistic."

Some people look at me a bit funny, and some people give me very big smiles.

Only one person comes to say hello. She is a tall, thin lady, who has got short yellowy-brown hair and is wearing a long red skirt. She has got some glasses on too, and a woolly jumper because it is cold in the village hall. She says, "Hi, you must be Matthew. We were expecting you. My name is Gillian, and I am the class coordinator; I don't like the word 'leader'."

I wonder why she doesn't like the word 'leader', because it isn't a naughty word.

Gillian says, "Your younger sister telephoned about you coming. I take it this isn't her?" She looks at Brenda with a funny smile. What a silly thing to say. Of course Brenda isn't my younger sister; she is old.

I say, "No, this isn't Hannah."

Brenda says, "I'm Brenda. I'm one of his carers; for my sins."

Gillian laughs a little bit, but I don't know why. Then she says, "Well, Brenda, you are more than welcome to join in with us tonight; we don't bite."

Brenda says, "No thanks, I don't go in for all this la-di-da stuff. Just tell me when it's time for me to take him home."

Gillian looks a bit cross at her and makes a little coughing noise. Then she shouts, "Starting time everyone; get a chair please, and make a circle in the middle." She smiles at me and says, "You too, Matthew."

I get a chair, but I don't know what she meant when she said 'make a circle in the middle', so I wait.

Brenda is now sitting on a chair by the door and she is looking at her mobile telephone.

I can see everyone else moving their chairs to the centre of the room, and sitting them in a big ring facing the middle, so I think that maybe I should do the same, but I do not know what Gillian meant by 'make a circle'.

I wait until everyone is quiet, and then Gillian looks at me. She is not smiling now. She says, "Come on, Matthew, we are supposed to have started. Bring your chair to the middle and sit down please."

So I do.

"Okay everyone, we have a new member with us here this evening. Matthew, this is everyone. Everyone, this is Matthew."

Everyone looks at me.

Gillian continues, "Matthew, would you like to tell us all a little bit about yourself?"

I look around the room. There are about thirty people here. Some are men, and some are ladies. Some are old people, and some are just children, and some are ages in between; like me. I do not want to tell them anything about myself so I say, "No."

"I beg your pardon?" Gillian looks at Brenda, but she is still looking at her mobile telephone.

I say, "No," again, a bit louder this time because she didn't hear me the first time. She looks cross, so I add, "Sorry."

She pauses for a minute, and some people in the room laugh. I think they are laughing at me, but I don't know why. Then she says, "Can you tell us why you want to be an actor, Matthew?"

I say, "Yes, I want to be an actor because I want to make movies in Hollywood, in the United States of America, and also because I like plays like the Peter Pan play, and the Lion King play."

"The Peter Pan play? Sorry, I'm not familiar. Is that a play now?"

Other people laugh again.

I am not sure why people are laughing. I am feeling quite hot, so I take off my coat and put it on the floor in front of me.

Gillian looks at it, and more people laugh.

I answer, "Yes, Peter Pan is a play, because I saw it one Christmas-time."

She smiles again and says, "Oh I see, and was Peter played by a lady, and was there an Old Dame played by a man, by any chance?"

I say, "Yes," because she is right.

She looks at me, making a little smile, and she says, "Right." Then she lifts up some folders that are lying on her legs, hits them back down onto her thighs, and looks around at everybody else. "Okay, shall we get started then? Into pairs please. Ian, you can go with Matthew."

I did not know that Ian Hobson came here. Mum never told me that. I look around the room for him, but I cannot see him.

A man who looks about the same age and the same height as me walks over to me. His face is a bit red. He says, "Hi, I'm Ian." He doesn't sound very happy.

I say, "No you are not," because he is not Ian Hobson. He is a young man, like me.

He says, "Alright, I'm not. Whatever."

I look at him funny, because I think he is very strange.

Then Gillian claps her hands. "Okay," she says, "we will start with some trust exercises. Into your positions everyone."

The man who said he was called Ian stands in front of me, facing the other way. He turns his head around to look at me and says, "Make sure you catch me, okay?"

I don't know what he means when he says, 'make sure you catch me, okay?' because it doesn't make any sense.

Then he turns back to face the other way.

Gillian shouts, "Three, two, one - go."

Suddenly, pretend Ian starts to fall backwards. It is so fast that I don't have time to think about what to do, and his body hits mine. We both land on the floor, and he is crushing me. He looks at me with an angry face. "You said you were going to catch me," but I didn't say that.

Gillian walks over to us.

Everyone else is standing up, and is watching us.

"You don't seriously need me to explain trust exercises to you, do you?" Gillian asks me.

I look at her.

"Well I'm guessing you know what it's all about now. Up. We are doing it again. Swap over please."

I stand up.

Pretend Ian says, "I am so tempted to side step out of the way now."

I don't know what he means.

He makes me stand in front of him and says, "When she says fall, you fall back, okay? I'll catch you - not that you deserve it."

I don't like this. I stand in front of pretend Ian, ready to fall back when Gillian says go, but I do not want to fall back because I might hurt myself. I start to breathe very fast.

Gillian shouts, "Three, two, one - go."

But I don't go. I am too scared. I do not want to fall backwards, because it would feel horrible, and I might get hurt.

Pretend Ian shouts, "Fall, you idiot," and everyone in the room turns around and looks at me.

I look around to Brenda, but she is still looking at her mobile telephone.

Gillian says, "Is there a problem?"

"I don't want to fall."

Then one person in the room shouts, "Fall," and then another person shouts, "fall." Soon, everyone in the room is shouting, "Fall, fall, fall, fall," and they are clapping their hands.

Now I am making my train noise. I cover my ears to stop all the shouting and I close my eyes, but I can still hear them. I feel really hot. My head hurts, and I know that it is about to start screaming. I breathe faster and louder through my teeth, and then suddenly I feel something. Some hands are on my chest and are pushing me backwards. I start to fall, and I am very scared. I scream because I am going to hit the floor and hurt myself. I open my eyes, and Gillian is stood in front of me with her arms stretched out. I think it must have been her that pushed me. All of a sudden I feel something soft on my shoulder blades, and I am being pushed back up again. I land on my feet and wobble forwards a bit, and then I stand still.

Everyone cheers.

I was so scared and I want to hit Gillian, but I know that that would be bad, so I don't. But I was so scared, and my heart is beating very fast, like I am having a heart attack again. I think that my eyes have gone red, because I feel like I am starting to cry.

Gillian says, "Pull yourself together, Matthew. It wasn't that hard, was it?"

I don't answer because I am still a bit frightened.

Then Gillian stands back and claps her hands again. "Groups of six or seven, please. We are going to do some improvisation activities." While everybody is getting into groups, she comes up to me again, and she says, "As you're autistic, I am assuming you are no good at improvisation?"

I do not know what 'autistic' means, and I do not know what 'improvisation' means, so I do not understand Gillian's question. "I don't know," I answer

She smiles and says, "Right then, a little test. Imagine you are a woman with three young children - you have just found out that your husband of twelve years has been cheating on you - I am that husband, and I have just got in from work. Go."

I look at her.

She folds her arms, and tilts her head to one side.

I keep looking at her. "Go where?"

She says, "I'm waiting," but I don't know what she is waiting for. She stares at me for a few more seconds, and then she says, "That's what I thought. Matthew, I'm sorry, but I really don't think acting is going to be the thing for you. Maybe try an easier career choice, like sharpening pencils, perhaps? Something where your own incompetence doesn't affect other people."

I say, "I don't understand."

"Maybe I should explain better? You need to go over there, and tell your friend, Brenda, that it is time to go home now, and that you can't come back because you will never be an actor, okay?"

I feel like my chest is hurting a lot. I think I am definitely having a heart attack now, because heart attacks make your chest hurt a lot, like mine does. I look around the room, and people are standing in small groups. At the other side of the room I can see an open hatch into the kitchen, and I can see a kettle.

"Matthew," I hear a voice say, and I think it is Gillian. The door into the kitchen is held wide open by a chair. "Are you listening to me, Matthew?"

I look quickly at Gillian, and then I turn my body towards the kitchen, and I run.

I hear a voice shout, "Where do you think you are going now?" and I think it was Gillian again, but she is far away from me now because I am running very fast.

"No!" I hear another voice shout, and it sounds like Brenda's. Maybe she is not looking at her mobile telephone anymore. "Not the flaming kettle," she shouts.

I squeeze quickly past the chair that is holding the kitchen door open, and I feel it falling over. I hear a crash, and I can see that the door is starting to close behind me.

Through the open hatch into the main hall I can see a fat person, who I think might be Brenda, running to the kitchen too.

I slam hard into the kitchen cupboard that has got the kettle on top of it, and it stops my running. Then I quickly pull the kettle from its base. The base sticks to the bottom of the kettle for a second, and then seems to jump off it and lands on the kitchen worktop. The kettle is plastic and not metal, but it is very heavy, which is good; that means that it is full. I stretch out my left arm and quickly tip the water through the spout and onto my skin.

I hear a scream from Brenda, and I hear someone shout, "What does he think he is doing?"

The water stings for a second as it floods over my arm and falls to the floor. I take a quick, deep breath to help the shock. Then, straight away, the stinging stops, and I realise that the water is not hot. The water is very cold. I do not think that the water in this kettle has been boiled for a long time. I am very cross, and I throw the kettle across the room towards the door.

I did not know that Brenda would open the door as I threw the kettle. I see it hit her on the right side of her face, and I hear her scream again as it happens. The kettle falls to the floor and makes a bit of banging. Brenda puts her arms up over her face and closes the door, but I do not know why, because the kettle is on the floor now, and it cannot hurt her when it is on the floor.

***

Brenda has got a very red face. She has got a red face because I hit her face with a kettle, but it was by accident. She is very, very cross with me, but I don't think that she should be because I said sorry to her, and when someone says sorry to you, you should forgive them and say, 'That's okay.' She didn't say that it was okay, but she said that I have got only one more chance with her. I do not know what that means.

Gillian was very cross with me too, because I made the floor in the kitchen very wet and I broke the kettle. She said that I was going to have to pay for the kettle, but I do not have a job to pay for it. Gillian told Brenda that if I couldn't pay for it, Brenda would have to pay for it herself, so she said that she would take it out of my benefits. I do not know what that means.

I am very annoyed, because me and Brenda have not gone home yet because we have had to come into town first to get some money so that we can pay for Gillian to buy a new kettle for the village hall. I want to go home because I want to watch a DVD of The Simpsons, but we cannot go home until we have got the bus back to Billsford Village Hall and given the money to Gillian.

Brenda and me have been to the bank, and Brenda took three hundred pounds out of my bank account, because she says that kettles cost three hundred pounds. She put a little bit of the money into one of the pockets in her jeans, and she put the rest of the money into her purse. I am sad to lose three hundred pounds, because that is a lot of money, but

Brenda says that it is my own fault for being silly and losing my temper.

I do not like it when I lose my temper, but I feel like I am going to lose my temper again soon because I am feeling very cross. It is very busy in town because it is a Saturday, and I don't like it when places are very busy. There are lots of people walking around me, and I can hear lots of people talking as they walk past me, but I can not tell what anybody is saying because they are all talking at the same time. My head starts to hurt, and I feel like I am very hot, so I pull my coat off.

Brenda says, "Don't be silly, you'll freeze with those wet clothes," and she puts my coat back on for me, but I am really hot. Brenda doesn't have her coat on, so I wonder why she is making me wear my coat. I try to take it off again, but she says, "No, you must wear your coat," so I put it on because I have to do what I am told.

We keep on walking, but I am feeling very hot, and my head is hurting me. The streets are very busy and loud, and I keep walking into people coming the other way.

Someone says, "Oy, watch where you are going."

I am watching where I am going. I am watching as lots and lots of people walk towards me, very fast. My heart is beating fast too, and my head really, really hurts. There is so much noise, because lots of people are talking at once so I can't tell what anyone is saying. I put my hands over my ears and blow air through my teeth. I hope this will make everyone go away.

Brenda pulls my hands away from my head and shouts, "Stop being so silly, Matthew. You're embarrassing me."

I don't like it when people shout at me. It makes me feel very sad. I put my hands back on my ears and fight against Brenda trying to pull them off.

Lots of people are looking at us and are pulling funny faces as they walk past.

I feel very hot. I think my face must be bright red because I feel so hot and cross. My head is hurting, and there are lots of loud noises in my ears. I keep bumping into people. Suddenly, I hear the loud screaming noises in my head again, so I let them out of my mouth, holding my hands against my ears as hard as I can. I close my eyes, and I stamp my feet, and I keep screaming.

I can feel that Brenda is still pulling at my hands to get them away from my ears. I feel like I might explode. I take one hand from my ear and throw it out towards Brenda to get her away from me. I can feel it hit something, but I can't see what because my eyes are shut tightly.

In my uncovered ear I hear a loud scream that is not my own, and Brenda's other arm lets me go. I open my eyes, and see Brenda falling to the floor. Her face is red, and there is blood coming out of her nose. I think that I must have hit Brenda in the nose, but I don't remember.

At this moment there is a big gap around Brenda and me, but then I hear some voices shouting, "Oy," and two big men start to run towards me.

Lots of people run to see Brenda on the floor.

The big men look very cross with me, and I am scared of what they will do to me because one shouts, "I will kill you, you... (and then he calls me lots of rude names that I don't like to think about)"

I don't want him to kill me. I shout, "Sorry," and then I turn and run away from the men as fast as I can.

One of the men shouts, "Stop him," but I am a very fast runner, so I think that it will be hard for them to stop me.

My body is shaking as I run, and I feel wet with all the sweat that is coming out of my body. My head isn't hurting or screaming anymore because I have already exploded and now I feel better. I turn down a thin alley, and I run very, very fast.

I turn my head, and I can see that the two men are chasing me, but one of them is a long way behind. I come to the end of the alley, and it is a road, so I turn to the left and start to run along the pavement. I turn my head again, and see that one man is still following me, and he is getting closer. The other man must have given up chasing me, because I can't see him anymore.

I keep running. My legs start to feel like I am not controlling them anymore, they are just moving superfast underneath me and I can't even feel them. I can see that the pavement I am on is about to disappear on this side of the road, but the pavement on the other side carries on, so I need to get onto that bit. I will have to cross the road. I slow down until I stop at the edge of the road. I look right, and I look left, and I look right again. I am listening for cars. Nothing is coming, so I decide to cross.

Suddenly, I am thrown backwards against a big building. I think the man has caught up with me, because he has grabbed me and pushed me against the wall. I am very scared of this man, because he is very big and muscly, and he is pressing his body against me on the wall. His big arm is trapping my throat, which is making it very hard to breathe (and I need to breathe fast because I am very out of breath from running). His other hand is holding my right arm to the wall. He puts his face right in front of mine, and he shows me his teeth. He looks like a dog that is angry and snarling. I am very, very scared of him.

I still feel very hot in my coat, and I wish I could take it off.

The man shouts lots of rude words to me, and calls me lots of very rude names. He says, "Make you feel like a big man, does it; punching helpless women in the face?"

I cannot talk because my throat is squashed, but I want to say sorry to stop him from being so cross.

Then he says, "You make me sick," and he spits in my face. It is horrible. I do not like it when people spit in my face, because I think that they might have got germs in their spit. He says, "Give me one good reason not to put you in hospital."

I don't really understand what I am supposed to say, but I cannot talk anyway. My throat is really hurting, and I wonder if he has broken my neck.

The man says, "I am calling the police," and then he lets go of my throat, puts his hand over my face, and grabs it. He pulls my head forwards, and then pushes it very fast back into the wall. It hurts a bit, but only for a second, and then I can't feel anything.

John Pickering
November 2009

I am in two minds. In some ways, being arrested seems like a rite of passage that every young boy should have to go through – I certainly had it happen to me when I was a teenager – but there's a world of difference between 'drunk and disorderly', and 'Actual Bodily Harm'. Mind you, I have wanted to clock that Brenda in the nose for a good while myself – irritating cow, so, while I'm not entirely impressed at being called from work to collect my only son from a prison cell, I am not about to murder the kid. Besides, it *may* have been me that has encouraged him to stand up for himself for all of these years.

I am taken into the tiny room by a skinny male officer with a too-neat haircut. The cell is grim. It's cold, smells faintly of urine, and is no larger than my bathroom at home. And my bathroom isn't big. My breath is taken away - not by the smell, but by the sight of my son, cowering in the foetal position in the corner of the room. His head is buried in his knees, and he is visibly shaking. There are crusts of deep red blood attached to the hair on the back of his head. I can hear him comforting himself with his blowing noise, although it is muffled through his legs.

"Matthew," I say calmly, getting to his level by kneeling in front of him.

The look of relief on his face as he looks up at me breaks my heart a little. His eyes are red, and his face is pale and tear stained. "Dad."

His breath quivers, and I can't resist throwing my arms around him and pulling him into a tight embrace. He is freezing, despite being wrapped in his thick winter coat, and his whole body quakes underneath my arms. "It's okay, Son," I say, almost brought to tears myself, "there's no need to be frightened anymore. I'm here."

"I'm going to prison, Dad," he says, beginning to cry.

"No, you're not."

"Yes I am, because I did some Actual Bodily Harm to Brenda, and then the police came and put handcuffs on me and put me in a van, and now I am going to prison."

"Miss Richardson dropped the charges," says the officer, in an unexpectedly deep voice. "You are free to go."

Matthew pushes himself back, and looks at me to explain.

"It's okay, Son. Brenda has told the police to let you go home. She's not going to make them send you to prison."

His mouth opens wider, still quivering. "Has she forgiven me? Like you did when I broke your nose?"

The officer coughs pointedly. I ignore him.

"Well, I don't know about forgiven, Mate, but she's not pressing charges. I think that's the best you can ask for."

And right there in my arms, my baby boy begins to cry uncontrollably.

I hug him tightly, and make a promise to myself never to let go. A promise that I have to break two minutes later, when he calms down a little and I see the officer tapping his watch. I release him, and help him to stand up. "Has anyone seen to his head?" I ask the officer.

He merely shrugs at me.

Right, let's get you to the hospital; just to get you checked over. What happened? The police said they found you knocked out after they had received the call.

"I can't remember," he says, looking utterly confused.

"Never mind, then." I wrap my arm tightly around him as we walk out of the cell.

* * *

"Sweetheart, what's happened?" Sue practically runs Matt over in her rush to greet him as I drop him at her and Ian's that evening. "Your dad called and said you were at the hospital. Then Brenda phoned and said that she'd, 'dropped the charges,' but that she won't work with you again."

"Good riddance," I mumble, closing the door behind me and throwing an acknowledging nod towards Ian.

Sue moves her gaze to me - a rather angry gaze. "What did she mean about dropping the charges, John? You didn't mention any charges."

"I'm sorry, Mum," Matt says, his shaky voice returning. "I was a bad man, and I gave Brenda some Actual Bodily Harm."

"You what?" Ian looks - for want of a better word - flabbergasted.

Sue's gaze flits from me to Matt, and then back again. "You gave her some... what?"

"He broke her nose, Sue. But you know the old bag as well as I do; she had it coming to her."

"John." Her eyes are wide. Anyone would think it was me that had done the dirty deed. I'm just standing up for my son, just like she has always wanted me to. "Matthew, what happened, Darling? Did she do something to you?"

It occurs to me that I haven't even asked what caused him to hit her; I just assumed that she deserved it.

"I was sad because I had a sad day," Matt says, removing his shoes. "I was not allowed to stay at BATS, and then I broke the kettle so Brenda had to take three-hundred pounds out of my benefits to pay for it, and then - "

"What?" I look at Sue, and she looks at me. Then I focus back on Matt. "Sorry, go back a bit - Brenda did what?"

"Did you say she took three-hundred pounds from you? For a kettle?" Sue's face is turning the darkest beetroot colour.

An angry burning begins in my chest, and I feel my eyes protrude a little from their sockets.

Ian continues to look flabbergasted. He doesn't say a thing.

"Yes," continues Matt, "and that made me feel sad, and then there were lots of people, and it was loud, and I got stressed - "

"Come on, Son," says Ian, removing him from my arms and directing him into the living room. "You've had a long day. Let's leave your mum and dad to chat."

"Okay." He follows Ian into the room and out of sight.

Ian closes the door, with a quick glance towards us as he does.

"The cow!" says Sue, banging her fist forcefully into the wall.

I do not wish to repeat the series of swear words that fall out of my mouth following this. I am cut off my spiel as thick, angry tears begin to fall from my Susie's eyes. I pull her towards me and wrap my arms around her.

She screams into the shoulder of my shirt and hits both of my arms simultaneously.

I kiss her forehead. "It's alright, Suse. Calm down."

"Calm down?" she shouts into my chest. "How could we have employed someone so evil? Paid her – actually paid her to *look after* our son. The utter, total, complete cow!"

The smell of my Susie's hair is intoxicating. I kiss her forehead again. "We are going to get this sorted, okay? We are going to call the police station right now, and we will make her pay for this. No wonder she wanted to 'drop the charges'. It's okay, Babes, calm down. We will sort this."

Susie cocks her head upwards, and I wipe a tear from her eye. "Do you promise?"

"I promise." I kiss her gently on her lips, and then, although she doesn't protest, I pull back instantaneously – an inch.

She is looking at me with her beautiful wet eyes, and my heart shatters.

I hold her gaze, continuing to hold her in a tight embrace.

Her lips twitch, just a little.

The front door suddenly opens again, into my back.

"Only me, oh, sorry," calls Hannah's voice. "Oh - Dad?"

I jump back from Susie, and she does the same.

Hannah grins. "Don't mind me," she says, "I'm not really here." And with that, she begins to make her way up the stairs.

Matthew Pickering
February 2010

I am at a place that I have never been to before, and I have come with my mum. We have come to see a lady that Ian Hobson knows, and she is called Sara. Her job is called a counsellor, and I am going to talk to her about some things. Mum said that it might help me to feel happy and calm again, because I feel sad and cross lots of the time now.

Sara's room is nice. It smells like flowers, because there is a vase of flowers on the windowsill, and the walls are painted a light blue colour. Blue is my favourite colour because I am a man. There are three comfy chairs in the room, and Sara is sitting in one of them. She points to the other one and tells me that I can sit down, so I do. My mum is waiting for me outside this room.

Sara looks like a nice lady. She has got a nice smile, which makes me think that she is not a bully, because bullies don't have nice smiles. She has got lots of short, spiky hair, which is browny-red coloured with some grey bits in, and she has got some very thick glasses on. She is wearing a yellow top, a red cardigan, a red skirt, and some brown boots on her feet.

"Hello, Matthew," she says to me. "Is it okay to call you Matthew, or do you like to be called Matt?"

"My name is Matthew," I tell her. Most people call me other things, but that's a bit silly because my name is Matthew.

"Okay, Matthew, that's fine. My name's Doctor Sara Bingham, but you can call me Sara if you like."

"Okay," I say.

She opens up a file that is sitting on her knee, and she looks down at it. Then she looks at me again and she smiles her nice smile. "So, how are you feeling today, Matthew?" she asks me.

"Okay," I tell her. I do not feel poorly today.

"Do you feel happy?"

I think about how I should answer her question. "I never feel happy," I tell her.

She doesn't pull a face, but she keeps on looking at me. "Don't you? Why don't you feel happy?"

"I don't know." I think. Maybe I do know why I don't feel happy. There are lots of reasons why I don't feel happy. "There are lots of reasons," I tell her.

"Could you tell me some of those reasons?" She smiles at me. I like Sara.

"I miss Rose," I tell her. I do miss Rose. It makes me very sad that Rose went away and died, because I loved her very much, and she was my only friend that I had left. I miss having her sleeping on my bed at night and protecting me, and I miss playing with her in the garden. I miss stroking her, and cuddling her, and taking her out on walks. Rose used to love me lots, and I miss being loved lots.

"Who is Rose?" Sara asks me.

"She was my best friend, other than Raine."

"And what happened to her?"

"Mum and Dad killed her."

She looks like she is surprised. "I'm sorry?" she says.

"It's okay."

She crosses one of her legs over the other, and pulls a bit of a frowny face. "Do you want to tell me a little bit more about Rose?"

"Yes," I say, because I like talking to Sara. I wait for her to answer me.

"You can tell me then. Go on."

"Rose was Nana's dog, and then she was my dog and she was my best friend."

Sara nods her head and smiles a little bit.

"But my mum and dad took her to the vets and killed her. They said she was very old, but she wasn't very old because she was only twelve, and that isn't very old at all."

"That must have made you sad. Are you cross with your mother and father?"

"Not anymore," I tell her, "because they told me that they were sorry, and when somebody tells you that they are sorry you have to forgive them."

"Well, I think that's very noble of you, Matthew. So do you think you will get another dog?"

"I want to get another dog," I say, "and Nana told me that I should before she went away, but Mum says I couldn't look after a dog by myself. Hannah thinks that I could, though."

"And who's Hannah?"

"My little sister."

"Oh, I see. And what is your relationship with her like?"

"I love my little sister, because she looks after me lots. But she is going to move a long way away soon, to a place called University, and that will make me even more sad."

"And when is she moving to University? Is it this year?"

"I don't know," I tell her, because I am not sure when Hannah is moving to university but I know it will be soon, and that makes me feel sad.

"I see." She writes something down in her folder. "So, you mentioned another best friend, what was he called, Ray?"

"Raine was my other best friend, and my girlfriend."

Sara's eyebrows go up a bit. "Oh, I see. So tell me about Raine. Is she not your girlfriend any more?"

"I don't think so," I tell her, "because Raine disappeared away and I have not seen her for two and a half years."

"She disappeared?" She looks at me with a frowny face on.

"Yes."

"Do you know where she went?"

"No." I think that is a silly thing to ask. If I knew where she went I would have said that. I would have said, 'she moved to London,' or, 'she moved to the United States of America,' but I do not know where she went.

"And has she contacted you since she disappeared?"

"No," I answer.

"Okay. How does that make you feel?"

"Sad," I tell her, which is the truth. "And angry, too. When you have a girlfriend they are not allowed to disappear for two and a half years."

"And do you think it is all these sad and angry feelings that are making you hurt yourself, and lash out at other people?"

"I hurt myself because it makes the other pain go away. My train noise doesn't help me enough anymore."

"What pain does it make go away?"

"The pain that is in my chest when I think about things that make me sad or angry. Or the pain that goes in my ears or my eyes when things are too loud, or too bright or too busy. And it helps the screaming in my head to go away."

"Okay, I understand. So, how do you feel when you have finished hurting yourself? Do you feel better?"

"Sometimes," I tell her. "Sometimes it makes me feel calm, but other times it makes me hurt more, because it makes me have real pain, and that can take a long time to go away. I don't feel very better when I have hurt somebody else, either, because that is not a very nice thing to do, and I want to be a nice man."

"Of course." She nods her head, and she smiles at me. Then she pauses for a long time and looks at me like she thinks I have got more things to say, but I don't. "Can you tell me, is there anything else that you feel sad about right now?"

"I feel sad that I can't be an actor."

She lifts her eyebrows up. "You want to be an actor, do you?"

"Yes, I want to be an actor in the movies, and I want to live in Hollywood, in the United States of America."

"Wow, that's quite an ambition. And why do you think you can't be an actor? Has somebody told you that?"

"Gillian told me that."

"Who's Gillian?"

"A lady who runs Billsford Amateur Theatrical Society."

She nods her head, and pulls a bit of a frowny face. "Ah, I know the place you mean, actually. Would you ever like to try going to a different drama class, Matthew?"

"Yes, I would like to try that," I say, "but only if they are nice to me."

"Yes." She taps the end of her pen against the folder on her knee. "I might have a word with your mother about that in a little while, I might be able to help a bit. But for now, is there anything else that is making you unhappy?"

"Lots of things make me unhappy. And scared."

"What makes you scared?"

"Loud noises," I answer. "They make me scared. Lots of people all together at once, that makes me scared too. And bullies make me scared."

She is nodding her head as she writes something down in the folder.

"Bright lights scare me as well; they are daggers in my eyes. And I get scared when I don't understand things."

Sara smiles at me. "I think we all do, a bit."

The sun is shining through the trees outside, and it is sending a line of light into the room. I can see lots of bits of dust floating in that line.

"Do you ever do any visualisation, Matthew?"

"I don't understand," I tell her.

"Okay, try this then. Can you tell me something that makes you feel calm? Really at ease."

"Rivers make me feel calm," I say.

"And why is that?"

"Because they are gentle, and they have soft sounds. I don't like rain because it can be loud and scary and it makes me wet, but then the rain makes rivers and that means that a bad thing becomes good."

"Wow," says Sara, "you're good at this."

I smile, because I am pleased that Sara thinks I am good at this.

"So, the next time you feel angry, Matthew, why don't you try and visualise a calm, flowing river?

Something that you can throw all of your troubles into and it will just carry them away from you - calmly and peacefully."

I am thinking about a calm, flowing river, like Sara is telling me to, and it is making me feel calm too. I think it is a very good idea to visualise that when I feel upset or angry, because it might help me to feel better. "Okay," I say.

She smiles at me. "Excellent. Well, for your homework I want you to try that all week, any time that you feel stressed, okay?"

"Okay," I say.

"Lovely. Well done, Matthew. I think now might be an ideal time to bring your mother in. Is there anything else you want to talk to me about before we do?"

I say, "No."

Sara nods her head again, and then walks to the door, opens it, and says, "We're ready for you, Susan." Then she walks back into the room, and my mum follows her.

Mum sits down on the empty chair next to me. She is holding her hands tightly together and twisting them round and round. I don't know why she is doing that. She looks at me and makes a little smile.

"Thanks for joining us, Susan. Matthew and I have been having a good chat. Before we really start, Matthew expressed an interest in attending a drama class, is that something you would approve of him doing?"

"Oh." Mum starts to talk, but her voice is sounding a little bit shakier than normal. "Well, it's not that we didn't want him to go. I mean, he did go to one a couple of months back, but they - well, it wasn't a very nice place for him - but please don't think we are trying to hinder - "

"You misunderstand me, I don't think anything of the sort, I just know of something that may be of some help to you, if you have no objection to him attending such a class?"

"Oh. Well, no, of course not."

"Okay, well this isn't exactly the time, but I have a niece, Jodie, and she is on the autistic spectrum also. She's something of a drama queen, and she actually attended the same drama class that Matthew went to - horrible place. Anyway, she now goes to a new, disability-friendly class, which she absolutely loves, and they are fantastic with her. She's really happy there. I will give you the details later on if you would like me to?"

Mum is tapping her fingers against her thighs. "Erm, yes. Thank you, that would be good."

"Quite alright. So, Susan, would you like to tell me anything about how *you* are feeling at the moment?"

Mum looks at me and takes in a big breath.

"Would you feel more comfortable if Matthew were to wait outside while we talk?"

Mum looks back at Sara. "I don't... I'm not sure he would be al - yes, yes I would, really." She smiles a funny smile at me.

Then Sara looks at me, and she points to the door. "Matthew, do you like magazines?" she asks me, but I don't know why.

"Sometimes," I say. "I like the ones that have got movie stars in them."

She smiles. "I think there might be a few of those just outside the door in the waiting area. Would you go and look at them for ten minutes while I speak with your mum, please?"

"Okay," I say, and I stand up.

Mum reaches her hand out to me and puts it into mine. "I wont be long, Baby. You promise me you won't walk off anywhere."

"Okay," I say, and I drop her hand and walk out of the door.

Matthew Pickering
March 2010

It is seven pm, and I have just arrived at the acting class that Mum is taking me to. It is a very nice acting class that I have been to two times before, and the people here are kind to me, and do not make me do scary things like falling backwards when I don't want to.

I have made a new friend called Jodie at my acting class, and she has got an auntie called Sara, who is my counsellor. I like Jodie a lot. She is eighteen years old, and she is a little bit shorter than me, which is probably because she is younger than me. She has got dark brown hair that goes down to her shoulders, and she has got very big green eyes. I think that Jodie is very funny, and we have got a lot to talk about because we are very good friends.

My new acting class is called, 'Saint Paul's Arts Club,' and it is held in a church, which I think is a little bit funny because we don't do any praying, although we do do some singing. We are in a long room that has got a wooden floor and lots of chairs, but the chairs are all stacked together against the walls. There is a funny smell in this room, and I do not know what it smells of, except that it is the same smell that was in the sports hall at school. It is not a horrible smell, but it is not very nice, either. There are some windows in the room, but they are very high so I can't see out of them. I wonder what is the point of having windows if you can't see out of them. There is a big window at one end of the room that has got lots of colours and pictures on it. I like that window. I wish the windows at my flat had got lots of colours and pictures on them, too.

I am looking at the window now, but something makes me jump, because someone has put their hands on my shoulders from behind me and jumped up and said, "Boo."

I scream and turn around, and someone is laughing very hard.

It is Jodie. She is bent over because she is laughing so hard, and she is shouting, "I got you, I got you."

I say, "Don't do that, Jodie, you made me scared."

Jodie laughs again.

Mum says, "Hello, Jodie. How are you?"

"Hello, I'm fine, Matthew's mum." She has nearly stopped laughing now.

"You can call me Sue, Sweetheart."

Jodie says, "Hi, Sue. Matthew is my best friend." She starts singing a song about best friends, and then she stops and says, "That's a song by 'All Stars'."

My mum smiles at her. "That's a nice song, you've got a nice singing voice." Then she looks at me. "You didn't tell me Jodie was your best friend, Matty."

I say nothing, because she is right, I did not tell her that she is my best friend because I forgot to tell her.

"We have been best friends for ages, Sue. Nearly two weeks."

Mum laughs a bit, but I don't know why. Then she says, "Is your mum here tonight, Jodie?"

Jodie says, "No, my Granddad John is here tonight instead of my mum."

I look at Mum because I know what she must be thinking. I say, "It is not the same John as my dad, Mum. It is just someone else with the same name as my dad. Do you understand?"

Mum laughs. "I think so."

Jodie looks at me and she says, "Hello, Matthew"

"Hello, Jodie".

Then we are quiet for lots of seconds.

Mum says, "Good luck with your class, Angel," to me, and then she kisses me on my cheek and sits down on a chair at the side of the room to watch me because it is time for the class to start.

I am standing with Jodie, and we are quiet for two minutes. I think it is really nice to have a best friend like Jodie. She is looking very pretty tonight. She has got a purple top on, which has got pink flowers on it, and she has got her hair tied up in a ponytail. There is some purple make-up on top of her eyes, which matches her top, and she has got some pink lipstick on too.

The leader of Saint Paul's Arts Club is a man called Robin. He is a tall man, and he is wearing some brown trousers, a red shirt, a brown waistcoat and some glasses. He is a bald man, because he hasn't got any hair. I like Robin because he is a nice man to me. He says, "Good evening, everybody, I hope you have all had a nice week. I have been away, as you know, escaping the frost. Beautiful weather, but those mosquitoes were murder - I'm covered in bites - absolutely covered. But never mind that now, I hope you have all been practicing our songs this week. We are going to start now with a little bit of singing practice. Into your positions, please."

I know where my position is, because I was told where my position is when I came last week. My position is at the back of the group on the right hand side, next to Jodie. That is very nice, because it means that I can hear her singing, and Jodie's singing is very beautiful - just like she is.

John Pickering
April 2010

A quick shot to the head, perhaps? He wouldn't suffer too much - barely at all, really. I wouldn't even have to do it myself; I could hire a hit man, or something. Although, that would cost a fair whack, so perhaps it's not the best option. Maybe I will just have to let him live, and accept that if my girl really wants to be with me, she will just leave him. It can't be that difficult. I mean, she's been married to the guy almost ten years now - that's how long she lasted with me. Perhaps she has a ten-year cut off point in relationships? Though that would mean she would finish with me again in another ten years if that were true. Oh well, I don't plan on being alive in ten years, anyway - I plan to drink myself to oblivion long before my good looks fade away.

I can't wait to see her later on. I've got the kids for the day (I say 'kids', it was Hannah's sixteenth birthday last week and Matthew will be in his twenties by the time the years up. Hold do I feel?), so I will be seeing her when I drop them off. I hope clever Mr Doctor Man is at work so we can chat.

I'm not sure at what age it stopped being cool for Hannah to hang out with her old, grey daddy and her big brother, but by the face on her today, that time has clearly passed. "Dad, I've told you, the girls are shopping today, can you *please* drop me at Meadowhall? I am *actually* begging you."

"Don't be so melodramatic," I chastise throwing her a box of nails. "Put those back in the drawer for me. There you go, Matt - knock one into there." I hand Matt a long nail and the hammer, pointing to the roofline of the birdhouse.

He hammers it in, surprisingly hitting the nail every time and his thumb not once. I have finally taught him something.

"So, that's a no, then?"

"That's a 'maybe after me and your brother have finished this'."

She lets out a loud groan. "But that will be *ages*. I didn't put on my best outfit to sit in a shed with you two all day."

"That's your best outfit?" I marvel at the plain jeans and grey t-shirt/cardigan combination she has on, wondering how I got so lucky as to not end up with a short skirted, low necklined sixteen year old daughter.

"Thanks, Dad." She rolls her eyes at me.

"No, I like it. Believe me, I like it. Don't ever change, Babes, okay? You've finished that, Matt? Good man, that's all the nails in. Next, it's time to sand."

I pass him the sandpaper, and he knowingly takes a pair of thick gloves from the bucket next to him.

"So, Han, you haven't filled me in on this new boyfriend of yours - don't look at me like that - your mum told me. So, when do I get to meet him?"

"Why would you want to?"

"Interrogation, of course." I begin to pick up the dozens of bent nails that have fallen to the floor, while Matt gets started on smoothing down his masterpiece.

"In that case, never."

"Oh, don't be like that, I've already bought the lie detector and thumb screws. Do you want all that good money to go to waste?"

"Oh, ha ha," says Hannah, not laughing; not even smiling. "When I want to see a comedian I'll go to a show." Cutting.

"Who says I'm joking?" I reply with a grimace.

***

"There you go - two children, each in one piece."

"I am not a child," protests Matty, removing his shoes at the door and thus blocking the entrance for myself and Hannah, "I am a man."

"Yeah, and FYI, I'm not five years old any more either, Dad." She doesn't need to tell me that.

Matthew finally removes his shoes and begins to make his way upstairs.

"See you, Mate," I shout after him.

"Goodbye, Dad," he calls back, before disappearing into his bedroom at the top.

Hannah quickly kicks off her shoes and begins her own climb up the stairs.

"That's fine," I call. "I didn't want a goodbye kiss, anyway."

"Don't be gross," comes her reply.

Susie looks at me with a knowing grin, and I reciprocate.

"Kids," I say.

"Teenagers," she responds. "Are you coming in?"

"Where's Ian?" I say this quietly, in case he appears in the hallway at any second.

"Night shift."

Excellent. "In that case..." I enter the house and, brainwashed by Matthew, remove my shoes as I close the door behind me.

"Juice?" she asks.

"Anything stronger?"

"Well, you know the situation with the coffee, and beer is *far* too unsophisticated to have in this house, and all the wine we have is about eighty years old, cost the earth and is saved for 'the most special of occasions'." Is she really trying to put on Ian's voice? It isn't quite working.

"Ah," I answer with a slight grin, "juice is fine."

* * *

"So, I took Matt to that acting class tonight." I wrap my arms around Susie's waist from behind her as she reaches into the fridge for the juice.

She turns her head and sort of nestles it into my shoulder as she closes the fridge door. "What did you think?"

I snigger. "A bit poncey, but they seem like a nice bunch, I guess. And Matthew was loving it."

"Yeah, he does. Did you meet the famous Jodie?"

I kiss the side of her cheek, and feel her give a little shudder. "Oh yes, you can't miss that one, can you?"

She turns in my arms to face me, and places her hands onto my hips. Bliss. "Oh, don't," she reprimands, "she's a lovely girl."

"I didn't say she wasn't."

"So you're not going to kick off about how it's 'not normal' for a nineteen year old boy to go to an acting class, then?"

"Don't, Suse. You know I'm not like that anymore."

Her eyes drift away from mine.

"You know I'm not."

They drift back. She gives the slightest of smiles and nods her head once. "I do know." Those eyes are definitely inviting me. Her whole body language is inviting me.

I take a breath, and then slowly lean forwards and press my lips against hers.

She lets me.

A whole spring of electricity bounces through my entire body.

Her lips are soft and warm, just like my Susie is. But before the electric bolt reaches the tips of my fingers and toes, it fizzles away again as she pulls back and pushes me away from her. "Ian," she says.

"No, I'm John."

She doesn't laugh. "Exactly. You're not my husband. Don't do this again. Please? I think it's best that you go."

"But you were doing it, too," I protest. A childish argument, I am aware.

"I know I was, and I'm sorry." She looks distressed. "I'm a horrible person. Please, just go."

"Why are you doing this to yourself, Suse?"

She sighs, and turns her body away from me. "I don't know. It's like we're polar opposites and you just magnetise me towards you."

"Not that. Why are you staying with him? You know it's over between you, you just have to admit it to him. And more importantly, to yourself."

"But he's been so good to us, John. I can't just get up and leave him. What sort of person would that make me?"

"An honest one," I tell her.

Her eyes are filling with tears, so I decide that now may not be the time.

"Just promise me you will think about it?"

She looks out of the window, but I see her nod her head, just a little.

John Pickering
August 2010

Life is good. I have got myself a new pair of wheels; the flashiest, most expensive pair I have had in a long time. In reality, the Harley I had when I was barely an adult was an old, smashed up piece of junk, but this - ooh - I cannot wait to take this bad boy out for a spin.

Adding to this, Susie is finally coming back to me. She is telling the old man tonight, and then she is packing all of her stuff up and moving back into here with Han. My life is finally sorting itself out. Things really are great.

Probably best of all, I have never had a better, more healthy relationship with my son than I do now, and I am so excited to take him out on the bike. He is going to love it.

"Where is my surprise?" he asks me continually as we cross the car park outside his flat.

"We're almost there."

"Come on, John, stop teasing us." Sue and Ian (the poor beggar) are following us. Had I known they were at Matt's today, I might have saved this little surprise for next weekend. As it stands, they are just going to have to lump it. Ian has no say anyway, being that I am Matthew's dad and not him.

We finally reach the beautiful machine, and I stop us next to it. "Tadaa," I say, melodically.

"What?" asks Matt. Is he not a man?

Susie's eyes are wide, and I'm sure I can see a sparkle behind them. The same sparkle I saw all those years ago when she first rode on the back of the original beast. "John, what is this?"

"It's an ice cream van," I answer.

Matt is looking confused. "No it's not, it's a motorbike."

"Oh, so it is. How did you tell?"

I see Sue grin.

Ian just looks concerned.

"Because ice cream vans have four wheels, and that has two. And because ice cream vans sell ice cream, and that doesn't. And because that is a motorbike."

"Ah, silly me." I throw my arm around my son in a manly embrace. "So, what do you think?"

"Those things are very dangerous," Ian answers.

Was I asking you, Old Man?

"I'm serious, John - the amount of fatalities I see from motorbikes..."

I ignore him. "Matt, what do you think?"

"I don't know," he answers.

"Well, come for a ride with me now, see if you can make up your mind."

"Oh, I don't know about that," says Sue, her expression suddenly matching that of her husband.

"I don't want to go for a ride on it," Matthew tells me. "Ian Hobson says they are dangerous."

Flaming Ian.

"Don't listen to him, Mate. You want to come for a spin, it's amazing."

"No, I don't."

"John, he said no." Sue is frowning now.

"Come on, Mate. Don't you want to spend the afternoon with your old dad?"

"No," he says.

Bullet straight through the gut.

"I want to watch The Simpsons with Ian Hobson like I planned to do this afternoon."

"Don't be silly, Son; you can watch that anytime. Would you rather spend your afternoon with him, or with me, your dad?"

"I would rather spend my afternoon with Ian Hobson watching The Simpsons."

I feel very hot. "No, you wouldn't," I argue.

"Come on, Son, let's go inside." Ian puts his hand onto Matty's shoulders and is steering him away from me.

"He's not your son!" I shout, unable to control myself.

"John, calm down."

I shake Sue's hand from its new position on my bicep. "I said, 'he's not your son'." I am shouting louder as they walk further and further away from me.

"Why did you have to go and buy a silly thing like that, John? Is it a mid-life crisis thing? Ian's right, they are so dangerous. I wouldn't let you take Matt out on it."

"Oh, wouldn't you?" I ask, spinning around to face her. "Because you're the expert on these things, right?"

"Don't shout at me."

I take a deep breath. "I'm not, I'm sorry. I just *hate* that he's taking my son away from me."

"He's not. No-one could ever take Matty from you, he loves you."

"Not as much as, 'watching The Simpsons with Ian Hobson.' Susie, please. Go and tell him that it's over. Go and pack your bags, and get Hannah, and come home to me."

Sue is not looking at me, but at the bike. "John, I -"

"Please, go and tell him. Now."

"John, I can't."

"What?"

"I can't tell him that. I can't do that, I'm sorry."

"What do you mean, 'you can't'? You're leaving him tonight. You're coming back to me tonight."

"I, I can't. I'm so sorry." She is crying. Why is *she* crying? "He's just been so good to me, and he's safe, you know? He gives me safety and security, and at this time in my life that has to come before excitement and..."

"And what? Excitement and what?"

"And love," she finishes, almost silently.

"So you're saying you love me? For the first time in more than a decade you are telling me that you love me, and at the same time you are saying that you don't want me?"

"It's not that I don't want you, John - don't ever think that."

"You liar!" I kick the bike with all the force of my right leg and it tips over before me, making a heavy, crashing noise on the floor.

Susan screams.

"You flaming liar. You said you would come back to me - liar. You said you love me - liar. You said no-one could take Matty from me - liar, liar, liar." I kick the carnage of the bike again with every lie I retell. Then I reach down, and heave it back up again.

"John, what are you doing?"

"Just what you do all the time. I'm leaving you." I throw my leg over the bike and myself onto the seat, lifting the floor stand off as I do.

"Just calm down. Stay here and we can talk. I don't want you to go like this. At least let me explain to you."

"I get it," I shout over the loud purring of the engine.

"No, you don't."

"Yes I do, I get it. He wins again. Got it." I rev the engine hard, and then release the beast.

As I am racing away I am almost certain I hear her shout, "But, I love you."

Matthew Pickering
August 2010

Andrew is my support worker today. He is a nice man that started working with me after Brenda decided not to work with me anymore, and that was a very good thing. Now I have Andrew and Brian as my support workers, and I like them both very much. My little sister, Hannah, says that Andrew is gorgeous, but I do not know if she is right or not. He is twenty-nine years old, and he has got yellow hair that is short, but longer than most men's hair, and it is a bit wavy. He has got lots of muscles on his arms, because I think he does a lot of exercising, and he has got a very good suntan on his skin, even in the wintertime. Andrew is very fun and funny, and I have a good time when I am with him. He takes me out on lots of adventures, and he takes me running with him sometimes, which is fun, but it makes me tired. I am a very fast runner and I can run faster than Andrew, but I get tired more quickly than he does, which is not a good thing.

Andrew has taken me out today. He said that I need to dress in something comfortable, but not smart, and that I need to wear my trainers. I am wearing my comfortable jeans, a red t-shirt, and a green hoodie top, and I am wearing my new trainers that Brian took me to buy last week. I have come for my first day of my work placement at Hamington Dog Shelter today. Hamington is a village that is four point three miles from my flat, and it only takes ten minutes to get there on the bus. I have been excited about my placement because I like dogs a lot.

Andrew isn't allowed to come to do my placement with me, which I think is a bit silly. He has brought me here on the bus, and he came inside with me, but the people that run Hamington Dog Shelter told him that he could not stay with me and that he would have to go away and come back to collect me at three pm.

At first I did not like being here by myself, but the people that work here are very nice to me, so now I think that it is okay. There is a lady called Sandra who runs the shelter. She is quite short and a tiny bit fat. She has got light brown hair that is a little bit curly, and she is wearing green wellies, jeans trousers and a fleecey coat. There is also a man that works here, and another lady, who has a long ponytail of brown hair. They are both wearing jeans and wellies, and they are also wearing hoodie tops like me. The man is called Sam, and the lady is called Sam too. That is so silly, because one is a man and one is a lady, but they have the same name. I don't understand how that happened.

The man Sam says to me, "My full name is Samuel, but I like 'Sam' for short, and the other Sam's full name is Samantha. Do you get it?"

I do get it, so I say, "Yes."

Me and Samuel are out in a field and we are walking two dogs. I am walking a dog called Rufus that is black and white, and he is a Shih Tzu dog. Samuel is walking a little white dog that is called Mitzy, and she is a girl dog, who is a West Highland White Terrier. Samuel calls her a Westie for short.

There is another dog that lives at Hamington Dog Shelter that I have decided is my favourite dog because he is a brown greyhound, just like Santa's Little Helper on The Simpsons, and a bit like Rose, except that he is brown coloured and not black, and he is a boy dog and not a girl. He is called Ned, which is like the name of Ned Flanders, who is my favourite character on The Simpsons. I think that is very funny. I am going to take Ned for a walk next, and then I am going to eat my packed lunch in the staff room. This afternoon Samantha is going to teach me how to clean out a kennel so that I can clean out kennels by myself on the other times that I come. I am glad about this because I like learning to do things by myself.

I am having a very nice day at my placement at Hamington Dog Shelter, and I wish I could get a real job that is like this.

* * *

It is twenty past three pm in the afternoon, and Andrew has picked me up from my day at my placement and taken me to Mum and Ian Hobson's house. That is because Mum telephoned him and asked him to take me there after my placement. I do not know why she wanted him to do that, because she did not tell him why.

When we walk into the house we take off our shoes, and Hannah says from the living room, "Matty, is that you? Come in here. Is Andrew with you?"

"Yes, it is me. Okay, I will. Yes, he is with me," I answer.

I am surprised by what I see in the living room. My mum is sitting on the edge of the armchair, and she does not look very comfortable. Her face looks pale coloured and her eyes look very funny, like they look when she is crying, but she is not crying. She is staring at the wall opposite her, but there is nothing on the wall so I do not know what she is looking at.

Hannah is sitting on the arm of the chair, and she has got her hand on my mum's shoulder. Hannah does not look sad or happy, but she looks a bit confused. Mum doesn't look up at me as I enter the room, but Hannah does. She says, "Look, Mum, Matty's here now so you can tell us what's wrong."

Andrew puts his hand on the top of my back, and guides me to sit down on the settee. He sits on one side of me, and Hannah comes and sits on the other side of me.

Now Mum is looking at me, and then she is looking at Hannah.

"Is everything okay, Susan?" asks Andrew.

Mum makes a small laugh, but she does not really look very happy. "Does it look like it is?" she asks.

I don't think that it does look like everything is okay.

"Mum, you can tell us now," says Hannah. "Are you poorly? Is there something wrong with you?"

Mum shakes her head.

"Then is it Ian? Where is he? Is he okay? Has something happened to him?"

"Please stop guessing, Han," Mum says, holding her hand up in front of Hannah. Then she gives a little smile. "Oh, my babies. How can I tell you this?"

"Are you leaving Ian? You're finally going back to Dad, aren't you? I knew it." Hannah claps her hands together.

"Hannah, please." Mum does not sound angry, or happy or sad. She does not sound like anything. "Okay." She takes a deep breath into her mouth. "This is so hard. Ian is fine, Han. He's at work. I didn't call him to come home; that would have made it too real. But it is real. It is. I only found out an hour and a half ago, I - okay..." Now Mum is looking at me. "Matty, do you remember yesterday afternoon? Your dad came to see you, didn't he? He wanted to take you out on his... his..."

"His motorbike," I finish for her, because she has forgotten.

She makes a funny, squeaky sort of noise. "Yes," she says, "that. Anyway, he got a bit upset, and he went off on it quite fast, and - "

"What happened, Mum?" Hannah asks, but I think that Mum us about to tell us what happened.

"He... well, he had a bit of an accident."

"What did he do by accident?" I ask.

"How much of an accident?" Hannah asks in a very quiet voice.

Andrew puts his hand onto my back again.

Mum's eyes go wide. "A big one," she says.

I wonder what my dad did by accident.

Hannah makes a little noise. "But, he's alright?" she asks. "Tell us he's alright."

Mum shakes her head. "No, Baby. He's not alright."

Hannah screams and makes me surprised. She screams again, and I think I will have to cover my ears, but then she stops screaming. I look at her because she has picked up a cushion from the settee and has covered her face with it. It sounds like she is making a loud breathing noise.

"It's okay, Hannah," I tell her, because that is what Hannah tells me when I am screaming.

"Matthew?" Andrew says, turning me around to face him, "do you understand what your mum is telling you?"

I look at him.

"I don't think so," Mum says in a quiet voice. "Please, can you? I can't bear it."

Andrew is looking at my mum, and then he turns to look at me again. "Okay..." He takes a big breath into his mouth too. "Matt, I think your mum is trying to tell you that your dad has – well, he's died."

Hannah screams again.

I do not understand. My dad cannot have died because my dad is always alive, because he helps my mum and Ian Hobson to look after me. "My dad cannot have died," I tell him.

Andrew looks back at Mum, and I see her nodding her head.

"He has, Mate," he says to me, "I'm sorry."

I stare at him. I think that Andrew is telling me the truth and that my dad really has died. I cannot breathe, and I cannot move. I am very, very cold. I cannot feel any part of my body. The room looks like it is spinning around me, but I don't think that that is possible. I cannot hear anything. I feel like I am dead too, but I don't think that I am.

I see Hannah run over to Mum and give her a very big cuddle. I think Hannah is sad about my dad because she is crying, but I don't think that my mum is very sad because she is not crying.

Andrew puts one of his arms around me.

I feel like I am floating. I do not feel like anything is real anymore. There is a bit of a ringing in the air, and that is all that I can hear now. I do not want to scream, or hurt myself or shout. I do not want to make my train noise, or hit anybody. I do not want to do anything - I cannot do anything - I cannot move.

Hannah Pickering
January 2011

I throw another ball of paper into the bin with a frustrated squeal. Except it misses the bin and falls into the ever-growing mountain of scrunched up revision notes in the corner of my bedroom. My head falls forwards onto the desk in front of me.

It has become clear that, in the four months I have been doing my AS levels, I have not taken down one useful piece of information. Understandable, you'd probably agree, being that my dad was crushed into nothingness on the A57 less than a month before I started them. Understanable to you and me perhaps, but maybe not to the person hundreds of miles away marking my atrocious attempts at exam papers.

Mum tried to get me to postpone my A levels, and take a year out to get over it. Oh yeah, because it would be much better for me to mope around the house for a year, rather than actually trying to get on with my life. Even Matt's doing more than that; working two days a week at that dog shelter, and looking into training courses he can do.

Dad never did get to meet Ryan, my boyfriend at the time. That is something I am ever grateful for. I would have hated for him to go to the grave thinking I had ended up with that moron for the rest of my life.

Needless to say, we are not together anymore. He thought that straight after my dad's funeral was the ideal time to try to pressure me into seduction - 'if you really loved me, you would' - it's lucky he got out with all of his limbs still attached. That was the moment I swore off boys for eternity. So far it has lasted five months, and is still going strong.

Mum often asks me why I never cry about Dad. She cries all the time - funny that, seeing as she refused to be with him while she had the opportunity. I don't think Ian quite gets what Mum is so upset about; he never really noticed how much she still loved my dad. I think, at the moment, he is doing everything he can to avoid asking himself why she might be so upset about him now. I reckon he prefers the joys of remaining oblivious.

And me? Well, I don't cry anymore. I have done far too much crying for one person in this lifetime, and where did that get me? It's a new years resolution I guess; I don't cry. That doesn't mean that I'm not upset, or that I didn't love Dad as much as everybody else, but somebody has to stay strong, don't they? Apparently, in this family, that person is moi.

I hear a knock on the door downstairs and haul myself up to answer it, somewhat grateful for the interruption. As I pass the mirror in my bedroom I notice a large red indentation carved into my forehead from where I lay it onto the desk. I try to rub it clear as I hurry down the stairs.

When I open the door I am more than a little surprised at who I see.

"Hannah."

"Sorry, you've got the wrong house." I push the door closed again, but a hand sticks out and stops it. I give up, and allow it to open. "What do you want?"

"Can I come in?"

"No, I don't think so."

Raine looks behind me and into the house. "Is Matthew here?"

"Moved out years ago." I hold the door steady so she cannot pass me.

"Really?" She doesn't believe me. Come in and search the place, Hun. Be my guest.

"Really."

"Well, it's not actually him I'm after; although, I do want to see him - "

"But you can't."

"It's someone else I really need to see, though - John. Has he moved house or something?"

"What?"

"I need to see him. I went around to his old house, but there's this young family living there now. The woman I spoke to had never heard of a John."

"Come to sponge him for all he's worth in child support? Decide your sprog is his after all, now the money has run out?"

"You told him about that?"

A thick lump is forming in my throat. "No," I manage to squeeze out. "I kept your dirty secret."

She heaves a sigh of presumed relief. "Thank you, Hannah."

"He's dead." The words just fall out of my mouth; I cannot stop them. The brutality was not intended, but was the only way I could say what had to be said.

The sudden look of pasty horror on the girl's face is almost worth it. The last three and a half years have clearly not been good to Raine. She is skinny and pale, and her eyes look yellow and sunken. She is no longer caked in make-up, and today she has zero flesh on show. Even for January, that is impressive by Raine's previous standards.

"He's dead?" she repeats, he mouth wide. "Who's dead? John?"

"No, Michael Jackson."

"When?"

"Oh, a couple of years ago - didn't you see it on the news? It was everywhere – the King of Pop dying is big news. Although, you probably don't have a television on whatever park bench you have been living on."

"Are you being funny? Where is your dad?"

I sigh, and soften my stance a little. "Okay, Dad really is dead. I'm sorry. It happened last year. Motorbike accident."

She just stares at me.

"Raine."

She is still staring.

"You did hear me, right?"

"John didn't have a motorbike."

"No, well lots of things have changed since you've been away. So any child support you were after, no can do, I'm afraid. Inheritance, on the other hand - well, there you might be in luck; if you can prove your spawn's his, that is. Which I highly doubt."

She is not blinking. Perhaps she has had an aneurysm. What a shame.

"Raine? You still alive?"

"I can't believe he's dead."

"Yep, dead," I say, with a false air of nonchalance. "So you going to introduce me to your kid then? The one you came to tell me actually is my brother or sister. Or have you left them in a ditch somewhere? What am I saying? You probably live in a palace with all the benefits you will be on."

I see her swallowing. "You don't have a little brother or sister," she says finally. "I miscarried."

"Oh." I can feel my expression dropping.

"Yeah, oh."

"After... after that day when you fell?" I feel an intense stab of guilt.

"Er, yeah. That's life, though. You've got to carry on. Can you tell me where Matt is?"

I shake my head. I can't help the sinking feeling inside me.

Raine looks almost desperate. "Please, Hannah? Have a bit of compassion. I screwed up totally, but I'm here to sort it. I know I hurt him, but I want to make it better again. I have to see him. Don't look at me like that, please - just an address, or a phone -"

I close the door, lock it, and walk back upstairs.

Matthew Pickering
December 2011

Today has been a very busy day. I have had so much to do that I found it very hard to remember everything, so I have had to keep checking my visual timeline. My visual timeline is something that Andrew gave to me, and it helps me to always know what I am doing so that I don't feel stressed. It has got pictures of all the things I have got to do today, and it has got them in the right order. When I finish one thing I take that picture off my timeline so that I can see what is next. I have a little timeline that I take with me in my rucksack when I go on trips, and a big one that is stuck on my bedroom wall, right next to the photograph of my dad.

My dad has been dead for nearly a year and a half now, and it still makes me feel sad when I think about it. I miss him very much. Now I have nobody to do carpentering with, and that makes me sad, but I do still have all of the things that me and Dad made together. There are lots of little birds that like to live in the birdhouse we made, and that makes me a bit happy. I like to look at the photograph of my dad on my wall, because it makes me remember him, but sometimes it makes me feel a bit sad. Mum says that it is okay to feel sad about my Dad, and that she feels sad about him too. I don't know why Mum feels sad, because Ian Hobson is her husband now, and not my dad.

The first thing that I had to do on my busy day today, after I had my breakfast and a shower, was to take Ned for a walk. Ned is my dog. He is my favourite dog in the whole world, because he is a greyhound dog like Rose and he has got a name like my favourite character out of The Simpsons; Ned Flanders. I got him from Hammington Dog Shelter, which is where I had a work placement, and they said that I was so good with the dogs that I could adopt one for free. I chose that I would like to adopt Ned as a dog, and he lives with me in my flat. He has Rose's old kennel that me and dad made, but he sleeps on my bed every night so he does not really use it.

Mum said that it was not a good idea to have my very own dog, but Hannah told her that it would cheer me up after my dad dying made me feel sad, and she was right. I am a very good owner of Ned. I look after him very well, and take him for lots of walks and give him lots of nice food, and baths and cuddles. I love Ned very much.

After we had taken Ned for a walk this morning, it was time for my second ever driving lesson. I like learning to drive, even though it is very, very hard, and I hope that I will be a very good driver one day and have my very own car. One day, I would like to rent a car on the east coast of the United States of America and drive all the way to the west coast of the United States of America, which is Hollywood. I am training to have a good job so that in the future I will be able to afford to do that. I am also saving up the money that I got from my dad when he died so that I can do something very good with it in the future. I do not know what that very good thing will be yet.

I am getting very good at driving now, and I know how to use the clutch and the brake and the accelerator pedals, and I know how to use the steering wheel, and the gear stick up to gear two. Today we drove around an empty car park, and I practiced going faster and slower, and getting up to gear two. I also learned how to reverse my car, but I am not very good at that because it is confusing; it feels like you have to turn the steering wheel the wrong way. I bet that I will be a very good driver when I pass my test.

As well as saving the money that I got from my Dad, I am also going to spend a bit of it on a very exciting holiday next August. Just before Hannah goes away to University, me and her are going to go on an aeroplane to the United States of America. That is very, very exciting to me, and I think that Hannah is excited too. We are going to visit New York, which is where lots of movies are made, and then we are going to go down to Washington, District of Columbia, where the president lives. I wonder if we will meet the president when we are there. I wish we could visit where The Simpsons live, which is a place called Springfield, but there are too many Springfields in the United States of America, and I do not know which one they live in. And also, the Simpsons are cartoon characters, so I don't think we will meet them when we are there. I am very, very excited about my trip.

Since three pm this afternoon I have been practising for my play, which I am going to perform at seven thirty pm tonight. I am doing a play with my acting class, Saint John's Arts Club, and the play is called, 'The Traveller's Kiss.' It is about a man who is going on a journey around the world because he wants to find a girlfriend. He wants to see every girl in the world before he decides who he wants to be his girlfriend. The leader, called Robin, wrote this play, and he wrote lots of songs to sing in the play as well, which we have had to learn. One of these is a song called, 'Tokyo's Offering', and one is called, 'Dancing with a Stranger'. I really like the song, 'Dancing with a Stranger', because half way through it we have to start dancing with the person that is standing next to us, and I am standing next to Jodie so I get to dance with her. She is a very, very good dancer. I don't know how to dance, but Jodie shows me how by holding my hands and waving them up in the air.

I wanted to be given the part of the traveller in this play, but instead, I have got the part of a man who runs a bar in Canada, and I have to say, 'If you are going to fight, you had better take it outside.' Robin asked me to play another part too, but I didn't want to do that because I can't play two different people; that would be very silly.

I am very, very good at saying my line, and I know everybody else's lines too. I hope that nobody forgets their lines tonight when we are performing our play, because that would be terrible. I don't think that I will forget my line, because I know it very well.

Jodie has got some lines to say in this play too, and she is a very good actress because she talks very loud and Robin says that she is very dramatic. I think it is good thing to be dramatic, because acting is called drama.

There are some people coming to watch me in my play tonight. My mum is coming, and so are Ian Hobson and my little sister, Hannah. My mum said that Dad and Nana Brady would have loved to have seen me in my play tonight, but I know that they can't come to watch, because they are dead.

***

The play is starting now, and I am standing in a line of people waiting to go onto the stage. An old lady called Marjorie is standing in front of me in the line, and Jodie is standing behind me. I get to stand next to Jodie a lot in this play, and I like that.

Some music starts to play, and we all walk onto the stage. We have to walk through a door into the big audience room, and then up some stairs onto the stage. I get into my place. I am on the front row of people on stage, and that is good because it means that the people that have come to see me, like my family, will be able to see me very well.

Suddenly I can see Hannah in the audience, because she is wearing a bright yellow top. She is sitting on the left side of the room, on the second line from the front, so she is very close to me. I think she sees me looking at her, because she smiles and waves at me. I do not smile or wave back, because that is not in the script. My mum is sitting next to Hannah, and next to my mum is Ian Hobson. They are both smiling at me as well, and Mum is waving at me, but I don't wave back.

Then I forget about looking at my family because the first song starts, and I have to start singing.

All the men, including me, sing the first bit of the song. It goes,

> "No man, no man, no man is an island,
> I don't want to be alone no more.
> So I will travel, travel, travel every island,
> And search for my love on every shore."

Then the ladies start to sing the next line, and after that we all sing together and we move around the stage in a circle, putting our hands to our foreheads, and looking like we are searching for something. After that song is finished, the audience clap, and lots of us walk off the stage, down the steps, and out to the back room. The person who is playing the traveller, and five of the girl actors stay on the stage to act in the next bit of the scene.

* * *

My line in the play went very well because I remembered it all and I acted it very well. I heard some clapping after I said my line, and I looked at the audience and my little sister was clapping. I think that maybe she was clapping for me.

It is now the very last song in the play, and I am on the stage again for the last time. The actor who plays the traveller starts to sing the song, because the first bit is him singing it all by himself.

He sings,

"So goodbye to San Francisco, a real good friend to me,
Goodbye to old Orlando, my favourite place to be.
It's goodbye to Kenya, and goodbye to France,
Goodbye to Venice, city of romance.
I travelled every country for my Traveller's Kiss,
But now I realise that the one I really love –
Is the one at home that I miss."

Then we all sing,

"And now he realises it's the one at home he misses.
She's his true, true love,
She's the one at home he misses."

He sings,

"So goodbye to Rome, although you did me well,
Goodbye sweet China, though my time with you was swell.
I met some fine girls and I almost fell in love,
But they made me realise that they're not the ones I love."

Then we all sing,

"No, as hard as he tried, they are not the ones he loves."

He sings fastly,

"So I'll get onto that plane,
Take a thousand or more trains,
Take a bus, take a car,
Walk; don't even care how far.
I will find my way home, I will find my one true love,
I will take her by the hand and I will show her my true love."

Now he sings slowly,

"I will go back home to the one I really miss - "

Then we sing,

"And he is going to give her his Traveller's Kiss.
Yes he is going to give her his Traveller's Kiss."

Then we all stand to each side of the stage while the actor who is playing the traveller stands in the middle with a girl actor. Then they see each other, run together, hug each other, and spin around.

Then he sings slowly,

"Yes, I am going to give you my Traveller's Kiss."

And then he kisses her, and we all say, "Aaaah."

Then the lights go darker because it is the end of the play. We have to stand still for lots of seconds while we wait for the clapping to get a bit quieter, and then we have to walk to the front of the stage in turn, and bow down. The crowd claps a bit more every time some more people bow.

When it is my turn, I walk to the front of the stage in my line of actors, and I am holding hands with them. Then we all lift our hands up and bow forwards.

There is lots of clapping, and I hear Hannah's voice shout, "Yeah, Matty."

Then I hear a whistle and I look up. There is a young lady at the back of the room who is standing up, and she has got her fingers in her mouth and is whistling. She is the only person in the room that is standing up. It is a bit dark, so it is hard to see who it is, but when I look carefully I can see some long blonde hair and a very pretty face... and then I know who it is. I can see that it is Raine. Raine has come to see me in my play.

* * *

I have got changed back into my normal clothes now, and I walk into the audience room to find my family. I wonder if Raine is still here, and I wonder if she will speak to me. I cannot believe that Raine came to see my play. I do not know how she got here, and I have not seen her in lots and lots of years. My heart feels like it is bouncing when I think about her.

I am looking around the room to see if she is still here when I hear someone shout, "Matty." It is my sister, Hannah's voice, and then Hannah is jumping on me, and she is giving me a very big, squeezy hug. She says, "You were brilliant, brilliant, brilliant. Well done, you."

I say, "Thank you," and she lets go of me.

Then Mum gives me a hug and a kiss, and says, "Baby, you were amazing. Next step, Hollywood."

I do not know what she means when she says, 'Next step, Hollywood,' but I smile anyway, because I think that she is very proud of me.

Ian Hobson sticks out his hand and I shake it. Then he says, "Well done, Son. Great show."

Mum says, "Did you enjoy it, Matty?"

I say, "Yes," because I did enjoy it.

"It was very good, wasn't it?"

"Yes, it was very good."

Then I hear someone coughing behind my family, and a lady voice says, "Excuse me, is it okay if I just come and have a word?" It is Raine.

Mum and Ian Hobson are looking at her, and their mouths are open wide.

Hannah turns around and looks at her too. "No," is what Hannah starts to say, and she grabs onto my arm with both of her hands. She is looking at Raine. "No, you have done far too much damage. Get away from him."

"Hannah," Mum says to my sister, and then she looks back at Raine.

"Where on earth have you been?" is what Ian Hobson says to her, with a cross voice. "Your Grandmother has been worried senseless. She phoned us up almost every week when you first went - crying down the phone she was - to find out if we had seen you. That was until she finally gave you up for dead after a couple of years."

Raine is not looking at Ian Hobson; she is just looking at me. "I left her a note," she says quietly.

"You think a note is sufficient for the woman who practically brought you up? Who gave up so much for you. Your mother would be turning in her grave if she knew what you had done."

Raine does not look upset that Ian Hobson is shouting at her, but she suddenly looks like she has remembered something, and she says to me, "I'm so sorry to hear about your dad, Matt."

"It's okay," I say, because she said she was sorry; even though it is not Raine's fault that my dad is dead.

"Can we talk?"

"Yes," I say

"Why are you here, Raine?" is what my mum says.

Raine looks up at her.

"How did you know about the play? Why did you decide to come now, after all these years of hurt for him?"

"I'm sorry about that," Raine answers, "I will explain everything to him." Then she looks at me again. "Will you come with me? I have seats at the back of the room. My, er... things are there."

"Okay," I say, and I follow her, pulling Hannah's hands away from my arms as I go.

Raine takes me to some seats at the back of the room, and there is a little girl sitting on one of the chairs. She is holding a book, and flapping the pages open and closed.

The noise is a bit annoying, but I am sensible now, so I do not make my train noise.

"You okay, Babe?" Raine asks the little girl.

"Okay, Babe," she answers.

Raine sits down, and taps the chair next to her. I think she wants me to sit down there, so I do.

"You were really, really good in the play, Matt. I always knew you'd make it as an actor."

"You told me I would never be an actor," I remind her. "In the shed, that's what you said."

She smiles. "I forgot about your Polaroid memory."

I don't know what she means.

"Anyway, I was flicking through the local paper at the end of last year, and I saw your picture from that other play you were in. I missed you so much, and I tried to come and see you then but I – well - I wasn't able to find you. So I kept an eye out for any other adverts for 'Saint Paul's Arts Club' plays, and I saw this one. I thought you might be in it, so I came on the off chance." She reaches her right hand out and strokes the bottom part of my cheek. "And you were. I'm really proud of you."

"Where have you been?" I ask her, because I want to know the answer to this question.

"Not far," she says to me. "I got a place from the council. That helped me out a lot. I couldn't face my Gran, but I know I'm going to have to. It's not easy, though." She drops her hand from my face and starts to play with the ribbons on the bottom of her top. "I've hurt so many people, Matt. Probably you the most. I am so sorry."

"It's okay," I tell her.

Her eyes look back up at me again, and she is smiling a little bit. "You are so good and so kind," she tells me. "I have missed you so much."

"I have missed you so much, too," I tell her back, because that is the truth.

She takes a deep breath, and then she sits back on her chair so I can see the little girl again. "This is River," she says to me, putting her hand on the little girl's shoulder. "She's my baby."

I look at the girl. She is not a baby; she is a child. I frown at Raine. "She is not a baby."

Raine laughs. "She will always be my baby. But you're right; she will be four years old in January." She looks at the girl, who is called River (which is a silly name), but River is still looking at the book that she is opening and closing lots of times. "Say hello to Matt."

"Hello to Matt," says the girl.

"Why is she called River?" I ask. "I think it's a silly name for a person."

Raine smiles at me a little bit. "I'm from a silly family." She puts one of her arms around the little girl, but the little girl pushes it off again. "But you know, rain makes rivers. I'm Raine... plus she's a free spirit, a bit like a river. A bit like me... and you."

I don't understand.

"Me and you are alike in so many ways," Raine tells me, but I am not sure if this is true. "We were always meant to be together. You know that, don't you?"

I nod my head. I think that we were meant to be together, and I was very happy when Raine was my girlfriend.

She closes her eyes and makes a very long breath out as she touches her chest with her hand. "I'm so glad you feel the same." She opens her eyes again, and moves her hand from her chest to my leg. I look down at it. It feels funny. "River is so like you, by the way," Raine tells me. "It's scary how like you she is. Even the doctors agree that she's like you."

I am confused. No doctor has ever seen me and River together, so how could they know that she is like me.

"We need you, Matt," she continues. "River needs you to show her the way, and how to survive this life. And I need you to... I just need you." She is looking at me again, and puts her hand that is not on my leg back onto my cheek. "I love you."

I swallow some saliva from my mouth.

"I think I always have, but I didn't want to admit it. I'm here to turn my life around, and to get what I really need. I want to be with you; I love you. Do you love me?"

I feel like my heart has stopped beating, and I am finding it hard to breathe. It feels a bit like I have died, but I don't think that can be true. Raine loves me. She loves me again. "Yes," I answer.

Raine takes a big breath, smiles a very big smile, and then pushes her face to mine. I think that she is going to kiss me.

Her lips get to mine and I feel like my body cannot move. I am like a statue. Raine loves me, and wants to be with me, and is kissing me. I close my eyes. Then I open them again and I push Raine away from my face with my hand, but only gently; I do not want to hurt her. "I do love you, Raine," I tell her, "but I don't want to be with you." I hold her away from me with my hand. "I do love you, but I love someone else more."

Raine's eyes go very big. "Oh," is all that she says.

Then, in the distance, I can see Jodie looking for me, and I wave my hand at her. She sees me, and walks over to us.

Raine is looking at her.

When she gets to me, I hold her hand, and I say, "Raine, this is my girlfriend, Jodie. I love her very much. Jodie, this is Raine. She is my old best friend."

Jodie looks at her and smiles. Then she reaches out her hand that is not holding mine for Raine to shake.

Raine does not shake it.

"It's nice to meet you," Jodie says to Raine, as she moves her hand back again. "You have a very funny name, it's like the weather." Jodie starts to laugh, and I start to laugh too, because she told a funny joke. Jodie is a very funny person.

"Er," is all that Raine says.

"It's funny that you are Matt's old best friend, because I am his new best friend, and I am his girlfriend. Who's that?" she asks, pointing to River. "She's being silly with that book."

"This is River," says Raine. "She's Matt's little si - she's my little girl."

"River?" says Jodie. "Like the rivers?" She laughs again, and so do I. Then Jodie sits on my knee and I put my arms around her for a cuddle.

"Er, yep," says Raine. Then she looks at me, and not at Jodie anymore. "Matt, I'm sorry about before. I shouldn't have just assumed. I'm happy for you. I am. Can we..." she stops talking and looks at Jodie again, and then back at me, "can we, maybe, be friends again?" she finishes.

"Not best friends," says Jodie, "because his best friend is me."

"How about second best friends?" Raine smiles at me.

"Okay," I say.

"Okay," Raine nods.

Matthew Pickering
August 2012

"Killer's owner is in the waiting room, Matt," says my boss, Michael. "Go and talk to him. Tell him what's happening, and then get yourself home. No need for us both to stay late on a Friday. You've got a holiday to pack for."

"Okay," I say, nodding my head and giving the ginger cat one last stroke before closing up his pen for the night and throwing my disposable gloves into the bin. I open the door into the waiting room, and am a bit scared to see who is there. I close my eyes, take a deep breath, and imagine throwing the past and all of my scaredness into a big river, and watching it float away from me. I feel instantly better, and open my eyes again.

I have not seen Billy Robin for five years, and he looks a bit different to the last time that I saw him. He is looking very fat, and his forehead has got a bit bigger, but I don't know how that happened. I am surprised to see that his eyes look a bit red coloured, like he has been crying. I did not know that bullies cried. I do not want to talk to Billy Robin, but I have got to talk to him because he is Killer's owner, and my boss wants me to tell him what is happening.

I walk into the room and close the door, feeling a bit frightened of what he might do to me. Then I remember the river taking all of my frightenedness away with it. "Good evening, Mr Robin," I say, because you have to call clients by their title and surname, like they are teachers.

"Yeah, hi," he says. He is not really looking at me, so I don't think that he knows who I am yet. "You've got to give me some good news about that dog, Mate. The kids are going nuts without him."

I am surprised. "I did not know you had kids."

He looks up at me, and his red eyes go very big. "Flaming Nora, its Pickers, isn't it? What are you then, a nurse, or something?"

I take a deep breath. "I am a veterinary nurse, yes. And I know that you will say to me that nurses are ladies, but that is not true, because nurses can be men too, because I am one."

"Right, whatever." He has folded his arms across his chest. I wonder if he is going to bully me. "How's the dog?"

"I am very sorry, Mr Robin, but Killer is a very poorly dog."

"Yeah, the guy on the phone said he needs a tumour removing, or something. I've come to say just do it. What's it going to cost me?"

"The operation will cost five-hundred and thirty-six pounds."

He looks cross. "What? On top of the fortune I've already spent?"

"Yes, that's right, Sir. I'm sorry."

Billy Robin makes a loud roaring noise and kicks the coffee table in front of him. It makes a loud bang, jumps up in the air a bit, and some of the magazines on it fall onto the floor.

I take a step backwards because I am scared that he might kick me too.

"It's a flaming outrage. How much do they think I get on benefits? And I bet it goes straight into your pocket, doesn't it? Go on then, what do you earn for doing basically nothing? I bet it's loads, isn't it?"

"I earn fifteen-thousand, seven-hundred, and ninety-nine pounds a year," I tell him, "but I don't do nothing, because I do lots of things."

He just stares at me, and then puts his head into his hands.

"Are you okay, Mr Robin?" I ask him.

He stands up. "Stop with the flaming 'Mr Robin' act, would you? Just give me my dog. I can't afford that, so just give him to me."

"I don't think I am allowed to -"

"I don't care what you're allowed to do, he's *my* dog. Just give him to me." He kicks the table again.

"I can't," I tell him. "He will die if he doesn't have the operation."

"Well, I can't afford the operation," he shouts. And then he coughs. And then he is crying, and he turns away from me.

"Mr Robin?"

He does not answer me.

"Are you crying, Mr Robin?"

"No," I hear him say through a crying voice.

I feel a bit sorry for Billy Robin, which is very weird, because I am usually very scared of him. I feel sorry for him because I know what it is like to have a dog that you love and that dies, because that happened to my dog, Rose. "Let me help you," I tell him.

He turns around, and wipes his sleeve over his face to rub away his tears. "What?"

"I can help you get some money to help pay for Killer's operation. I know some people you can call, because I heard you say that you are on benefits, so there are some people that might help you."

He makes a frowny face, but I don't know why because I am saying a nice thing to him, and not a horrible thing. "Get lost. Why should I accept your help, you spaz?" is what he says.

My heart hurts a little bit when he calls me that name, but I don't think it is a heart attack. "Because you can't afford to help your dog live," I answer.

"I can afford what I want; I don't need any help from you." I think he is telling me a lie.

"Okay. Can we have five-hundred and thirty-six pounds, please?" I ask him.

He makes a long, blowy sound, and shakes his head. "Just keep the wretched dog," Billy Robin says. "He's no use anyway; who wants a bulldog that just lazes around the house all day, being soft?" And then Billy walks out of the front door, and slams it very hard.

I hear a cough behind me, and I turn around.

Michael, my boss is standing there. "You did your best," he says.

"I don't want Killer to die," I tell him.

He makes his shoulders lift up and down again. "What can you do if people refuse to accept help?"

"Maybe he will change his mind," I say, hoping that this will happen.

"He might, but he will have to do it quickly. If we don't get this operation done a.s.a.p. the poor thing won't last until Monday."

I have got an idea. "What if I pay for his operation?"

Michael pulls a funny face. "Why would you do that? That kid was awful to you."

"Because I love dogs, and I want Killer to be alive."

"You're going to live a pretty skint life if you spend all your wages on saving other people's pets."

"I don't care," I tell him. "And it's not my wages, it's money from my dad. He wanted me to do something special with it."

Michael laughs. "You're something else, Matthew. Has anyone ever told you that?"

"No," I answer.

"If you want to do something special with it you should open up a whole animal sanctuary, or something. You could save as many dogs as you liked then." He laughs again, but I don't know why he is laughing, because he is not telling a joke; I think he is telling me a very good idea.

"Okay," I say, "I will do that."

Michael's mouth is open wide. "Hang on, I wasn't serious. I don't want to lose the best nurse I've ever had."

"You should have been serious, Michael, because it is a very good idea. I will set up an animal sanctuary, and when my little sister has become qualified as a doctor she can help me look after all of the animals and make them better."

He laughs again. "I don't think it works like that, Matt. I think she might want to be a doctor for people."

"Oh," I say. "Well, my second best friend, Raine, wants to save animals for a job, too. Maybe she would like to work in my animal sanctuary with me."

He smiles. "Just go on your holiday, Mate. And when you get back I want you to have forgotten I ever suggested this, and come back to working with me, okay?"

"I will come back to work with you, Michael," I say, because I like working with him.

"Good man - "

"Until my sanctuary is ready."

He smiles at me again. "Enjoy America," he says.

I smile too. "I will."

-- The End --

Learn more about the author and her upcoming projects at

www.laurenwoodcock.com

Printed in Great Britain
by Amazon.co.uk, Ltd.,
Marston Gate.